D1766286

WOUND FOR WOUND

WOUND FOR WOUND

Janie Bolitho

This first world edition published in Great Britain 1995 by
SEVERN HOUSE PUBLISHERS LTD of
9–15 High Street, Sutton, Surrey SM1 1DF.
First published in the USA 1995 by
SEVERN HOUSE PUBLISHERS INC of
425 Park Avenue, New York, NY 10022.

Copyright © 1995 by Janie Bolitho

All rights reserved.
The moral rights of the author have been asserted.

British Library Cataloguing in Publication Data
Bolitho, Janie
  Wound for Wound
  I. Title
  823.914 [F]

  ISBN 0-7278-4739-2

All situations in this publication are fictitious and
any resemblance to living persons is purely coincidental.

Typeset by Hewer Text Composition Services, Edinburgh.
Printed and bound in Great Britain by
Hartnolls Ltd, Bodmin, Cornwall.

Life for life,
Eye for eye, tooth for tooth, hand for hand, foot for foot,
Burning for burning, **wound for wound**.

Exodus 21:23

Chapter One

He stood on the corner of Oakfield Road on a patch of grass worn bare by many footsteps. Under the streetlight it looked greener than it actually was. He could see most of the houses on the even-numbered side, including his own. But it was not his own which held his interest. To his left, out of his line of vision, was an identical row; behind it a block of flats, all, unmistakeably, council-built.

The edge of the pavements were lined with a strip of equally worn grass and a row of trees – horse-chestnuts. The original oaks, after which the road had been named, had been cut down and their roots excavated in order to build the houses.

Colin Mitchell glanced expectantly to his right, but it was too soon and he knew it. His eyes flicked back to the even-numbered houses. They were semi-detached, each with a small front garden divided from its neighbour by mesh-linked fencing. At the back were good-sized gardens in varying states of attention. His own, for instance was rarely touched whereas May Wilkes had neat rows of vegetables and masses of dahlias in the summer.

It was not an ugly estate, having been constructed before space was at a premium. The bricks were pinkish red and the roofs tiled. Running between each pair of houses was a narrow, concrete access path leading to the rear.

Colin kicked impatiently at the leg of the seat which had been donated by the widower of one of the first inhabitants of Oakfield Road. The plaque, dedicated to his wife, had been prised off and the wood was scored with hearts and initials. At weekends, and on warm evenings, youths congregated here, talking or revving their motor bikes or smoking. At this hour on a damp, chilly night, Colin was alone, as he mostly preferred to be, his adenoidal breath steaming from his mouth and disappearing in the glow of the streetlight. There was enough illumination to read his watch. Eleven-thirty. Soon she would come. Before that, though, so would his father, but an evening in the pub would render him incapable of recognizing his own son.

Laughter drifted through the stillness of the night, coming from the direction of Marlborough Road which ran parallel to where he stood. Teenagers mucking about. The laughter became fainter. They were not coming his way. A dog barked as if seeing them off the premises. There was a low, spasmodic roar from traffic on the motorway, too distant to be a nuisance here but unfortunate for those living on the other side of town and whose bedroom windows were the same height as the flyover.

Overhead, competing with the few stars not hidden by cloud, the lights of a plane winked as it gained height and banked away. None of these things registered with Colin. With the cold creeping further and further into his body he felt the waiting was worth it, just for a glimpse of her.

He sensed, before he saw, his father rounding the corner. Frank Mitchell bounced off the wall and stumbled between two parked cars as he negotiated the kerb. There were cars on both sides of the road because the tenants who also rented garages tended to fill them with broken furniture and boxes of junk which would probably never see the light of day again.

His father made it to the front door. The gate, no longer a barrier, stood drunkenly on its hinges as if in imitation of the man passing through it. The hall light came on and shone through the ridged glass of the top half of the door. Seconds later it was extinguished. Colin was safe now. He released his breath, unaware he had been holding it.

Several minutes later he heard the tap-tapping of high heels on the paving stones. She reached the first streetlight. Colin thought she was the most beautiful girl he had ever set eyes

2

on, far better than anything on the nude calendar his brothers had hanging in their bedroom.

"I'm here, darling," he whispered to himself, as he would never have dared to her face. "I'm here, watching out for you. And I'll wait for you forever if I have to."

His hands were in his pockets. He edged his fingertips as close together as the stiffness of the denim of his jeans would allow, then squeezed gently, imagining they were her hands. He felt the familiar excitement.

"Hello, Karen."

"Oh!" Startled, her hand jerked involuntarily towards her face. Her high heels no longer tapped. "Oh, Colin, it's you. You made me jump."

He blushed, furious with himself for causing her even a moment's anxiety. She had not been expecting anyone to be around, he should have made some sound to warn her.

"You'll catch your death standing there in this weather. You ought to go in." Encouraged by her soft voice and kind words his arousal swelled further, uncomfortable now in his restricted clothing.

"You're right. It's not very warm." But he wasn't sure if Karen heard, as she was already walking up the short path to her front door. He wasn't even sure if he had spoken aloud.

He waited until she was inside, watching until lights were first lit, then extinguished. Then he moved away, towards the alley which ran down the side of Karen's house, bounded on one side by trees and undergrowth, on the other by the blank walls of the rows of houses between which ran narrow paths leading to the back gates.

In this direction lay relief.

The girl did not move, could not move, for several seconds. By then it was too late. It was unexpected, but she cursed herself for not taking more notice of the newspaper reports, for not guessing by his behaviour.

The man came to her late, and he seemed in a hurry, not even taking the time to remove all his clothing. It happened

3

like that sometimes, the excitement, or nervousness being too much for them. They would unzip themselves and pull their clothes down as far as their knees and then it was over. Hardly worth the money, in her opinion.

She had let him in, told him her name was Candice, which it wasn't, and named her price. He did not argue. Once the money was safely in her dressing-table drawer it seemed all that was required of her was that she lay on the bed and opened her legs. That was all right by her.

There were no preliminaries, no play-acting, no special requirements. Nothing but the act itself. She wished it was always so.

Her client rolled off her, stood up, at the same time doing up his trousers, then leant towards her. For a fanciful second she thought he was going to kiss her on the cheek. She gasped, staring at him, seeing nothing. He was gone before she realised what had happened.

There was wetness on her forehead which trickled into her eyes. There was no pain, not immediately. Only when she reached up and touched her face and saw the blood on her fingers did she scream. She could not picture his face, only his smile when she gasped and although she hesitated before she went to the police, not sure of her own position, she did so because she was not the first and there were other girls out there in danger.

The description she gave was next to useless. The man was of average height and weight and his hair was "ordinary", by which she meant somewhere between dark blond and medium brown. There was nothing outstanding about his features, apart from which, she rarely took much notice of the "johns". It was their money, not their appearance that interested her. She remembered the smile, that was all. And his voice? Sort of gruff, with no particular accent, but he had spoken no more than a few words.

She was thanked for her time, although she felt it was done in rather a sarcastic manner.

Candice, as she called herself, left the hospital with several butterfly strips over her wound and went back to work.

The man, whoever he was, did not strike twice in the same place.

SOPFORD MAIL

'CARVER' STRIKES AGAIN –
FIFTH PROSTITUTE ASSAULTED

A 23-year-old Sopford woman, who wishes to remain anonymous for fear of reprisals, became the fifth victim of the man dubbed 'The Carver' in the early hours of Thursday morning. She was taken to Sopford General Hospital where she received treatment for a deep cut to her forehead. The woman discharged herself, although she was reported to be suffering from shock.

As in the four previous cases, police believe the injury may represent a letter, possibly an L or a C, which might be an initial of the perpetrator. These injuries are not serious but will leave permanent scarring.

Prostitutes, and any women out alone at night are asked to be extra-vigilant and to report anything suspicious immediately.

It is now known that the knife used by this man is narrow-bladed, possibly a stiletto. Anyone with information regarding the identity of this man or who knows anyone in possession of such a knife, is requested to telephone Detective Constable Jeffries on 87390. All calls will be treated in the strictest confidence.

"I'm surprised they haven't got him yet," Karen's mother, Doreen Turner, commented to her husband over breakfast on Friday morning. She turned to an inside page of the local paper and continued reading, her gold-rimmed glasses on their serpentine chain wedged firmly on the bridge of her nose.

"It says here there may have been more than five; that others could have been too frightened to come forward in case they lay themselves open to charges, or in case the man went back and did them more harm. I can't believe that, not if they needed hospital treatment. Does it say anything in your paper?"

"What's that, dear?" John Turner, his grey hair still damp from the shower, glanced over the top of his own glasses. His, though, were bifocal, framed in plastic tortoiseshell.

"About these prostitutes. Does it say anything?"

"Oh, sorry." He flicked through the news pages of the *Daily Telegraph*, a paper which he privately thought was occasionally more prurient than some of the tabloids. Page 3 guaranteed sex and violence without resort to exaggeration. He paused for another spoonful of muesli which he detested but which Doreen had taken to buying recently, along with granary bread and skimmed milk. He pushed the oat mixture around his mouth with his tongue until it resembled something he could comfortably swallow. It was easier than querying Doreen's ever changing dietary decisions.

"Only a small paragraph. Here, you read it."

Doreen reached across for the paper, neatly folded to the relevant passage. "Um, you're right, it doesn't say much."

"There isn't much *to* say. These girls aren't badly hurt. It's bound to make more of a splash locally; not much else happens around here."

"You'd be surprised," Doreen informed her husband, enigmatically.

John often wondered what his wife talked about all day long with her staff and the all female clientele she pampered at her beauty salon. It seemed he was not about to be enlightened.

"Toast?"

"No thanks, I'm not very hungry."

"In that case I won't bother either. And I'd better be off, my first appointment's at quarter-to-nine today. See you later. Oh, and don't forget, we're going to the Frasers' tonight."

"No, dear." Or should it be yes, dear? The grammatical correctness of his answer hardly mattered. Doreen took his compliance for granted. At least the Frasers were not going through a phase of healthy eating, sharing his preference for

6

a good piece of meat and a decent bottle of claret to wash it down. "I'm going to pop in and see Karen on my way home – don't worry, I won't be late. Any message for her?"

"No. Just give her my love." Doreen was rummaging in her capacious handbag for the keys to her Mini. "I really don't know why you go over there so much. I don't mean to Karen's, although I think she could come here a bit more often. It's those other people, they're awful."

"They're all right once you get to know them." This timid piece of defiance was ignored.

"Ah, here they are. Why do they always drop to the bottom?" Waving the car keys at him she left by the back door of their modern house on the outskirts of town, which Doreen loved, and John, secretly, hated.

A few minutes later, after stacking the dishes in the dishwasher, John did likewise, locking up behind him.

As he drove the two miles to his office he gave some thought to what was interesting, and concerning, his wife. He recalled what she had read to him from the *Sopford Mail*. The article, for want of facts, had consisted mainly of comparisons with other serial crimes, and was padded out with editorial speculation.

Nevertheless, the reporting of these assaults had left John increasingly concerned for Karen's safety. She was undeniably pretty, and the right age. Working at that club and going home in the early hours might give someone the wrong impression. But Karen was not like that; never had been. All right, when she was on a late weekend, her boss paid for a taxi, but that was no guarantee of safety nowadays. The Carver might even be a taxi driver. He'd know where various girls lived and would legitimately be on the streets in the small hours.

John knew he must stop torturing himself. He would speak to Karen again tonight, try to get her to change her mind about the job, although it was doubtful he could overcome her stubbornness. Since Dave left her she had developed a streak of independence not noticeable before. But the least he could do was try.

*   *   *

7

Doreen parked the yellow Mini in one of the two parking spaces replacing what had once been the back yard of the premises she used as her salon. She had dismantled the wooden fence herself without bothering to inform the council or apply for planning permission to turn it into anything other than a garden. They, in turn, had not bothered her with demands for extra community tax or whatever else they deemed it necessary to charge for, because they were totally unaware of this improvement to the property.

She let herself in through the back door, switching on the sun-beds in the two secluded booths to warm them ready for her early customers. Unless they were hot they didn't believe they were getting their money's worth. Next she raised the blinds at the front and turned the sign on the door to "open". Sheila, one of her two assistants, was waiting punctually outside. Unless she was on holiday there was no one but herself who held the keys. The question of illness had never arisen and it seemed unlikely that any germ would invade Doreen's well-upholstered body.

"Good morning, Sheila, not too bad today, is it?"

"No, not now that awful drizzle's stopped. Did you hear there's been another one? I can't believe this is going on, on our doorstep."

"Hardly that," Doreen commented dryly. "They've all been on the other side of town." She did not add that it was where her daughter lived.

"Well, it's put me off going out alone at night, I can tell you."

Doreen's eyes swept over Sheila's skinny form and wondered how she could possibly think any man would be interested. "Put the kettle on, would you dear? We've just time for a cup of something." Doreen began to arrange the trolleys of nail varnish and trays of different sized rollers ready for the day's action, then she checked her own appearance in one of the many mirrors.

The rather-too-black hair was neat in its uncompromising French pleat and her make-up was reminiscent of the 'fifties, but she was still a handsome woman, and she had the sense not to let her own preferences influence her clients' choice. If they required softly waving hair, subtle highlights and cosmetics so delicately applied as to seem nonexistent, then that was what she provided. And she made good money doing so.

Her second assistant arrived, breathless and apologetic, at almost the same time as their first client. Her tardiness was forgiven as the hectic day progressed, throughout which the sole topic of conversation was "The Carver" and the shocking realisation that there were prostitutes in dear old Sopford.

Chapter Two

Leonard Murdoch viewed his customers with amusement. From Tuesday to Friday, in this bar, they were mostly youngsters, some of them underage. But his conscience did not trouble him. If he did not supply their booze, someone else would. He might as well be the one to profit. Saturday offered some variety, in that the teenagers used the upstairs disco. The larger dance floor below converted into more of a proper nightclub, in that tables and chairs were set out, properly laid for eating. Here, the older residents of the town could enjoy a meal, a drink and middle-of-the-road music; mostly stuff from the 'fifties up to the 'seventies.

When he first proposed this innovation, people laughed, saying he'd never see the over thirty-fives patronising some-where like "Lenny's Place", yet it had worked. The two groups did not come into contact with each other, and both areas were soundproofed. Saturdays were also more profitable. The older generation, many of whom, he supposed, had children in the upstairs bar, even if they didn't know it, were not so inclined to nurse a bottle of foreign lager for an hour or more, and they generally had a meal. There was money in food. Of course, it helped that there was free entry for anyone who might be influential: there was a local councillor and his wife, that cocky detective inspector and his various floozies, and anyone else who might be prepared to turn a blind eye or grant him favours, favours which he always repaid.

The profit on the food was more than adequate to pay for whichever mediocre band was churning out the golden oldies, and his drink prices were the dearest in Sopford. And still they came.

Murdoch was resourceful in every aspect of business. He had recently done a deal with a new firm of Asian cab drivers. He had an account with them, for his own use and for taking the staff home. In return for a cheaper rate he had a direct line to their office which his customers could use free of charge. They did not get a cheaper rate. Murdoch grinned. People were so gullible. They saved ten pence on the free 'phone but paid more for their ride home. He was fair enough to make sure the firm was not summoned for drunks or potential troublemakers.

Friday night and business was good. He congratulated himself again as he took it all in. Six bar staff: three here in the disco; another three upstairs where tonight there was a bar only. All were busily employed and there was no chance of fiddling. The tills were the latest state-of-the-art technology, connected to the actual pumps and most of the drinks were bar-coded, the prices clearly displayed on screens the customers could see – if they ever bothered to look. No system was unbeatable, but this one was the best available.

Beyond the sea of customers waiting to be served, some three or four deep, were steps which led down to the dance area. Bodies gyrated, some with natural rythym, but for the most part, clumsily, with too much drink inside them to pick up the beat. The flash of alternating coloured bulbs and bursts of strobe lighting gave the scene an eerie quality. Faces and clothes suddenly startling white, movements jerky, the dancers looked like animated puppets.

What pleased Leonard most at the moment was not his self-made wealth but the way his relationship with Karen Wilkes was developing. She had come to him in desperation when her husband had walked out, leaving her with a baby less than a year old. He had been astonished when she had turned up in response to his advertisement, for she was not the usual run-of-the-mill. At once he had seen that she was beautiful; minutes later he had realised she was also intelligent. She could have done a lot better for herself.

"I need the job badly, Mr Murdoch," she had admitted, honestly. "I understand what you're thinking, but I'm not going to turn around and leave as soon as a better offer comes up. I want to be with my baby son during the day, you see, and this way I can do that."

"How come?" Leonard had wondered if he had misjudged her, if she was the kind of woman who would leave her child alone overnight.

"My mother-in-law lives a few doors away from me. I can take him there just before bedtime, put him to bed myself, then I'll collect him in the morning. It's perfect, you see, and I've already spoken to her. She agrees to do it." Karen had then licked her lips nervously. At the sight of those even, white teeth and the pink tongue, Leonard Murdoch had felt his loins stir.

He had taken her on, on a trial basis. Looks and brains did not necessarily mean she would make a good barmaid – or waitress – which she was definitely in line for on Saturdays because she would appeal to the older clientele. They had discussed hours and wages. Karen was to work from eight-thirty until midnight on Tuesdays and from nine until the club closed on Wednesdays, Thursdays and Fridays. On alternate Saturdays she would work from nine until eleven or two a.m.

The club did not open on Sundays and Murdoch used Mondays for another money-making venture. He hired out the rooms for meetings which ranged from political to protest, from touring evangelists who seemed to have no compunction about holding their rallies on licensed premises, to bird-watching societies who would not dream of doing otherwise. On these occasions, if required, he provided a skeleton staff from one or other of the bars, made up from part-timers.

Out of gratitude, Karen had agreed to go out with Leonard. They had had a couple of drinks and a curry, then he had dropped her home. Even with that sad expression she was lovely to look at, and he wanted her but knew better than to rush things. She was still raw from the break-up of her marriage.

They made an incongruous pair. Karen, slim and dainty

with a mass of auburn hair; Leonard, at forty, sixteen years her senior, stocky, springy hair showing through the expensive, open-necked shirts he favoured. Karen had refused his second invitation. The evening had been pleasant, no more than that. It was Trot, the chef, who fascinated her with his accurate mimicry, and the crinkles round his eyes when he smiled. She felt something inexplicable in his presence, yet he treated her no differently from the other girls. Even at her lowest ebb he could make her smile, although his temper, at times, made her nervous.

"Can't you get your mother-in-law to babysit?" Leonard kept asking.

"No, she does enough. Besides, I enjoy my evenings off at home. Maybe later, when I'm more sorted out." But she had already decided that, had Trot asked her, a babysitter would be no problem as there was always Mary Langley.

Lenoard took heart from her excuse. It was not a definite refusal, more of a postponement. He had been a long time without a wife. He needed one to complete his image, and Karen would be such an asset; apart from which, he wanted her.

Her watched her now, smiling at one of the customers, pouring foaming lager without any spillage. Yes, for her he could wait.

He retired to his office, his presence unrequired, as the place was running smoothly enough. His bouncers were hand-picked, but he was always in the foyer at closing-time in case there was trouble. The stories of the bouncers and a drunken idiot did not always coincide. And Leonard Murdoch could handle himself; a spell in the army had ensured that.

He poured two measures of gin over ice and angostura bitters then added a bottle of low-calorie tonic water. Pink gin. No longer fashionable, considered by some to be a woman's drink, but he liked it, and no one laughed at Leonard Murdoch.

Whilst he sipped his first and only drink of the evening, he looked over some paperwork. There was little need; he had a good accountant, but he needed something to take his mind off Karen – especially the fact that she and Trot, his chef, seemed to have something going between them. Not that they were going out; he'd have known. But there was an almost tangible spark between them. How did it happen, he pondered, that Dave Wilkes came to leave a wife like that? Perhaps she's difficult to live with.

Karen Wilkes was no more difficult to live with than any other well-balanced wife and mother. She was mostly contented, occasionally ecstatically happy, sometimes irritable and, on rare occasions, downright furious. The problems which had beset her marriage to Dave lay not in her personality but in Dave's character. He was overawed by Karen's efficiency and capability, and this had been exacerbated when Danny was born. She had coped with pregnancy, childbirth and looking after him as if it was the most natural thing in the world. To Karen it was. But Dave, despite his mother's impartial upbringing of both her children, lacked confidence, and felt unloved unless the attention he received was undivided. Throughout her pregnancy, Dave had cared for his wife, been extremely proud of her, but with Danny's birth the balance of Karen's attention had shifted. It had not been excessive; she had not, like some new mothers, lavished all her love on the child, but there had been times when she was tired, that she refused his advances in bed, and he had mistaken this for lack of love. He could not understand that she was able to get up in the night to feed the baby but not always able to respond to his touch.

Karen had some inkling of his feelings; she had been aware of his jealousy if she spoke to other people when they went out. She had loved him to the best of her ability but had been wise enough not to act as the dependent, or even helpless, little wife. As an only child she had been brought up to think for herself. At school she had been bright and popular and somewhere along the line had acquired a certainty about her place in the world. She knew she possessed no outstanding talents, but that she had other things to give. No matter

14

how she had tried to explain these things to Dave, to try to convince him that her loving Danny and talking to other people did not detract from what she felt for him, he seemed unable to accept it. He had accused her of not loving him any more. It was easier than asking himself some painful questions.

Eventually he had sought comfort in the arms of Julie Beechcroft, a plump, bespectacled typist he had met in the supermarket where he worked. Julie thought him wonderful; so handsome and attentive. She had gone out of her way to further the relationship. After a very short time she had allowed him to move into her flat and then made it her business to ensure his every need was catered for.

Dave felt this was exactly what his marriage had lacked. There was no doubt about Julie's feelings. If only he did not miss his son so much. Access was not the same thing as being under the same roof. However, Julie's obsession went some way towards making amends and, what was even better, he did not have to worry about anyone else chatting her up.

Plump Julie Beechcroft bolstered up Dave Wilkes' shaky ego by anticipating his every need: physically, sexually and emotionally. And, she was very good with Danny.

Late on Friday night he lay in bed cooling off after an energetic session of love-making. Julie's arm was flung heavily across his naked belly, her other arm propped up her head as she gazed down at him. Without her glasses she had a tendency to screw up her eyes. Idly, he wondered if this was a habit which might eventually irritate him.

"It's Danny's birthday soon, will you help me choose him a present?" He stared at the ceiling rather than look into her eyes.

"Of course. We can get it tomorrow, in your lunch-hour."

"No, Saturday's too busy. Monday'll do."

Julie had planned to have lunch with an old school-friend on Monday. She would cancel the arrangement. Dave's needs came first. She would also think of something nice to do with the child on Sunday afternoon. It was good practice

15

for when they had their own and he wasn't always harping on about this one.

Neither Dave nor Karen had consulted solicitors about divorce proceedings, so consequently there were no court orders for access, custody or maintenance. Even so, or perhaps it was because it was so, they had come to an amicable agreement. Their discussions usually took place in front of Dave's mother, May, who was not only sensible, practical and down to earth, but cared deeply for the three people involved.

Voluntarily, Dave gave Karen twenty-five pounds a week for Danny's upkeep. Karen refused to take a penny more because from the moment he had left, she had determined to get a job. Dave had not wanted her to work, but he was no longer in a position to voice his complaints.

He was to have Danny every Sunday afternoon, or the whole weekend if he wished. This sounded reasonable, but Karen was well aware Dave worked every Saturday and rarely took his second day off in the week, when he could have seen his son, because he was dead set on promotion from deputy, to manager of the store.

If he wanted to call in and see Danny in the evenings, that too, was all right by Karen, as long as it was before Danny's bedtime and he rang in advance to say he was coming. He would have done so more often if it were not for Julie's influence, Karen sometimes thought.

"Daddy's coming," she would tell Danny.

"Daddy." Danny always said the word solemnly, as if he was seriously thinking over the matter. To him, Daddy was someone who took him out in the pushchair or the car and gave him things to eat he didn't like very much. It was much better with his mother, or Nanny. Nanny always had chocolate buttons hidden somewhere.

"I suppose I ought to do something about a divorce," Karen said to May. "It does seem as if they're a permanent couple now."

16

May Wilkes agreed with her. "Best get it over with as quickly as possible. You've been apart, what? Bless me, it's over a year already. You're young, Karen, but time has a habit of slipping away, especially when you've got a child. Don't leave it too late; don't go spoiling your own life on account of my son. I still don't understand why it happened, really I don't." She sighed deeply. "Still, like they say, these things run in families. My old man scarpered and left me with three of them to bring up."

"I know." Karen had heard the story numerous times, especially in the early days after Dave had left. May used her own example to show her survival was possible.

Karen loved May almost as much as she loved her own mother; at times, she thought it might be more so. May was totally approachable, if a little parochial. But Karen would never dream of hurting her by saying so. Besides, who would look after Danny while she was at work if May suddenly started embarking on adult education classes or taking up judo or hang-gliding.

"What is it, dear?" May was puzzled at the sudden chuckle.

Karen was imagining May Wilkes' body, encased in her usual black, stretch trousers, her bosom like a bolster, suspended in harness, way up in the air. "I was just thinking how strange life is."

"You're right there, you are. Come on, look at the time girl. You'd better get Danny to bed and run along."

Once Danny was settled, Karen set off for the bus stop. It was getting dark earlier and earlier. She would be glad when Christmas was over and the lighter evenings returned.

"Hello, Karen," the bus driver said as he took her money. "How's the boy?"

"He's fine, thanks." She smiled to herself as she sat down. Since she had been on her own she had come to know many more people than when she had been with Dave; people like the bus driver, who was regularly on this route, to whom she would never have spoken if Dave had been with her. It made her feel alive, part of the community.

*   *   *

17

All that evening Karen was aware of Leonard Murdoch's eyes upon her. It unsettled her, but she dared not upset him; she needed to keep the job. Later, she fell into bed exhausted. Tomorrow would be better, she thought. It was "Grab a Grannie" night, as they privately called it at the club, though never in front of Leonard. A band would perform on the small stage normally reserved for the disc jockey. Now and then there was a decent singer and even the comedian could occasionally make them laugh, although the customers seemed to relish the smutty innuendos which seemed like old hat.

Saturdays at the club were so different from the rest of the week. There were quicksteps and waltzes, then, when things began to warm up, Elvis and Beatles' numbers. Saturday waitressing was kinder on the eardrums, but harder on the feet. Once people started dancing, negotiating the tables became hazardous. The drinks on Saturdays were more likely to be bottles of brown ale and large gins and tonic, the wine more overpriced than the lager. The menu offered no more than steak and scampi, gammon and chicken, all served with chips and frozen peas and a prettily carved tomato for colour. Anything better would have been wasted; it was solely to soak up the drink. Karen knew how much Trot resented having to turn out such food but he had been pushed for a job when he started at "Lenny's Place".

Karen sank down into the warmth of her double bed, Trot still in her thoughts as she drifted off to sleep.

On Saturday morning, at nine-fifteen, and almost an hour later than usual, Karen threw on jeans and a sweatshirt then, having opened the front door, went back for a jacket. Through the window it appeared the weather was grey and misty. Outside she realised that the fine drizzle had returned, the sort that clings to clothes and hair, deceptively light, but soaking you just the same. She sprinted the short distance to May's house, six doors away.

"Mummy. Cuddle." Danny held up his arms but made no effort to get up from the floor where he had been busy with plasticine, much of which was stuck to the vinyl floor-tiles.

Karen bent down and hauled him up by his armpits. He was getting very heavy. "Was he good?"

"'Course he was. Good as gold for Nanny, aren't you, pet?"

"Good as gold," Danny repeated to his mother, smiling with a beguiling innocence she sometimes suspected was false.

May patted his head. In looks he favoured his father; dark haired and pale skinned but his temperament was Karen's. Despite her auburn hair she was calm and placid.

"There's been another one," May said, shaking out the pages of the *Sun* newspaper. "Look, there's even a bit in here."

"I know. Someone told me at work last night," Karen replied. She glanced at the article over May's shoulder, catching at Danny's wrist to prevent him from tearing the paper. "It doesn't tell us anything we didn't already know."

"No. I suppose it's because he doesn't kill 'em. Different then, it'd be on the front page, along with all the gruesome details. Are you bothering to go into town this morning, dear? Look at it." May nodded towards the kitchen window. The drizzle had finally made up its mind to rain properly. "Only if you are, there's a few things you could get for me."

"Yes. Write them down, I'm sure to forget if this one distracts me." Karen was pleased to be able to do something in return for the baby-sitting, even if it meant lugging extra carrier bags back in the tray under the pushchair, or draped over the handles. May refused to accept money for having Danny so Karen had to make do with slipping in an extra twenty cigarettes or some luxury item of grocery along with May's genuine purchases.

"You shouldn't have," May always said. "You know I love having him." But it eased Karen's conscience a little, and May knew it did.

19

She picked up the short list and stuffed it into the pocket of her padded jacket. She could shop any day of the week but Karen liked Sopford on a Saturday, bustling and busy with traffic whatever the weather. It had a definite "weekend" feeling.

"Have you thought any more about what I suggested, love?"

"What, the divorce?"

"Well, yes, that too, but I meant playschool or something for Danny. Not immediately, but he'll be two next week, you'll need to get his name down."

"Yes, I hadn't forgotten."

May saw the answer for what it was, an evasion. It was all very well for Karen to want to do things right, to be with Danny during his formative years – May wished more were like her – but Danny was missing out. He had no company of his own age. There were Sandra's two, his cousins, but they were much older.

Karen pushed Danny's arms into the sleeves of his anorak, pulled up the hood and picked up the bag which contained his night-time nappies. May had gasped in astonishment when she had learned that a delivery van came every day to collect them and provide clean ones.

"It costs less than disposables," Karen had explained, "and no more than doing them yourself by the time you take everything into account. And, it's better for the environment."

"How come? Or is that just what they're telling you?"

Karen had smiled. "I can't remember all the details. Something to do with industrial machinery or something."

May would never be convinced. To her mind there was nothing better than a good boil in the Baby Burco and a nice drying wind. "Go on, off you go. I'll see you later. There's no hurry for my bits."

May shut the door and went to make herself a large pot of tea. Saturday morning was the only time she had to herself and, much as she loved her family, she looked forward to an hour or two of solitude.

*　　*　　*

Karen walked quickly, both arms around Danny and the nappy bag, protecting him as best she could from the rain. Because her head was down she almost bumped into Sue, May's next-door neighbour but one, as she stepped onto the pavement after locking the boot of her car. "Hello," she said cheerfully, "awful day, isn't it?"

Sue Trent barely nodded but her eyes softened as she looked at Danny.

Karen shrugged mentally. Everyone knew about the Trents' misfortune, but it had all happened some time ago. If Sue was ever to find happiness, Karen thought, it was time she started speaking to her neighbours, none of whom cared about her past or looked down on her, as Sue seemed to believe.

"'Morning, Karen."

She looked up again. "Colin. You haven't been there all night, have you?" Although she was a bit wary of him she tried to behave in a friendly manner. Colin Mitchell and his family were neighbours and Karen believed they should try to get on. She genuinely liked Mrs Mitchell, Colin's mother. Besides, after Sue's snub, a pleasant greeting was welcome. It occurred to her that Colin had never spoken to her when Dave had been around. How much he had influenced her life.

"All night?" Confusion caused Colin to blush. "Oh, I see what you mean." Did she know he watched her? Perhaps she was just making a joke. Roughly, he pushed back a lock of darkish hair.

Today Karen was wearing tight jeans and a short jacket. At the neck he saw the pale blue of her sweatshirt. She looked good in anything and never wore skirts up to her arse like his brothers' girlfriends. He stared at his shoes to prevent himself from staring at the outlined curves of her buttocks as she bent to put Danny on the doorstep while she got out her key. Her hair, which she mostly wore loose, was tied back today. At some unspecified time in the future he would run his hands through it. His reverie was interrupted as two bikes roared around

21

the corner and skidded to a halt a few feet away from him.

"Hi, Col, how're you doing?"

"Not bad," he replied sullenly. He hated being called Col, his name was Colin.

"Where's Mickey?"

"I dunno. Still in bed, I expect."

"Go and knock him up for us, will you. We've got plans for today."

Colin hesitated. He was not an errand boy, but he knew Darren and the other bloke were banned from entering the Mitchell household after it was discovered one or other of them had taken a fiver from his mother's purse. His brother, Mickey, was no better; he'd always been lightfingered. Hiding her purse had become second nature to Gloria Mitchell.

Karen was still on her doorstep, trying to untangle her key-ring from the cord of Danny's anorak.

"Go on, Col, fetch him for us, we haven't got all day."

Colin was slightly afraid of Darren who had once threatened to beat him up, but the threat had come to nothing. He fingered the knife in his pocket wondering if he'd ever have the nerve to say he carried one. "In a minute, Darren."

"Brave all of a sudden, aren't we? You hear that, Rob?" Darren shouted over the noise of Rob's motorbike as he performed a wheelie. "Col says he'll go in a minute. Ah, now I see it." He followed Colin's eyes. "Got the hots for her, haven't you?"

Colin was saved further embarrassment by the appearance of Mickey as he came from round the back of the house, pushing his own bike. He watched them disappear, unable to understand how they, with their weasly faces, unkempt appearance and insulting comments about, and to, females, had no trouble pulling girls, yet he could never get one at all. Not that it mattered, it was only Karen he wanted. They'd smile on the other side of their faces when he and Karen and Danny were all together as a family. How proud he'd be, pushing that pram. Perhaps it was time he said something. Watching her was lovely, but it was not enough.

He waited until Karen reappeared with the pushchair, Danny strapped into it. Once she turned down the alley which was a short cut into town, he went home.

Chapter Three

From the moment of their various conceptions the Mitchell boys were trouble. There were four of them, spaced at eighteen month intervals, and Gloria thanked God there had not been more. It was no thanks to Frank, that was for sure.

Having suffered the drunken gropings of her husband, Gloria then suffered a further nine months of discomfort which consisted of all the minor ailments associated with pregnancy. Often she wished it was something serious enough to put her in the hospital for a few weeks. There was morning sickness almost from start to finish, and heartburn and swollen ankles, high blood pressure and painful iron injections. None of these things were life-threatening although they caused misery, and none of these things were worth the end result. She was rewarded with four layabout sons, three of them still at home and, in her opinion, far too old to be there.

Dean, at twenty-four, was the oldest. At least he was married and off the premises. He was the only one in employment and she often wondered how long that would last. There must be temptation hidden in those boxes he conveyed in his long-distance lorry; things like television sets, surely asking to be nicked. Maybe his extramarital affairs were enough to keep him occupied and out of prison. Gloria knew about them; she had heard him boast to his brothers, but she kept her mouth shut. She did not want his wife and two children to be hurt, but neither could she bear the thought of the marriage disintegrating and Dean turning up on her doorstep with his suitcase.

Mickey, Colin and Spike remained at home, although more often than not Spike spent the night with some girl or other. This suited Mickey, who shared a bedroom with him. No one was sure how this arrangement came about because Colin was the middle brother of the remaining three, yet it was he, nearer in age to both of them than they were to each other, who had a room to himself. It was never admitted that they thought Colin peculiar.

Spike's name was actually Jason, but whilst still in primary school he had misguidedly believed he could jump off the flat roof housing the extension containing the boys' toilets without hurting himself. He bounced off some railings surrounding the playground, very fortunate not to have been impaled. The name had stuck. He still proudly showed his scar to anyone who was interested, adapting the story to suit the audience.

Gloria was not yet past childbearing age; perhaps not for another ten years if her own mother was anything to go by, but she was looking forward to the relief the menopause would bring. It would take some of the dread and revulsion out of Friday and Saturay nights when Frank staggered home from the pub. In the days when he was still at the factory, he and three hundred or so men, clocked off and made large inroads into their wage packet before they reached home. Unemployment had not altered him. Frank thought Gloria was unaware of how much redundancy he had been paid. She had found out from another wife but knew it was better to keep quiet.

At weekends she would lie in bed waiting for the inevitable. In summer, windows open, neighbours or a late passer-by would be the unwilling eavesdroppers on his grunting exertions as he sweated out the beer with little regard for his wife's feelings. In winter, hot-water bottle at her feet, she would have warmed the bed up. On a couple of occasions, when she had pulled her nightdress between her legs and said no, he had slapped her and forced himself inside her. It was his right, he said. Well Frank might be a pig, but so were his sons.

25

Last night had been a blessing because he'd drunk so much he'd fallen asleep on top of her. Gently she had rolled him off and fallen gratefully asleep herself.

On Saturday morning she was still in her dressing-gown as she drew the living room curtains and looked out at the dreary sky and the droplets of water collecting and swelling on the mesh fence before their weight, and gravity, made them fall. A spider's web between the dustbin and the gate seemed studded with diamonds. Gloria took pleasure from such small beauties. And then she turned her head. Down there on the corner was Colin. Whatever was the matter with the boy? "Ah, well," she sighed, "there's no point in worrying." That was a lesson she learned years ago. "None of it'll matter in a hundred years," was one of her favourite sayings.

She fried bacon and eggs and slid a piece of white, sliced bread into the pan. She was dying to know how much longer Frank's redundancy money was going to last, but did not dare ask. The landlord of The Cherry Tree must be rubbing his hands with glee at the moment. Fifty of them had been laid off, all with money to spend. And they did that all right.

She heard Frank's footsteps. It was early for him, considering how drunk he had been last night. His head and paunch both seemed to appear round the kitchen door at the same time. She turned her back so he would not see her smile. She hoped he felt as bad as he looked.

Frank sat down. He was unwashed, unshaven and clad in pyjama bottoms and a vest, the clothes in which he slept. He scratched his flabby stomach through the vest.

"Here you are." Gloria handed him a plate containing his high-cholesterol breakfast and plonked a bottle of brown sauce next to his elbow.

I've got my job, she thought, and at least the boys do chip in if I nag them enough. We'll cope, however little money he's got left. Secretly she decided to pay a visit to the DHS to see if they could do anything to help out. Frank would never get another job; you only had to look at him to know that. Besides, what difference would one more useless male make around the house?

"Dean's coming over later," she said. "It would make a change if we could all eat together."

"What's he coming here for? Can't that wife of his feed him?"

"Oh, don't be so bad-tempered, Frank, of course she can. I invited them, they're all coming. It's ages since we've seen them, and they're your grandchildren too, you know."

"Humph." Frank declined to comment further as he wiped egg yoke and brown sauce from his plate with another slice of bread taken from the packet on the table. Colin chose that moment to come in through the back door. Father and son ignored each other.

Better than a row, I suppose, Gloria silently told the soapy dishwater.

Frank took the newspaper, delivered free of charge because his wife worked at the newsagent, and went through to the living room, which was warmer now as the fire had been on for nearly an hour. He sat down and applied himself to the sports pages. Only when it was time to go to the pub would he wash and get dressed.

In the kitchen Gloria sponged down the stainless steel draining board and the chipped and scratched formica table and placed the cereal and tea packets in the standing cabinet with its pull-down flap which acted as a work surface. It was second hand when they bought it, not long after their marriage. With Frank's redundancy her hopes of anything more modern had finally vanished. "Have you eaten anything, Colin?"

Colin shook his head. "I'm not hungry."

"What're you doing today?"

"I'm not sure. I might go up the town."

"I wish you'd get a hobby or something."

"Like what?"

"I don't know. What do other people do? Watch football, anything. You must get bored."

"I don't," Colin shrugged.

Despite his lumpishness and the untidy lock of hair he was forever brushing back, and his habit of wearing his father's clothes, Colin was Gloria's favourite child. The best of a bad lot. He was less trouble, even though eleven years of the state education system had failed dismally where he was concerned. He had left school at sixteen with only the rudiments of any subject. He might be a bit simple, his mother thought, but he's the only one who hasn't brought the police to the door.

She gave one last flick with the dishcloth then slung it into the bowl under the sink before she sat down to her own breakfast, which consisted of several cups of stewed tea and as many cigarettes. Bill Haines, her boss, let her buy them two hundred at a time, at cost price. This generosity was not solely due to his knowledge of her financial predicament, but also because he had a soft spot for her. Unfortunately, his own wife also helped out in the shop so mostly he had to keep his feelings to himself.

Gloria sipped her tea and looked forward to going into town for the weekend shopping. At least it got her away from this lot. She watched the ash on the end of her cigarette grow longer and knew it was odd to find such a perverse pleasure in managing to make the money stretch far enough to feed and clothe the five of them.

When the teapot was empty she threw the leaves down the sink and left it on the draining board, ready for when she returned. She dressed then retrieved her purse from the empty soap powder container where she hid it. The last place any of her idle family would think of looking for it was anywhere connected with housework.

"I'm off now," she called out as she buttoned up her raincoat. "Back about twelve." She may as well not have bothered.

As she walked down Oakfield Road she saw Sue Trent staring out of her front window as if the rain was the most fascinating subject on earth. Gloria waved. Sue ignored her, but was given the benefit of the doubt. Perhaps she had not seen Gloria.

*   *   *

Karen was back later than she had anticipated. She had met a girl from school she had not seen for two years, and they had gone for a coffee. Maggie was married now but had no children; a pity from Danny's point of view.

"How do you cope, Karen?" she asked. "And don't you miss the sex?"

"I do, actually, but I've almost stopped missing Dave."

"Someone else?"

"Not exactly. No, not really. But there is a man I work with. His name's Trot. We haven't been out or anything, but . . ."

"But you'd go if he asked."

Karen smiled. "Yes. I can't explain it, there's something about him. I just like being in the same room. He's never said anything but, oh, I don't know."

"You don't always need words to know when something's right. Have you thought about asking him out?"

"What? You're joking. I couldn't possibly."

But as she had walked home she had thought she might, if Trot remained silent. She was sure she wasn't misreading the situation. Perhaps he was holding back because she was still married. But she was young and what she really missed was going out with people her own age, and, she had to admit it, a little romance would not come amiss. Blast him, she thought, I wish I could stop thinking about him. The job may not be ideal but seeing Trot five nights a week made it worthwhile. She would not allow herself to think she might be falling in love, yet those curious surges of euphoria ought to have told her she was.

"Bless you," May said, taking a Tesco carrier containing her groceries from Karen. "I don't think I could've faced the shops this morning. Have you got time for a cuppa?"

"Not really. I'd better get Danny something to eat. May? Are you all right?" She had just noticed her mother-in-law's pallor.

"Yes, I'm fine, just a bit tired. I'd better get moving myself, they'll be back from their swimming soon." May smiled reassuringly, her face, slightly jowled, matched her generous body. The gash of pink lipstick emphasized her paleness. "Bless me, I thought I'd turned them down." A large pan of potatoes, enough for herself, her daughter and her husband and their two children was boiling over on the stove, the gas spitting in protest.

A second saucepan containing chicken stew simmered obediently and smelled delicious, making Karen wish she had something similar for Danny. But May's house was always welcoming and warm. She enjoyed making her family comfortable. With five of them, including two ever-hungry children, there was always something cooking. No wonder she's tired, Karen thought guiltily, knowing Danny was an extra burden. It was a mixed blessing, Sandra being pregnant again because now the council would have to find them a place of their own.

She let herself into her house which was at the end of the row. It was two-bedroomed, and with Danny being of the opposite sex, she did not think the council would move her somewhere smaller.

Gloria Mitchell had offered some sound advice when Dave had left: "Look, you're in. Pay the rent and keep your nose clean and they'll leave you alone." So far this had proved to be true.

Karen grilled some fish fingers and felt another twinge of guilt as she poured hot milk and water onto instant potato powder. But Danny was grizzling and obviously starving.

When the doorbell rang she was surprised to find her father on the front step as he'd only called in to see her the previous night.

"Sorry I couldn't stop long yesterday," he said, kissing her on the cheek, "but we had that do at the Frasers'." My, my, what's all the row about?" He picked Danny up and he instantly stopped crying, smiling as the last few tears still ran down his pink cheeks.

"Do you fancy some lunch? I'm just doing it."

"No thanks . . . Karen?"

"Sorry, I was miles away."

"I could see that."

Stop it, she told herself, staring at her sheathed kitchen knives, seeing in her mind Trot wielding his amongst the stainless steel and tiles of the kitchen at the club.

"You carry on, I had a good breakfast," her father said.

They smiled at each other, sharing a small duplicity. On Saturdays, once Doreen had taken herself off to the salon, John went to the butcher on the corner and purchased sausages which he cooked, carefully washing up and leaving the windows open to get rid of the smell of frying. Karen was convinced her mother knew what went on; she didn't miss much, but allowed John to believe he was having one over on her.

John accepted a mug of instant coffee. "I'm sorry to keep on about it, love, but I do worry so about you being out late at night. I always have, but it's worse at the moment with this Carver chap about. Look, why don't you reconsider—"

"I know all the arguments, Dad, but it's no good. There's no way my coming home would work. You know what Mum's like, and it wouldn't be fair on you both having to look after Danny at night."

"It's all right for May to do it though?"

"No, it isn't. Not really. But Sandra's usually there as well and May doesn't go out in the evenings. She enjoys it. I know, you would, too, but Mum would come to resent it in the end. You know that."

John did know. When his daughter's marriage fell apart he had offered her the spare bedroom. It had never been her own room as the Turners had moved there after Karen's marriage. John let the matter rest as he leant forward to wipe a smear of tomato sauce from the corner of Danny's mouth before taking him from his high chair and placing him on his knee. He kissed the soft folds of his grandson's neck, smelling the sweetness of his skin and baby powder, wondering how long it would be before there were no signs of the innocence of babyhood.

31

Karen wiped down the table then took Danny upstairs for his nap. When she returned she made them both more coffee. Her father had already washed up the few dishes. If Karen was stubborn enough to refuse all offers of a secure home and financial help, the least he could do was provide some domestic assistance.

"Karen . . ." He hesitated. What he was about to ask was none of his business. "Is there anyone else? I mean, it's over a year now, and I just wondered, well, never mind."

Karen laughed at her father's awkwardness and kissed him. "There isn't. I don't feel the need at the moment." But that wasn't strictly true. "And it's not easy meeting new people when you've got a baby to look after and a job to hold down. And before you say anything, that's the way I like it at the moment. I'm sure you only want me to find another man so's he can make sure I get safely home at night."

"Karen!" her father exclaimed, looking hurt.

"I'm only teasing," she smiled.

"I'll always babysit, you know that. You ought to go out more. You're still so young."

"You're beginning to sound just like Mum," Karen chastised. "She thinks women can only be happy if they're married, yet she finds it perfectly acceptable if men prefer being single."

"What happened with Leonard, your boss? I thought you went out with him."

"Once. That was enough." She grimaced. "Besides, I don't think my mother would approve."

"Oh?" John was pleased to see his daughter grinning.

"Well, you know how she felt about Dave, not being good enough etc. Len's forty, and flashy. He's the only man I've actually known who really does adorn his hairy chest with a medallion."

"He doesn't!" Playing along, her father looked suitably appalled.

Karen couldn't repress a laugh, now. "Not all the time. I've never noticed it at work. But he wore it when we went out. I was quite embarrassed. Can you imagine what she'd have to say about that?"

John could indeed.

"He's not so bad," Karen continued, "quite good-hearted in a way. It's funny really, whenever I think about men now, I always imagine them in the role of Danny's father. No one seems to pass the test."

"His own didn't do that well either," her father replied, frowning.

"I know. But Dave does love him."

John knew it was time to change the topic of conversation before they started arguing in a way neither of them ever argued with Doreen. He and Karen were similar; both were stubborn and liked to make sure they got their point across. "How're the rest of the Wilkeses?" he asked, to change the subject.

"They're fine. Oh, Sandra's pregnant again which means they'll be moved up the council house waiting list a bit sharper. But, now you've asked, May didn't look all that well this morning." Karen did not voice her worry that the extra burden of Danny might be making May ill.

"I'll drop in and see her," John said. "You're mother won't be home until after six and I've nothing else to do. Funny old time of year, this."

Karen knew her father was referring to the garden and the greenhouse where he spent many happy hours. There was little to do once the bedding plants were finished, and it was too early for seeds.

"She'll like that. You know she fancies you?"

"Karen! Really!"

"Go on, you know it's true," she teased.

John Turner ran a hand through his grey hair before leaving. Karen grinned at his vanity.

Chapter Four

On Saturday mornings a teenager from the nearby comprehensive school helped out in the newsagent's. On Sundays
Bill Haines only opened until twelve and he and his wife
managed adequately which left the weekends free for Gloria
Mitchell. At one point, when she knew he was looking for
extra help, Karen had thought of working there. Danny was
smaller then and could have remained in his pram. It would
be impossible now, he was into everything. It was Gloria who
had suggested it to her.

Gloria returned from the shops before Karen although she
had seen her through the window of a coffee bar. She felt
sorry for the girl. Her own sons were a nightmare, but Dave
Wilkes had always seemed a responsible sort of boy and he
held down a good job. How he could leave someone like
Karen was beyond Gloria. She had to hand it to the girl,
she kept her chin up and got on with life. She'd like to see
her meet someone decent.

On Monday she was going to ask Bill Haines either for a
rise or an increase in hours. A rise would be better as Frank
need not know about it.

The man in question was out when she got home and she
suspected he could be found in The Cherry Tree; not that she
had any desire to find him. She simply hoped he'd remember
Dean and the family were coming over this afternoon and not
stay there all day. She was surprised when he returned a little
after two.

"No bugger there," he informed her, "none that I know,
anyway. All saving their money in case they get laid off."

Gloria refrained from pointing out that perhaps they were

wise. She made him two sausage sandwiches which he ate in front of the television, then she began preparing a proper meal. Later she wondered why she'd bothered.

Dean and his wife and children turned up almost an hour late and hardly seemed to be there five minutes before they said it was time to go.

"He might be my son," Gloria complained to Frank, "but I think it's bloody rude after all the trouble I went to."

"Just as well, love, I couldn't stand much more of those bickering kids. Miserable lot, aren't they? And did you see the looks Michelle was giving our Dean?"

Gloria had not failed to notice the hostile undercurrents and hoped it was not due to Michelle discovering what Dean got up to on his trips away. She had to admit it, it was a duty visit, one repeated as infrequently as possible. And they all knew it. Dean, having left the claustrophobic atmosphere of Oakfield Road, did not like returning to it.

"Where's the rest of them?" Frank was not really interested but liked to think he knew what his family got up to.

"Spike went to football and he's going to spend the night at Jenny's. At least he's let me know this time. Mickey's gone off on his bike with his mates."

"I'd like to know where he gets the petrol money."

Gloria did not mention Colin; it would only lead to disagreement. He was more than likely in the shopping area. He often sat there, on one of the benches along with elderly people, watching the comings and goings. There were times when he blended in so well he might have been one of them.

Frank grunted and picked up a can of beer from the floor beside his chair and drained the last few drops. "What about Colin?"

"I don't know. He said something about going into town." Gloria was on her way to the kitchen.

"Pity you don't find out. He's a dirty little pervert, if you want my opinion."

Gloria did not bother to point out that some of his father's habits left a lot to be desired.

"I'm going to the pub. Want to come?"

He always asked her on Saturdays, it was traditional to give the wife an outing at the weekend. Mostly Gloria refused, as, over the years, did other wives, foregoing the dubious pleasure of listening to their men discuss work or sport in favour of a few hours peace in front of the television or a session of bingo down at what used to be the Savoy cinema.

"Yes. After that lot I wouldn't mind a drink. Let me finish the dishes then I'll just do my face." She was already wearing her best black skirt and a fairly new jumper; black with silver appliqué flowers, which she'd got cheaply in the market and had put on especially for her son's visit. "I'll be about ten minutes."

Frank was surprised and even a little flattered that she wanted to go out with him.

"They can damn well fend for themselves," she said when she returned, ready to go. She was referring to her other sons who treated the place like an hotel because she had allowed them to from an early age. It was too late now to change things.

"You're a bit of all right, do you know that?" Frank said, eyeing her up and down. He liked women with some flesh on their bones, not these skinny types you saw in the papers and magazines. And his wife had a wonderful head of hair, still dark, almost black, and it hung thick and shiny to her shoulders. There was something of the gypsy about her, especially when she was angry. Frank was not articulate enough to put a name to the aura of sexuality she exuded, and the effect it had on him. And other men. He'd seen them looking. Pity she isn't more of a gypsy in bed, he thought, little realising that the fault lay with him.

Gloria picked up her handbag and headed for the door. She knew what to expect later, she did not need an appetizer now.

They walked the half mile to The Cherry Tree, their last car having been repossessed because they could not keep up the payments. Gloria wasn't bothered, everything she needed was within walking distance and there were plenty of buses. Frank had cursed and grumbled at the time but soon became accustomed to travelling to work on his pushbike which now sat rusting in the shed.

By the time the second martini and lemonade was in her hand Gloria was reminded anew why she rarely bothered coming out with her husband. A couple of Frank's cronies came in and when they'd finished cursing the government, the management at the factory where they once worked and their own boss in particular, the conversation turned to football. Each man considered himself an expert, quoting the various commentators without forming any opinions themselves.

"Oh, come on," Gloria interrupted, "when did any of you last go to a match? And I bet none've you have played a game in your life."

There was a stunned silence at the sheer affrontery of a woman having views, especially on such a serious subject.

"Yeah, but you don't see any female experts, do you?" one of them finally said.

"They've probably got more sense. Or better things to do." At that moment she caught Frank's eyes and decided she'd better keep quiet. He would not take kindly to her making a fool of his mates, and that's precisely what she was doing because she had more brains than all of them put together.

Frank avoided making an issue of it by ordering a round of drinks, forgetting to ask Gloria if she wanted another one.

"I think I'll go on home, Frank," she said, aware of the general relief at these words. "You can drink mine if you want." She pushed the empty glass towards him. The sarcasm was lost on him.

"All right, if you like. I'll see you later."

"Never again," she vowed as she stomped home. "Bigots and chauvinists, that's what they are." But she wasn't really sorry to be leaving. The pub was so crowded it was uncomfortable, and she liked a bit of space to enjoy a drink, not having to move out of the way every few seconds so someone could get to the bar. And since they'd started doing evening meals in there the smells of food lingered and added to the oppressive atmosphere. Much nicer to be at home. She would make a pot of tea, or maybe see if there was some of that gin left from her birthday, then she'd have a quiet cigarette in front of the telly.

Rounding the corner by the garages she thought she saw a movement under the trees. Gloria was not afraid; not of shadows or of strange men lurking in them. She paused and stared hard at where she thought she saw the movement. She must have been mistaken.

There was no moon tonight and a damp breeze moved the nearly bare branches of the trees. As they swayed they cast their shadows in the orange glow of the streetlamp. There was no one there. She crossed the road and continued confidently to her front door.

It was Karen's early weekend. She got in and immediately ran a bath, desperate to get rid of the greasy smells. All her clothes she threw into the laundry basket. It was bliss, lying up to her neck in bubbles, no Danny to interrupt her pleasure. Finally she washed her hair in the bath water and rinsed it under the shower attachment. It was still only a little after midnight. She decided to watch an hour's television, a rare treat, if there was something worth watching, that was. No work tomorrow but there was still Danny to collect, so she couldn't be too late.

She watched the second half of an old black and white film, picking up the story easily enough and enjoying it for its simplicty. If only life was really like that.

In bed she thought back over her life and wondered how she had let it go so wrong. Whatever happened, out of it all she had Danny, the most precious thing in her life. The tenderness she felt when his little arms went round her neck was indescribable.

Her earlier conversation with her father came back to her. She was almost ashamed to admit that she did need a man; not just any man to satisfy her sexual desires, but someone to love. Though she valued her freedom and independence, she had come to realise quite young in life that she was the sort of woman she had thought she despised; one who really preferred having a man about the place.

Her thoughts turned to Trot. There was something about him which turned her legs to jelly. Something which excited and attracted her; some mysterious element of danger, which made her want to reach out and touch him. Not that she ever would. Yet they hardly exchanged more than a few words on any given night. Recalling the the way his dark, springy hair curled from beneath his chef's hat and the way, when he smiled, his mouth seemed to turn up more at one corner than the other, she felt herself becoming aroused. "This will not do, Mrs Wilkes," she whispered. "He doesn't even notice you're there unless you make a mistake."

At last she fell asleep, not realising that Colin Mitchell had remained under the trees, hidden in shadow, until her bedroom light went out.

It was no longer enough. He knew that. The sexual act itself was merely a release, the real enjoyment came from the gasp of shock as he carved his initial with the point of his thin knife. If only there was some way to make that expression of disbelief and horror last longer, some way to preserve it so he could see it any time he liked.

But how could he continue without risk of being caught? So far he had been lucky. No one had been able to give any real sort of description. He had been very careful about that, knowing instinctively how to make himself blend into the background, become one of those invisible faces that people see but can never recall. The police obviously had no idea who he was. He continued to wear different clothes and never undressed fully. His face he kept averted, or even covered. The girls did not find this strange, they dealt with far more eccentric things than that. And his voice. He did not speak unless it was absolutely necessary, and then he disguised it well. It was easy for him.

It was amazing how stupid they were. The last one had

been slightly suspicious but instantly believed his story about being badly scarred in an accident, and that he couldn't bear to have people looking at his face. "That's why I have to come to girls like you," was his hardly gallant explanation. "No one else wants me."

And the police, what did they really care? They were prostitutes, worthless individuals in some people's eyes. He'd heard various comments about how they deserved it because of the way they earned their living. And he didn't really hurt them. He had been surprised to find so many in Sopford. But it was time to spread his wings, to move to Bordfield, maybe, for his night-time enterprises. It was a bigger town, more anonymous. He hoped it would work, that he could keep it under control. He didn't want it to turn out the way it had in London.

But not today. No. He had other things to see to today.

Karen spent Sunday with her parents. It was not a weekly event because she liked that time to herself, when Danny was out with his father. This week she had anticipated the traditional roast which she never bothered cooking for herself. She was disappointed. Her mother's new healthy regime ruled it out, though it was still nice to be waited on, and to eat food she had not had to cook herself.

On Monday she caught up with the housework she usually did on Sunday, then took Danny to the park. It was too cold to stay very long.

On Tuesday morning she was looking forward to going in to work that night, and knew that Trot's presence was responsible for this feeling.

"My feet are like lead," she said later to Melissa, the barmaid she was mostly paired with. "It doesn't seem to matter how many hours I work, it's only during the last one that they play up."

"Psychological," Melissa told her in a no-nonsense tone of voice. "Same with me. Have you thought any more about what I said? A girls' night out?"

"I don't know, Mel. Maybe if I can get a babysitter."

Melissa realised it was an excuse but she liked Karen a lot and thought it was time she started enjoying herself.

To Karen, the idea was tempting but she knew that although she got on well with Melissa, that they shared the same sense of humour, it was because they worked in close proximity and their jokes were peculiar to their place of work. Under other circumstances she doubted that they would have become friends.

Tonight was unusual for a Tuesday. The downstairs area had been booked by a private party. Even now Karen wasn't sure who they were, but it was along the lines of a Saturday. She watched Melissa as she went through the swing doors balancing three empty plates loaded with cutlery. She returned a second or two later bearing three full ones which she deposited on a table occupied by a trio of middle-aged businessmen. Karen smiled to herself, wondering if it was really necessary to bend quite that low. Melissa's cleavage was more than adequately obvious when she was upright. Still, the girl made no bones about the fact she was after a man. Old, young, it didn't matter, as long as he'd got a bob or two and she could give up the lousy job. Karen envied her the simplicity of her ambition. She took another order herself and went out to the kitchen.

"Two scampies, a steak, well-done, and a chicken, please, Trot." He grabbed the slip of paper on which the order was written and thrust it roughly onto one of the prongs above his head.

"Two fucking scampies," he muttered as he chucked a handful of the breaded fish into the fryer. A chicken quarter followed, into an adjoining fryer. "And one steak. Well-done, naturally." The T-bone was slapped onto the griddle where it spat and sizzled, adding more heat and grease to the already suffocating kitchen. "Morons, the lot of them. Well-done steak, indeed. Still," he turned, giving Karen that half-sneering smile she could not take her eyes off, "with the quality of meat Murdoch buys, it's probably safer well-done." With several deft movements he halved tomatoes so that they resembled small, red crowns. Karen

41

leant against the tiled wall and watched him. He fascinated her, maybe because everything about him was alien to her own background. Or so she gathered from the little he told her. Maybe he was lying. His qualifications were genuine enough. They hung in frames on the wall to remind him, he said, that he was actually a lot better than this.

"Why stay here if you hate it so much?" she asked.

His glance was scornful as he turned the steak. "No choice at the moment. Restaurants are closing down all over the place, there's no money about. And those that are secure won't risk changing their chef unless it's an emergency. It's a job, and that's the way I have to look at it for the moment. But anyone could do this, you could, even Murdoch could if he was pushed. This is shit. Being a chef is an art." He stood, hands on hips, glowering at the slab of meat. Blue jeans showed beneath his whites. His face, under the harsh fluorescent tube, was more olive than sallow, his cheeks tinged with pink from the heat. Karen had to admit she liked him, for all his feisty ways. She had heard that all chefs were temperamental, and most of them probably acted up to the image. She did not think this was so in Trot's case. She had to go back outside to see if anyone else was ready to order.

"Table eleven's ready," Trot said when she came back again, "and I was thinking, if you fancied a decent meal some evening, let me know." He turned his back so did not see the look of astonishment and pleasure on Karen's face. She felt idiotic, like a schoolgirl being asked out on her first date. But what exactly did he mean by those words? She had jumped in feet first. He might simply be meaning if she wanted a decent meal he could recommend somewhere to go.

"Yes," she said, "I, uh, where did you mean?" That was a safe enough, noncommittal response.

"My place. Let me know." And with that he handed her a couple of plates and became busy at the sink washing more tomatoes.

"To Trot's place? You must be joking," Melissa said when she told her later. "He's weird, mad as a hatter. I wouldn't risk it." That was saying something, there were few men Melissa wouldn't have taken her chances with.

Now Karen had two things to consider, two options which might lead to a more interesting life. A night out with Melissa and her friends which she knew would entail drinks and a club similar to this one, and the possibility of Karen being left on her own if Melissa succeeded in finding a suitable man, and a night in with Trot, where, no doubt, the food would be excellent, but what about the company?

She made it just in time for the bus. For the past five years there had been night buses, running through the early hours, until the day-time service started again at five-thirty. It made life so much easier.

The bus lumbered up the hill behind her just as she reached the bus stop. Melissa and Gary, the barman from upstairs, had walked her there where they waited for their own bus. Karen held out her arm. There were quite a few passengers considering the time of night and the fact that it was a working day tomorrow. "Oakfield Estate, please," she said, holding out the correct fare.

The driver indicated and pulled out, noisily changing gears as the vehicle increased speed. Karen stared at the shop windows, not wanting to think about Trot, leaving that for when she was in bed and could savour the memory. There were Christmas decorations in some of the windows and it would only be a matter of weeks before the street illuminations went up. She could hardly wait until the time when she could show them to Danny. He was old enough to appreciate them this year. She pictured his face, beaming with excitement when he saw them.

She thanked the driver and alighted at the main road. Her short route home from here was well lit and she was nowhere near as concerned as her parents about her having to walk home unaccompanied from the bus stop. The girls receiving those injuries were prostitutes. There seemed to be no exceptions, and the incidents occurred under their own roofs. But though she did not feel in any particular danger, she was wary, just as she always was if she was out alone at night.

43

"Karen?" Tonight some sixth sense told her he was there. He often was but sometimes she forgot.

"What is it, Colin? I'm very tired."

"Can I talk to you, please? Just for a minute?"

She looked at him. Sometimes he seemed every bit his age, even older, other times, like now, he was more like an adolescent. She recalled May saying he was all right, just a bit simple, but harmless, and she should know, she had known him all his life.

"Another time. I've just finished work."

"I wanted to ask if you, if you'd . . ." She waited, wishing he'd spit it out.

"What, Colin?"

"Nothing. It doesn't matter." Karen sighed and walked up the path, opening the door with the key that was always already in her hand when she got off the bus. She had no idea it had taken Colin the whole day to summon up the courage to ask her and she had deflated him with a few words.

May's right, she told herself, he's definitely not all there.

She stretched, anticipating her bed, had a quick cup of tea, an even quicker wash and cleaned her teeth, then sank gratefully under the duvet.

He tried very hard to fight against his desires, but it was to no avail. He needed to do it again. There was always a pattern, the complete calm after he'd done it then a period of normality. It did not last long. Soon the vague urge to find another girl crept upon him – he could cope with that – but it built up, getting stronger and stronger until it was no longer a question of his having any choice in the matter. Sometimes he tried to analyse it, trying to pin it down to one cause. There was no single reason, it was an accumulation of many. The desire was there again, for power, for total dominance over a woman, any woman, it didn't matter, except that prostitutes were easy. He did not have to bother courting them or talking to them and, of course, if he did so, he would be immediately recognizable. He was not aware that his actions were motivated by

44

revenge. It was a consuming fire, eating away at him, unquenchable.

Tonight there was no need to change, he was already wearing jeans and a drab, greyish bomber jacket, the uniform of thousands. His gloves were in one pocket, his knife in the other. On his head was a cap, pulled down to shadow his face – perfectly acceptable at this time of year but what was he going to do in the summer?

As he walked towards the town centre the streets were quiet. It was very late, even the clubs had closed.

Down by the railway station he found a telephone box in working order, one in which he knew he would find the cards of several girls. British Telecom cleaners removed them regularly, but the cards always reappeared.

"Katherine," he read, "Disciplinarian." She would do, any of them would have done. He dialled the number and was answered by a sleepy voice. He spoke a few, gruff words and hung up. The idea had come to him as he spoke. Disciplinarian. Perfect.

"Do you know what time it is?" she had asked, but did not turn away the business.

A taxi was out of the question so he walked. It wasn't all that far but it took ten minutes to discover which block of flats Katherine inhabited. He hoped she had not given up and gone back to bed. At last he saw a light in an upstairs window. The building seemed remarkably respectable.

There was one, wide step up to the front door. On the right was a row of buzzers, beneath each, a name. He pressed the one which displayed the girl's name. The lock was released without his identity being asked for. On the second floor one of the doors had an oval porcelain plaque bearing the name Katherine surrounded by dainty flowers. He knocked and waited, his back to the door so she would be unable to see his face through the spyhole. He had told her his name was Pete.

The door opened. "Pete?" she said.

"Yes." His voice was low, almost inaudible. "Will you do what I want?"

"Of course. It's extra."

His request was by no means unusual, except that they normally waited until they were inside.

He felt the sexual excitement mounting at the thought of this averagely attractive woman who seemed full of confidence, in his power, terrified of him, submitting to his will, just as all women should. All but one.

Katherine came back to the door and slipped the thing over his head. It had a sweetish smell, reminding him of visits to the dentist when he was a child. "You've been extremely naughty, haven't you? I'm going to have to punish you."

What she said now was irrelevant. She could not see his face, except for his eyes. He followed her inside.

"Just how naughty have you been?" She could not hear his reply, nor did she care. She was wondering how many times she had said those words, or similar, and why so many men wanted to hear them. It was, she thought, a strange way to earn a living.

He looked at her close up and saw pitted marks in her skin, old acne scars. She had not bothered disguising them with make-up for her late night caller.

"Come here," she said, "I'm going to take your clothes off, then I'm going to punish you."

"No," he grunted, sweating behind the rubber mask. Katherine thought it was part of the game. She was wearing a red, nylon negligé under which was a corset affair. She picked up a cane.

"Do as I say." She rapped him gently across the knuckles, waiting for his lead, not knowing how much pain he wanted.

"No, I said. Get undressed." She was a little surprised, most of the punters wanted her to keep some of them on. Katherine smiled and brought the cane down harder.

"Naughty boy, mustn't disobey me."

He pushed her away roughly, his hand stinging, furious that she had dared to strike him at all. She regained her balance but in doing so the arm holding the cane became

46

raised. He mistook the action and slapped her before pushing her on the bed.

Katherine's face paled, but he was undoing his zip. It was going to be all right, she knew that as soon as she saw he had an erection.

He removed none of his clothing, the metal of the opened zip scratched against her skin as he forced himself into her, her head crashing into the headboard.

How dare she, he thought. How dare she. No woman was ever going to hit him again. He slammed his body against hers, his hands around her throat. Immediately it was over he stood up, sweat pouring down his back. His hand was already in the pocket of his jacket, gripping the handle of the knife.

He saw her face, bloated with blood, discoloured, and only then did he realise she was dead. In time he stopped himself from cutting her, from leaving his mark. A wave of nausea washed over him. There was no turning back now.

He left her as she was, not even bothering to cover her half-nakedness. The rubber mask had not been necessary after all; Katherine was no longer in a position to identify him. He kept it on until he was outside the building then pulled it off, welcoming the cold, night air, gulping in lungfuls. His brain was racing. The police had no idea who he was. He did not have a record, had never been arrested. But no disguise would be necessary again, he knew that now.

The mask he placed in a black bin liner full of rubbish which lay in the alley alongside the Chinese restaurant. Some glutinous matter clung to his hand as he withdrew it. He wiped it off on a piece of newspaper. Then he went home.

Chapter Five

Dave Wilkes sat back against the pillows enjoying his breakfast in bed, a pleasure he had not indulged in with Karen since
Danny was born. He was still not sure whether his feelings
for Julie Beechcroft were comprised of sexual attraction and
companionship, as they had originally been with Karen, or
whether he was simply enjoying being spoiled.

Julie was organised and knew exactly what she wanted out
of life. Her advantage over Karen was that she never let Dave
see it. The flat was small but it would eventually be hers, the
deposit having been a combined present for her twenty-first
birthday from her parents and both sets of grandparents.
She had made it her home. There were fresh flowers and
polished surfaces and never any signs of toothpaste splashes
on the mirror over the basin in the bathroom. Of course,
there was no two-year-old to create any mess either.

At five feet, three inches she weighed ten and a half stones
but was prettily plump rather than fat. Her features and hair
were those of a Botticelli cherub, apart from the glasses. Last
week, though, she had weighed ten stone thirteen.

"This is great," Dave commented, tucking into poached
egg, bacon and tomatoes. Julie got back in beside him and
started on her own breakfast which consisted only of orange
juice and black coffee. When, the previous Sunday, she had
first set eyes on Karen she had come to an instant decision.
She would make herself as attractive as Dave's ex-wife. There
was still some way to go but she would succeed and, when she
had saved up enough, she was going to invest in some contact
lenses and they would be a slightly darker shade of blue than
her own eyes. It was only fair to Dave, after all.

It was too late now, the term had started, but after Christmas she was going to enrol in evening classes; literature, or law, maybe, something a bit up-market. Dave was so handsome and clever she was determined to make him proud of her. The only thing which flawed their relationship was having to have the boy on Sunday afternoons; it was the only day they had together. It was so boring trying to entertain him. It also meant that Dave saw Karen every week and she wasn't keen on that arrangement either. However, she wisely kept these thoughts to herself and bought a few cheap toys to keep at the flat for Danny.

"Where shall we take him today?" Julie asked.

"We might as well stay in, look at the weather."

"Oh, no, Dave, that's not fair on him. He loves going out with you. I don't suppose his mother takes him anywhere very exciting." She had no intention of amusing the child while Dave sat and watched television which was what she imagined he would do.

Dave felt a twinge of irritation on Karen's behalf. She had Danny and the house to look after and then went out to work almost every night, and he knew she took him to the park and made sure he got enough fresh air. He said nothing. He did not want an atmosphere while his son was with them. "Is there any more coffee?"

"Of course. I'll get it."

Dave picked up the paper which Julie had brought in along with his tray. He could not concentrate on the words; his head was full of Danny. He loved him so much it almost hurt, but he found when he was with Julie he was inhibited with the boy. He did not use their special babytalk for fear she'd think him silly. Of course, if Danny was with them all the time, things would be different. He knew he and Karen would get around to a divorce at some point, but now it crossed his mind that if he married Julie it might be possible, as a stable couple, to get custody of him.

He started working out the practicalities. He earned a decent salary as assistant manager in the supermarket. If he got that promotion, so much the better, and he was pretty sure he would. If Danny was with them he would no longer have to fork out twenty-five pounds a week to Karen; quite a saving. And now Danny was almost two he could go to nursery school a couple of mornings a week, so Julie could still work part-time – if she wanted to. She might be happy to stay at home and look after them both. They would be a proper family. He knew Karen had never been satisfied just being a housewife. She had said often enough that she was wasting her education. Well, this would be a chance for her to use it. Working in a nightclub serving drinks did not require qualifications. It was a wonderful idea. Karen could have her career and still see Danny at the weekends, just as he did now.

"Julie," he said, smiling, when she returned with the refilled coffee cups, "how long does it take to get a divorce?"

Her round cheeks flushed with pleasure. This was a subject she had not dared to broach fearing Dave would think her pushy. "I think, with mutual consent, it's a year. I'm not sure, mind, you'd be better asking a solicitor. Why?" She held her breath.

"I think it's time I did something about it, for Karen's sake as well as mine." He didn't really mean this; the thought of Karen with another man made his stomach twist in knots.

"Oh, Dave, that's so typical of you, always thinking of other people. Even now you're concerned about her welfare, after all she put you through. I wish more men were like you."

"Well you can't live with someone for several years then simply forget about them, and she still looks after my son." He was flattered by her remarks, and playing up to them. "Supposing I get this divorce . . ."

Julie gazed at him, hoping he could not read the eagerness in her face. When he asked her to marry him she was going to say "yes".

"It'll take time, of course, but would you mind if I applied for custody?"

She bit her lip in frustration and disappointment. That

bloody child again. "No, of course I wouldn't mind." But she did mind, very much. Still, now she thought about it, it was pie in the sky. The courts would never take the child away from its mother, or would they?

"I couldn't do it without you, we'd have to get married."

At last he'd said it. She smiled without answering, no longer wishing to give him the satisfaction of a spontaneous reply. Once Dave was hers things would be different. They would have their own children and he'd soon forget about Danny. She certainly wasn't going to give up her job to look after someone else's kid, but she was not about to disillusion him if his crazy idea gave him the impetus to go and see a solicitor.

She cleared away the breakfast things and began to prepare the vegetables for lunch. Dave liked a good Sunday roast.

The week seemed to fly by for Karen. The days were spent doing all the chores that were connected with a small boy and most days they had gone for a walk. On Friday the weather had been awful, torrential rain and thunderstorms. It was half-term, and a Walt Disney cartoon was showing at the cinema. She had taken Danny; it was his first visit. At first, he had been fascinated by everything around him and for half an hour had sat quietly watching the film. But Karen soon realised he was too young to appreciate it fully when they had to leave, because he started being noisy. Still, it had made a change and had been a new experience for him.

It was the nights now which Karen looked forward to more and more. Trot had not said anything more about the meal, but he had made it plain it was up to her to make the next move. She could feel there was a mutual attraction each time their eyes met. On Saturday, amidst the heat and the rush she said, "I'd like that meal, Trot. Our next nights off?"

"Tomorrow?"

"No, I meant the next ones. I've got to arrange a babysitter."

"Fine. Took you long enough to make up your mind. Melissa, was it?"

"Melissa?"

"She's thinks I'm crazy."

"So do I sometimes," Karen replied. Trot could look a little mad at times, especially when he wielded one of his chef's knives, but it was all part of the act, she'd decided.

By Sunday the weather had changed for the better. It was still dull but the grey clouds scudded across the sky, driven by a northerly wind. The pavements began to dry up and Karen decided she could risk washing the kitchen floor again. The sheets from her double bed and the small ones from Danny's were flapping on the line. Almost everyone in Oakfield Road had washing out. It was such a drag draping things over the bath on the frame she'd bought for that purpose.

Because she was happy with herself and the world when Len Murdoch rang just after eleven, she agreed to go for a drive to the coast with him. Only when she replaced the receiver did she wonder why she had agreed. She shrugged. Too late now. What did it matter when she had an evening with Trot to look forward to? She could not understand why she'd hesitated so long. The babysitter was a genuine excuse, but perhaps she just wanted to make sure in her own mind it would be the right move and, silly though it seemed, she wanted to get Danny's birthday over with, as if it would make a difference somehow. Perhaps it was that when Dave had left she had decided to wait eighteen months to see if he would return to her before she gave him up completely.

"Mummy doing what?" Danny demanded to know when she hung up.

"Come here, you." She picked him up and swung him round and round until he was giggling. "You're going out with Daddy this afternoon."

"Daddy."

"Daddy and Julie."

"Duey," he said, still not able to pronounce every word.

"Yes." Karen was ashamed to admit she was pleased Danny had not really taken to Julie. It was an ungenerous thought. Julie did her best; it must be difficult with someone else's child. She carried Danny to the window and pointed to the last leaves falling from the trees opposite. Beyond them was a patch of blue sky. Ah, she thought, just the person I want to see. Mary Langley was trudging up the road.

Karen rushed to the front door, knocking Danny's head on the jamb as she flung it open.

He rubbed it with the heel of his hand and screwed up his face but decided against crying when he saw Mary.

Karen called out to her.

Mary turned round and smiled. She liked Karen and she enjoyed taking little Danny out in his pram. She crossed the road and came towards them.

"Come in for a minute, it's colder than it looks out there."

Danny stretched out his arms. Mary took him and rested him easily on her well-padded hip. She was more comfortable with children than people her own age.

"Are you doing anything next Sunday night?" Karen asked. "Only I wondered if you were free to babysit?"

"I'd love to. What time?"

"I'm not sure yet. Can I let you know on Wednesday? I'll make the arrangements Tuesday night. Oh, and before I forget, it's Danny's birthday on Tuesday as well. Would you like to come round for tea? He's not having a party." Guiltily, Karen recalled May's words. She was right, it was time she let Danny have some playmates his own age. "Do you want me to speak to your mum, about Sunday? I'll make sure I'm not late, I know you'll have school the next day."

"No, she won't mind."

"Oh, bother the kitchen floor. Shall we have some coffee?" Karen couldn't understand the change in herself lately. She was on a high, the smallest things giving her pleasure. Mary's face lit up. She loved being in Karen's house and she was so easy to talk to.

What a lot we are, Karen thought to herself as she put on the kettle. Here am I, so excited about one man, accepting a ride in the car from another like I'm used to going out with men all the time, and there's poor, dear Mary looking as if she's won the pools just because I've asked her to stay for coffee. She had not given Mary a thought lately.

"Here we are. Wait, Danny." Karen placed the mugs on the coffee table, holding Danny back by the straps of his dungarees before he knocked them over. "Get his cup, would you, Mary? It's on the side."

Mary returned with orange juice in Danny's plastic cup with a lid and a spout.

"This is your last year at school, isn't it?" Karen asked her.

"Yes. I finish next September."

"Any ideas what you're going to do?"

"Not really. I'll probably work in a shop or something. But I'd really like to be a receptionist in an hotel." For Mary, it was a job high on the list of sophistication and glamour, ever since she had seen a film based in an hotel.

Karen smiled kindly. It was a shame Mary's mother didn't offer her some advice on how to dress and make the most of herself. She would never get a job where she was the first point of contact. Apart from crippling shyness she was a mess. And it was so sad because she was such a nice girl. "What about working with children? You've really got a way with them, you know."

Mary flushed with pleasure.

"Why don't you ask one of your teachers about it?"

"I will do, thanks, Karen."

If Mary looked better, Karen was sure she'd gain some confidence. Unfortunately the attitude in Oakfield Road was that if anything needed doing or fetching, Mary was the one to do it. Mary always did. It was hard not to take advantage of her sometimes.

Delighted that she was going to Danny's birthday tea and looking after him next Sunday, Mary went home and celebrated in the privacy of her bedroom by greedily stuffing down two Mars Bars.

"Who's she going out with?" Mary's mother wanted to know. "Is is a boyfriend, do you suppose? She's pretty enough, that's for sure, and she's young, and no one would blame her, not with her husband walking out like that. You stay away from men, my girl. Take my advice, most of them are no good to you at all."

Mrs Langley's advice was tactless as well as biased. No boys, let alone men, ever gave her daughter a second glance.

Sue Trent knew what was wrong with her even if her husband didn't. She was also aware that her neighbours believed her depression to stem from the time of their misfortunes, when one disaster seemed to follow another. Yes, that was part of it, but not the crux of the matter.

How could Martin possibly understand what it was like to be a woman whose own, youthful actions were responsible for her present situation; one in which she had lived a lie for years. She should have faced up to things, told him before they were married. She was beginning to believe it would have made no difference. It was too late now; he would hate her for the years of deceit.

At one time she thought that what he had done to them equalled the balance, but still she couldn't tell him. Loss of money did not compare, and he was not a criminal. Only, as he once said, in her eyes. He had thrown away everything they had materially possessed. She had thrown away more. Now they were reduced to living here, in Oakfield Road, amongst a breed of people she would never understand for their petty lives and family squabbles. She had been used to so much better. They'd tried to befriend her, she knew that, but she lived in terror that if she responded, if she returned their friendship, she would become one of them, stuck here for the rest of her life.

To add insult to injury there was Karen Wilkes, young and lovely and liked by everyone, and with the most gorgeous little boy. She, Susan Elizabeth Trent, was barren, and would remain so.

Far, far better, she'd realised too late, to have incurred her parents' wrath than undergo that backstreet abortion. But she had been only fourteen and it was a miracle they hadn't found out. She had been quite ill afterwards. It had taken all her strength, all her powers of persuasion to get the money from the man responsible. He'd tried to deny it was anything to do with him until she had said she was going to tell both his wife and the police, because she was underage. She laughed cynically when she thought of how naive she had been. She had really believed him when he had said he would leave his wife for her. She had been totally infatuated with him.

And now, here she was, a few weeks past her fortieth birthday and Martin still believing that there was time. He'd tried to convince her that lots of woman had babies at her age now, but that they mustn't leave it too much longer. If she'd told him the truth, they could have adopted. Too late for that also. They were too old and no longer had their beautiful house with everything a child could need.

Martin had been a fool. He had taken bad advice and lost everything on the stock market. He'd dealt with large sums of money at work, and once his employers had found out what had happened they had discreetly asked for his resignation. He had been too proud to argue, to explain he would not dream of taking what wasn't his. He had simply sat down and written the letter on the spot.

Sue had not got over the humiliation of his taking a job on a building site, even though the money was far more than she had anticipated. At least he was going away soon, having been offered a long contract with better pay. She could not bear to see him in those scruffy clothes each day. She slammed down the iron having finished the pile she'd managed to get dry earlier.

"Where the hell have you been?" Dave stormed towards Karen from the car where he'd been sitting, waiting. It was dark and chilly but only a few minutes after the time he'd said he'd bring Danny back. Karen froze. What right did he have to speak to her like that?

"It's none of your business. Anyway, why're you sitting out here, why didn't you wait at your mum's? You know she doesn't see you very often."

"We did go there, that's the point. I brought Danny back early because he's a bit off-colour. I think he's getting a cold."

This was news to Karen but she saw no reason why Dave should invent such a story.

"And then I discovered my mother's in hospital."

"Oh, no, Dave! What's happened?"

His expression softened. He was not angry with Karen, it was worry which made him harsh. "She's had a heart attack. I couldn't go straight there, not with Danny being like he is, and they probably wouldn't let him in anyway. There was no one else I could leave him with."

There's Julie, Karen thought, but did not say. So that explained May's complaints of tiredness lately, and her grey-ish colour. How thoughtless she had been delivering Danny there every night without even inquiring how she was.

She unclipped Danny's harness and lifted him from the car-seat. He was asleep, his face hot. "I'm sorry, Dave, really I am. I had no idea."

"No. How could you have?"

"Look, you go straight to the hospital. Oh, where's Sandra?"

"She's already there, they all are. No one could get hold of you, and me and Julie were out with Danny. Trevor waited at Mum's until he could get hold of one or other of us before he went back to the hospital."

"Go on, Dave. Go." His white face and tight jaw showed how anxious he was. "I'll ring Julie for you."

"Will you? Thanks." He kissed her on the top of her head, an automatic action once, remembered now only because of his relief.

"And give my love to May." She could not bring herself to face her worse fears, that May might already be dead.

Only as she was settling Danny in bed with hot milk and some Junior Disprin did it occur to her she would not be able to go to work. At least there was still tomorrow to sort something out. Dave was right. Danny had a temperature and was snuffling, but Karen recognized it was nothing more serious than a cold. Satisfied he was asleep she went downstairs to ring the hospital.

"Thank God," she breathed when the ward sister told her May was out of danger, but required lots of rest and must not be subjected to any kind of stress. "Is she allowed visitors?"

Karen was informed that there were already too many this evening but she could 'phone at any time. "Please give her my love," she said, "and Danny's."

The sister said she would.

Karen was restless, unable to read or watch the television, desperately trying to think how she would cope. She had not taken any holiday since she started at the club and she had been there almost a year now. She must be entitled to some even if it was very short notice.

She had gone for a drive with Leonard Murdoch that afternoon, as arranged. They had driven to the coast, and as they walked along the sand in a biting wind coming off the sea, Leonard had made it plain to Karen that he was more than a little fond of her. She had been surprised at his subtlety, expecting any approach to come in a physical form or to be put more crudely. He had not so much as tried to hold her hand. She liked him more for that. He had also, unexpectedly, made her laugh, but she was more ready to laugh lately.

She did not find him in the least attractive and knew the relationship could develop no further. But if she asked him now for a favour, so soon after their outing, would he expect something more in return?

It was impossible to ask Sandra and Trevor to help her out. Sandra had her own two to cater for, and another one on the way, and now her day would be even busier with visits to May.

She went to the telephone. Better to do it now, on Sunday, and get it over with. It gave Len a bit longer to find a replacement. She dialled the number of the club, knowing the line was automatically transferred to his home address.

"Karen, how nice." There was genuine pleasure in his voice.

It was only the second time she had spoken to him over the telephone, the first being that morning, which seemed a lifetime ago.

She explained the problem and asked if she could take the time as holiday until she found someone else to look after Danny.

"Take as long as you want, sweetheart, the job'll still be here for you whenever you want to come back. Take two weeks leave, paid, then we'll take it from there."

"Oh, Len, I'm so grateful. Thank you."

How grateful? he wondered, when they had both hung up.

Karen jumped when the doorbell rang an hour later.

It was Sandra and, drawn and pale as Dave had been, she looked very much like her brother. "She's going to be all right."

"I know, I rang, it's great, isn't it. Come on in, you look shattered. Tea? Or something stronger?"

"Something stronger. It won't hurt, I had the odd drink when I was expecting the other two."

Karen found some vodka and poured half an inch for Sandra and twice as much for herself before adding ice and tonic.

"How're you going to cope?" Sandra asked.

"That's the last thing you should be thinking of, you've got enough on your plate," Karen replied.

"Look, if it helps, you can still bring him round, only a bit later. It won't make a lot of difference; either Trevor or myself has to be there to look after our two."

"No, Sandra, no way," Karen insisted. "Besides, I've just spoken to my boss. He's given me two weeks paid holiday so I've got plenty of time to sort something out."

"But after that? Mum won't be back on her feet for ages."

"I'll take it as it comes. Something'll come up."

"If you're sure. The other thing is, it looks like we'll be moving soon . . . I'm not sure if it'll be good or bad for Mum.

59

I know we're all on top of each other, but she'll miss us, and there won't be anyone there to keep an eye on her."

"I know, but I'll still be here, and she'll get plenty of peace and quiet."

But they both knew that was not the way May Wilkes functioned. Her family was her life. It was too soon to be thinking that far ahead; they would have to wait and see what happened.

Sandra stayed another fifteen minutes and they talked of other things. Karen watched her up the road until she was safely inside her own door then locked up.

From under the trees, Colin, in turn, watched Karen.

She shivered, the evening really was cold. In the living room she turned up the gas fire and went to draw the curtains. Across the road, under the trees, she saw a movement. Colin again. With a gesture of annoyance she flung the curtains together before pouring herself another drink.

· He fingered the knife in his pocket, the familiar smoothness of the handle a comfort. He would not be able to use it again, not after Katherine, but its presence was still reassuring.

This time his satisfaction was incomplete. He had been so furious at being struck that he had missed the moment of terror that Katherine must have experienced knowing she was about to die. Next time he would savour the moment. And there would be a next time, he was certain of that.

He loathed Sundays. Dead days. But at least there was Karen, his girl. He was sure now she would be his.

That other one, Katherine, if that was her name, there had been no mention of her in the papers, but her body may not have been found yet. Better to wait, to bide his time, until he knew how the police were going to deal with it. Far better to get on with everyday life, to act as normally as possible. And if the pressure started building up he would concentrate his thoughts on Karen.

Chapter Six

Colin Mitchell was forgotten when Karen drew back the curtains in the morning. Her first concern was Danny, who was thick with cold, miserable and whining. Trying to make herself heard over the sound of his continual grizzling she rang the hospital. "Will you tell her I'll be in this afternoon if I can find someone to look after my son, please?"

The sister had kindly pointed out that the last thing May needed was a head cold.

With Danny's overheated head nestling into her neck Karen had a sudden longing to see Trot. Of all the people she knew he was the one she wanted right now. Melissa was wrong, he was not crazy, and Leonard had made a few strange comments about him yesterday. They were both wrong, she was sure of it.

She smiled to herself as she gently rocked her son who soon fell asleep again, leaning uncomfortably against her. She was the only one at work who thought Trot good-looking. It was difficult to guess at his age. On the nights when he claimed he had not slept well he could be as much as forty; other times he was almost youthful. And his accents; he was a brilliant mimic. What was it about him that made people think him strange? He was just not like most of them, that was all; he was not satisfied with second best, and to Karen's mind that was a plus point.

She desperately wanted to see May but it seemed an impossibility at the moment. Mary was back at school in the day and it seemed unfair to both her and Danny to ask her to mind him as he was.

*   *   *

Gloria Mitchell went off to work having dished up four different breakfasts. The full bit for Frank, a bacon sandwich for Spike who had put in an appearance last night and actually slept in his own bed, toast for Mickey and cereal for Colin. She had done it almost in a state of shock, without making her usual protests, amazed at them all being up before she left the house.

She was well aware it was not the sudden urge to be first in the queue at the job centre which prompted this early exodus from the bedrooms but the sound of the torrential rain which had drummed continuously on the sheet of metal which covered the shed and the wind rattling the dilapidated window frames which prevented them from sleeping late.

"'Morning, girl," Bill Haines said by way of greeting when she arrived soaking wet and bedraggled at the shop. "Kettle's on, want some tea?"

"Love some. I'm just going out the back to change my shoes." She kept a pair of low heeled black pumps there which were easier on her feet. She was more than grateful for them this morning.

Bill grinned. "Need any help?"

"You behave yourself William Haines. Your wife's upstairs."

He slapped her playfully on the behind. "What the eye doesn't see."

"Get away with you." Gloria shook her head, secretly pleased at the attention.

Bil sighed. Gloria was all woman. She might be getting on for fifty but he'd rather have her than some of the younger ones you saw going about these days. And with all that hair and those sexy eyes, she always managed to look as if she'd just got out of somebody's bed. Bill Haines wished it was his.

His own wife was scrawny now and with her complexion, should not bleach her hair. And the tongue on her, it had to be heard to be believed. How he had ever come to marry her in the first place was a mystery to him, the key to it lost in the passing of time.

Two mugs of tea in her hand, both sweetly sugared, Gloria

came out to the front of the shop. "I made it whilst I was there. Thought I'd soften you up a bit first."

"Oh, yes?"

"I need a rise, Bill, or a few more hours work. I'll do Saturdays if you like."

"I wondered when you'd ask. I saw in the paper they're laying off another ten within the next three months. Cheer up, don't look so worried, I've already given it some thought. Things aren't perfect at the moment, but I can run to another tenner, will that do you? For the same hours." He knew if Frank got to hear of his wife's increase he would demand it from her and use it as another drinking voucher.

"You're all right, you are, Bill. I really appreciate it."

"Like to show me how much?"

Gloria laughed, used to his banter. Her brain was spinning. Ten pounds a week was more than she was anticipating; it would make an awful lot of difference. She tried to imagine how it would be if they were all in work but it was too much to hope that would ever happen.

Bill went upstairs for his breakfast. He saw to the delivery of the papers then got them ready for the paper boys, set out the rest in racks and on the counters and opened the shop at seven. When Gloria came in at nine he went up for a break.

As she dusted and rearranged the shelves, more for something to do than out of necessity, Gloria's mind flitted from one thing to another, finally settling on Colin. Once or twice she had allowed herself to wonder if he was homosexual, or "gay" as they called it these days. He had never had a girl-friend. If he was, and Frank found out, all hell would be let loose. Frank had no time for anything he did not understand. On reflection she did not think so. After all, he spent all that time watching Karen. Colin was different, certainly, but not in that way. It was more likely that because he didn't possess the usual brand of Mitchell cheek he had no idea how to go about asking a girl out, and he never went anywhere where he was likely to meet any. Mind you, she thought, it would be a strange sort of girl who'd want to go out with my Colin.

63

She never said anything, but it was rather odd the way he dressed up in his father's clothes, his old cap, for instance. It was like he was trying to be an old man before his time.

At a few minutes to ten Sue Trent came in. Her car was parked right outside so she wasn't in the least wet. Not a hair out of place, as usual, Gloria noticed as Sue approached the counter.

Sue had come in to buy cigarettes. She had had to give up or cut down on everything else, this was one little luxury she was not prepared to forego. They were for later, she couldn't smoke at work. It was a comedown to have to work at all but she found she quite enjoyed helping out at the sandwich bar. Danielle, a friend, owned it, but Sue was not averse to letting customers think they were in partnership.

"Hello, dear," Gloria said, "real change in the weather again, isn't it? The usual?"

"Please."

Her taciturn manner did not faze Gloria; she carried on regardless. "Terrible about Mrs Wilkes, isn't it? I mean, she isn't very old, not much older than me." That, in itself was a frightening thought.

"Mrs Wilkes? What's happened?" It took Sue a second or two to realise she was referring to the elder Mrs Wilkes. Politeness dictated she ask; she wasn't really interested.

"Heart attack. Yesterday afternoon. They took her off to Sopford General. I thought you might have seen the ambulance."

"No. No, I didn't." Thoughts rushed through Sue's head. If May Wilkes was in hospital, who would look after Danny? If she had ever had a child, one that lived, she would never dump it on someone else at night. Sue knew this was an act of providence. "How's her daughter-in-law going to manage?" She handed over three pound coins and waited for her change.

"I don't know, I haven't had a chance to speak to her yet. Oh, excuse me, dear." Another customer was waiting to be served.

Sue drove on to work picturing how it would be. Her and

Danny. That adorable little dark haired child with his winning smile. He would come to love her, more than his own mother perhaps, and that wouldn't worry Karen, a woman content to leave him with other people. There were endless possibilities, numerous scenarios. Martin was going away. He'd be pleased she had something to occupy her; their relationship might even improve because of it. There was one drawback: Karen might not agree to it. She cursed herself for not responding to her friendly advances.

"You're looking pleased with yourself," Danielle said when Sue arrived at the sandwich bar. "I think that's the first time I've seen you really smiling."

"Really?" was all she replied as she took off her coat and replaced it with an apron.

Later that evening Martin came home exhausted and wet, despite his oilskins. "What's for dinner?" he asked, hoping the tension that was between them this morning had evaporated.

"Stew." They still called it dinner although the evening meal now consisted of only one course and there was not often any wine.

The meat was tough and the carrots not quite cooked. Sue realised it was yet another failure. Hard as she tried she was never able to produce anything halfway decent. She held back tears of disappointment. Oh, for the old days when Mrs Willoughby came in to do the cooking; when the housework was done by someone else. This house was easily small enough for her to cope with, but she hated having to do it at all. Her earlier pleasure was a thing forgotten. The habit she had acquired over the last few years of finding fault with Martin was not so easily broken. She heard herself nit-picking at everything he said.

That night they lay in bed as far apart as was possible. There was no spare room here to sleep in. Martin might talk about having a baby but how he even considered it possible when it was so long since he'd made love to her, she didn't know.

In the morning he came down to breakfast in his working

clothes; torn jeans, a thick shirt and a sloppy jumper. Sue, still in her quilted dressing gown but washed, and her short, blonde hair neatly brushed, looked away in disgust.

When he had been with his old company he had worn one of his several dark suits, always with a white shirt and a suitable tie. Now, her stomach lurched each time she saw him like this, a constant reminder of what had been but would never be again.

"No bacon?"

"No. We ran out. Scrambled eggs and toast should fill you up." Sulkily she cracked the eggs and beat them with some milk. Ironically, now they had less money, Martin ate more. When he had been deskbound he had rarely eaten breakfast; occasionally a slice of toast. He'd had to watch his diet and had played squash twice a week. Now his weight remained stable and he was far more muscular. Another irony; he was definitely more fanciable but there was hardly any sex.

She looked at him at again. Her only consolation was that none of their old friends knew what they had become reduced to. As for their present neighbours, they seemed neither to mind nor to care. Most of them were pleased if they could find work at all.

"Sue? What is it? We can't go on like this for ever. I wish you'd talk to me."

"I am talking."

"You know what I mean. I can't remember when I last saw you smile."

"Smile?" She did so then, but it was a bitter grimace, a mockery of happiness. "And what exactly have I got to smile about?" She did not want to do it; it was as if she was outside of herself, watching someone else inside her body. Why on earth couldn't she be pleasant to him?

"Lots of things."

"Name one."

"We've got a roof over our heads, our health, we're both earning, and, despite everything that's happened, we're still together. That's more than enough for most people. I do love you, you know."

"I'm not most people." Typically, she chose to ignore all the plus points, especially his last words. "And we used to have our own roof, not a rented one. I loved that house. And I hardly think mucking about with bricks or whatever you do counts as a real job, any more than my buttering bread and rolls does."

Martin, tired of trying to reason with her, was stung into retaliation. "You're hardly qualified to do anything else."

"And whose fault is that? You didn't want me to work before."

"Oh, Sue, for God's sake, leave it."

"I see. First you say you want me to talk to you, then when I do, it's, 'for God's sake leave it.'"

"That isn't what I meant," he sighed. "It's no use going over the same old ground time and time again. You've got to face it some time: that life is over, certainly for the time being. I know I'm totally to blame, but I'm doing my best to make a better life for you. This job that's coming up, for instance, do you think I want to go away and leave you? I'm only doing it for the extra money, to see if I can build up enough capital to start something of my own. Sue, you must believe I love you, I'll do anything if it'll make you happy again. All I've ever done has been for you."

She could not bear his kindness, and his love was like a reproach. "Like gambling all our possessions away?" she said, hearing herself, hating herself and wondering if the kindest thing she could do for Martin was to cut her wrists.

"Oh, Sue." Martin shook his head, unable to hide the pain in his eyes. Yes, he had been more than foolish with his investments; he had suffered too, surely Sue had had her pound of flesh; surely after all this time she could forgive him.

"It's no use, Martin, I don't think I'll ever be able to accept it."

"Look, let's see how this job goes first. Perhaps in a year or two . . ." But he saw she was no longer listening. Her mouth set in a grim line and her mood was beginning to rub off on him. At times like this he felt like laying his head in his hands and crying. "I'm going to work now."

Sue tightened the belt of her dressing gown and flicked the switch of the kettle on to make herself another coffee. As she brushed back her hair with a slender hand, Martin noticed she had had the roots redone. It seemed then, that luxuries were affordable but the padded jacket he needed for work was not.

Beyond caring now whether he hurt her or not he said, "And if it's not too much trouble, if you're not too busy at the hairdressers or wherever it is you spend our money, perhaps you'd remember to get some bacon."

"Martin, please." But it was too late. The back door banged and he was gone.

Her hand shook as she placed her mug of coffee on the table. It continued to shake as she lit a cigarette. Martin was right. This had to stop. She was slowly killing both of them.

"Trot!" Karen couldn't believe it. She had not given him her telephone number.

"I had to ring. I hope you're not busy, but Leonard told me about your mother-in-law. He said you won't be back to work for some time."

"But how? It's Monday; you haven't been in."

"I know. He rang me because I mentioned I knew someone who was looking for work. It was a couple of weeks ago, she's found something now, but he thought it was worth trying me at home. Look, this is a bit of a cheek, and I'm sure you're all fixed up, but if you'd like me to look after Danny while you go to the hospital, I'd be pleased to."

"That's great. I really am stuck at the moment. He's got a cold though, he's not the best of company."

"I'll cope. When shall I come? Anything you want me to bring?"

Karen was overwhelmed. She had been right all the time. How many other men would make such a generous offer?

"About two? That'll give me plenty of time to get there."

He had said he would be there. Only after Karen put down the 'phone did she realise she had not given him the address. Which meant he must know it. No warning bells rang. For some reason she took his knowledge for granted.

"And to think," she told Danny who managed a feeble smile, "I was just wishing he was here."

Trot arrived at five minutes to two. Karen took a step back. This was not the man she knew at work. Dressed in smart grey trousers, with a loosish cream shirt and gaberdine raincoat he looked more like a high-powered businessman than a chef.

"Hello, Karen. Ah, this is the infamous Danny." He leant towards him and smiled.

Danny squirmed in his mother's arms and hid his face in her hair.

"My usual charm doesn't seem to be working." Trot grinned. "Don't worry, we'll be all right, even if he screams."

Danny seemed content to slump against the pillows of the settee whilst Karen got ready, his thumb securely in his mouth. He eyed Trot warily. Trot sensibly ignored him. It was always better to let a child make the first advances.

Karen was not gone long. May had woken long enough to recognize her presence and to thank her for coming. She had asked after Danny and apologised for being such a nuisance. After half an hour her eyelids had drooped and Karen had known it was better for her to sleep. She had kissed May gently on the forehead, had a few words with the sister then caught the bus back.

"Was he all right?" Karen looked at her son. He, too, was asleep but he was no longer flushed.

"Just fine. He's hardly moved."

"Oh, Trot, I'm sorry, I didn't even tell you where the tea things were. Would you like some?"

"I'd prefer coffee. Shall I help?" He followed her out to the kitchen despite her protests. He noted it was clean, surfaces shiny, but as they were mostly clear, it seemed she had very few appliances.

"You look tired, Karen," he observed.

"That's because I am. Worry about May, I expect. And Danny. He's on the mend though. And I've got to find someone to look after him. I don't know where to start. I'd prefer it if it was someone I know, but if everything else fails, I'll have to go to an agency. Just when I thought I was getting my life together."

"Hey. Chin up." His voice was gentle and brought tears to her eyes. Trot saw them and put his arms around her in a way that could not be misconstrued as anything other than comfort.

"Sorry," she said, "a touch of self-pity. Not a very nice trait." She pulled away and saw to the coffee.

This was not as she imagined her first social encounter with him would be; her place instead of his, day not night and drinking instant coffee instead of eating one of Trot's specialities. It did not seem to matter; she felt more at ease in his presence than she did at work.

He did not stay long but offered to look after Danny any afternoon if she wanted to see May. He left her a scrap of paper on which was written his telephone number.

"Call me anytime," he said, "and when all this is over, we will have that meal. Bye bye, little one," he said, patting Danny on the head. He turned to Karen, touching a finger lightly to her cheek, then made his way down the road.

Chapter Seven

It was Tuesday morning, and Sue Trent had three hours to kill before she went to work. The dishes washed, she had only to make the bed. She had a desperate need to talk to someone, the sameness of every day was depressing her more and more. Her sister was her only lifeline. She rang her, knowing the children would be on their way to school.

"Come over as soon as you like, you'll have to excuse the mess, though."

Sue replaced the receiver. Jill, who had everything, was the only one who did not look down her nose at their reduced circumstances.

As Sue dressed and put on make-up, she was once more aware that all her clothes were too smart for the job she did but she might as well get the wear out of them. Money was scarce and it had been inconsiderate to spend so much at the hairdresser.

Yesterday's bitter scene seemed to have been forgotten. The grey clouds had all been dispersed by gale force winds which continued to shake and lift every object not securely nailed down. Great gusts lifted her hair and threw it forwards, over her face and her coat flapped wildly around her legs. She unlocked the car, but faltered, as another realisation dawned. She could easily get a bus, or even walk, into town each day. Martin had further to go, and left earlier, in the cold darkness of these winter mornings yet it was she who had the car. How could she be so selfish when he went out of his way to make everything all right for her? It was time to make amends.

Outside Jill's Victorian terraced house she parked without difficulty then climbed the four steps up to the front door.

Jill flung it open before she had time to ring the bell. "I saw the car," she said, kissing her sister fondly. "Come in, quick." Jill was in jeans and a T-shirt, an apron over the top. Her face was flushed and her light brown shoulder-length curls more tousled than usual. "I'm spring cleaning. Don't laugh, I always do it at the end of the summer, it makes the house more cheerful for the dark days. If this weather keeps up I can get the windows done as well. Coffee?"

Sue envied Jill her ability to chatter happily and to actually appear to be happy no matter what the circumstances. On the other hand, Jill did not comment on the lines of discontent which seemed to be more deeply etched into Sue's face each time she saw her. She knew what her sister had been through and how hard she had taken it. Her own reaction would have been different, she would have found the situation a challenge, but financial superiority had always been a big thing with Sue, stemming, she was sure, from some insecurity. Strange, really, when she had always been their parents' favourite.

Jill's kitchen was large and untidy, bearing the tell-tale signs of three rapidly growing children and two adults. It was as far removed from the designer kitchen of Sue's huge house, set in its own grounds, as anything could be, but it possessed something hers had lacked; a welcoming warmth.

Sue thought about the children: two nieces and a nephew. Despite her overwhelming desire to have a child of her own, she had never been able to relate to them. Looking back, she had never known many children and their ideas, behaviour and noise were alien to her. She looked around, trying to find a chair not containing clothes waiting to be ironed or books belonging to the children. The arched recess, far too wide for the modern electric cooker it housed, cried out for a Raeburn. Jill had laughed when Sue suggested it saying she couldn't be bothered with all that solid fuel and mess, and she was sure she'd never be able to keep the damn thing alight.

"Come on," Jill said, "we'll go through. It's warmer. Gary's given in at last and put the heating on."

The lounge was just as cluttered, crayons and books everywhere and the table beside Gary's chair contained an overflowing ashtray and a dirty cup and saucer.

"I did warn you you'd have to put up with the mess. I've started upstairs, I did two bedrooms and all the cupboards yesterday."

Sue could not imagine how anyone could live in such chaos. Jill seemed to read her mind.

"It builds up somehow, no matter what I do. I don't know, what with helping at the playgroup, the wrinklies on Wednesday afternoons, and my lot, there never seems to be enough hours in the day."

Sue watched her sister's animated face as she spoke. The words, from another mouth, might have been a complaint. In Jill's they sounded only of the enjoyment she obtained from her various deeds. Jill, four years older, looked that much Sue's junior, but she was contented, running the large house single-handed and scraping by on Gary's teaching salary and income from foreign students in the summer. The two of them had always been different, ever since childhood. Sue always wanting the best and newest of everything, Jill, quite content to go to a birthday party in one of her sister's hand-me-down dresses as long as she didn't miss out on the ice cream and jelly.

Jill realised she had babbled on enough. Sue had come here to talk. "How's it going, down at the sandwich bar?"

"All right. I don't mind it too much, actually, it's Oakfield Road I can't stand. It's all so, I don't know, claustrophobic; the people, and the house."

"Better than the flat though." Jill was referring to what amounted to no more than a bedsit that the Trents had been forced to occupy during the first year after their financial collapse.

"I'm not even sure about that any more. At least everyone kept to themselves; not in and out of each other's places all the time, and it did have some character, dreadful as it was. But the neighbours now, ugh."

Jill raised an amused eyebrow. "Are you sure? Or is it a touch of the lady muck?"

"What do you mean?"

"Come on, Sue, don't be so crabby, you know what I mean. It's just the way you are. I know you can't help it, you've always been the same."

Sue rummaged in her handbag for cigarettes and lit one quickly, the smoke disguising her blush at the discomfort of the truth of those words. Yes, you are a snob, admit it, she told herself. But Jill was the only one who could get away with telling her so. "All right. Maybe. But they're what Mother would have called common."

Jill gave a little shriek of laughter. "Honestly, Sue. Here, can I have one of those? Derek took the last packet to work. I don't know why he couldn't wait until dinner time and go and buy his own. He can't smoke in school in any case."

Sue offered the packet. "It's always been different for you, Jill."

"Different, yes, but not easy," she replied quietly, "and I'll be quite honest with you, if you don't get a grip on yourself soon you're going to end up having some sort of breakdown. Martin must have the patience of a saint. It's what? Over four years now? And don't think I don't know what's really behind all this. You still haven't told Martin, have you? Because if you did I'm quite certain he'd understand. Think about it, Sue, it would clear the air. You could make a fresh start."

"It's too late." Sue had confided in Jill one late night when they'd both had too much to drink. Despite her disapproval, Jill would not betray that confidence. She had not even told Gary, from whom she had no other secrets.

"Look, I expect adoption's out, but what about fostering? There're hundreds of kids needing a good home, wanting to be loved."

"Well, now you mention it," Sue said, with the faintest of smiles, "I've a neighbour who goes out to work and needs someone to look after her little boy."

"A neighbour? You mean one of the common ones?"

Sue smiled fully then. "All right."

"That's great, it'll get you used to the little buggers. More coffee?"

She was tempted, enjoying the gentle teasing, but she saw Jill was anxious to get on with her cleaning, so declined.

She drove into Sopford and passed the remaining hour before work window-shopping, deciding on all the small things she might be able to afford to buy Danny if she finally got to look after him.

Karen strapped Danny into his pushchair. He was bundled up against the cold and the plastic screen fastened all the way around him. Being light, it was a struggle to keep the pram on a steady course in the wind. She set off for the small parade of shops which was much nearer than the town itself. She did not want to keep Danny out too long but felt she might go mad being cooped up in the house all day.

It was Danny's second birthday. Later she would prepare his birthday tea. Dave was going to call in on his way home from work, before visiting his mother, and Sandra's two children and Mary were coming. Sandra herself would not stay long because of visiting hours and May, the one out of all of them who would have gained the most pleasure, would not be there. Feeling brave and slightly reckless Karen had rung Trot and asked if he'd like to come. To her surprise he had accepted. She had not imagined a toddler's birthday tea would have appealed.

She had not mentioned her current dilemma to Dave; she would bide her time, give herself a week to arrange something and use him as a last resort as necessary. Last night he had totally surprised her by turning up unexpectedly and offering to run her and Danny to the hospital.

"I'll sit in the waiting-room with him while you go in," he had said.

She had never known him to be so considerate. On the way back she had realised his motives. He had brought up the subject of divorce. Suddenly, with her friendship with

Trot developing, it no longer seemed like such a traumatic idea. The finality of it no longer frightened her. And this morning, coming to terms with the fact that May was going to be out of action for a long time, she had picked up last Friday's local paper and scanned the vacancies column. The alternative to leaving Danny with a stranger overnight was either to find a job with a firm who provided a creche or one where she earned enough to pay for one. May was right, it was not fair on him having no other company than a single adult's all day.

She rounded the corner and almost came to a standstill as the wind funnelled between two roads and hit her full blast. Danny's clear, plastic hood crackled and he smacked its sides in delight. Karen's knuckles, gripping the handles, were white with the effort to keep the thing upright.

"Sweeties," he said as soon as they were in the small general store.

"No, Danny, not now." She tried to feed him properly, with sweets and chocolates and biscuits only as a treat. His tea tonight would be sugar-laden.

"Me want sweeties," he insisted, louder this time. Karen knew what was coming and was almost tempted to give in. It was his birthday, after all. But if she did so now, what about the next occasion? By the time she had picked up the few items she required, Danny's noise was deafening and embarrassing. "I'm ever so sorry," she said as she paid at the till.

"Don't worry about it, dear," the woman reassured her, "it only lasts a few months, although it seems like forever at the time. He'll grow out of it."

Karen placed her purchases in the tray beneath his seat, steadying the pram with one hand as Danny held himself rigid, his face red with fury. Half way home he gave up and Karen felt herself relax, glad she had not given in. Danny, too, forgot his displeasure when he saw Mary Langley ahead of them. He shouted to her.

"No school?" Karen asked.

"Dinner time. I left a book at home."

"Is that all? You're looking very pleased with yourself."

Mary's face was split with a wide grin. "Well, not really. I've got a boyfriend," she blurted out, dying to tell someone her secret. "Only don't say anything to Mum, will you? I haven't told her yet."

"Of course I won't. That's great news. Do I know him, does he live around here?"

"No." Mary paused. "I don't think so." She had no idea where he did live. Last night he had said he couldn't walk her home because he'd made other arrangements but as she hadn't told him where she lived either, how could he be sure it was out of his way? She'd ask him this afternoon, or tomorrow. If she hadn't been so stupid as to forget her text book she might have been with him right now. She was already in trouble for not handing in homework, she dared not risk attending the class without it.

"Are you still free to babysit on Sunday?" Karen asked. Trot had insisted that she deserved some social life and that she could visit May in the afternoon. He still wanted to cook her that meal.

"Oh, yes," Mary responded eagerly. She was not allowed out at night unless her mother knew exactly where she was. Her mother had made it clear that she thought sixteen to be old enough to start thinking about boys, not fifteen, and besides, this "Carver" was still on the loose. Other girls did not seem to have the same problems; some of her classmates had had boyfriends since they were fourteen. But now Mary could truthfully tell her mother she was at Karen's on Sunday night, and then ask her boyfriend to keep her company.

"I'm seeing him on Saturday afternoon," she confided. She hoped she had not said too much. She could get away with being out then, but it was difficult to keep such wonderful news to herself. She was sorry now she'd spent her pocket money on chocolate and magazines, she could have bought some eyeshadow – to be wiped off before she got home. "I'll see you later, Karen," she said and went happily on up the road to her house.

By Sunday Danny should be completely over his cold and therefore no trouble to Mary, Karen decided.

It was good to get out of the biting wind. She lit the gas fire, hooked the large guard around it and settled Danny down on the floor with some toys. May understood Karen would not be visiting today and had said to give her grandson a big hug and lots of kisses and that when she got out she would make it up to him for not giving him a present.

Karen made coffee and gave Danny some milk to keep him occupied while she prepared their lunch: scrambled eggs and toast soldiers for him, salad and a yogurt for herself. She thought about Dave as she went through these motions. Once they were the familiar, comforting actions which had got her through the bad times; feeding Danny, bathing him, reading to him. Now they were no longer used as therapy. There were times when she still missed Dave, but they were becoming less frequent. At least she did not feel that terrible pang each time she saw him; that desire to touch him. Did love, if not reinforced, simply fade away?

She supposed he wanted to marry Julie and that was why he had eventually come round to the idea of a divorce. Julie. Karen felt sure her ex-husband had no idea what he was getting himself into. He had resented any form of independence in herself; he seemed, so far, not to have noticed that her replacement was determined to keep hers. It was easier to see from a distance, no doubt. Julie had been more than cool when she telephoned on Sunday to explain why Dave was going to be late. Karen thought she suspected she was lying, that Dave was really with her. "She can think what she likes," she told the eggs as she stirred them in the pan, "it's no longer any of my business." Life was not so bad after all.

When Danny went up for his nap she got down to buttering bread, making jellies and placing two candles in the centre of the cake. She had bought it; her own attempts at sponges were miserable affairs, heavy and sunken in the middle. Trot was probably the only one who would notice.

Danny sensed something was up the minute he woke. His

eyes lit up at the spread on the kitchen table and the two gaily wrapped packages on the work top. Karen had to stay with him in the living room, the kitchen door shut, to avoid havoc.

At four o'clock Sandra arrived with Dean and Kirsty, still in their school uniforms. Karen had brought some wine for the adults and wondered if it was too soon to open it.

"Yes, go on," Sandra encouraged, "you only live once. Are your parents coming over?"

"Later. Mum doesn't finish until six. Dad should be here a bit earlier." She hoped that her mother would not embarrass everyone by buying some extravagant toy. Her father would know better than to do so.

Sandra and Karen sipped their wine while Kirsty, the elder of the two, lugged Danny up to his bedroom to play. Dean, at eight, only wanted to watch the television but was firmly told by his mother that he couldn't. With a long face he joined the others upstairs. A few minutes later Mary Langley arrived and almost died with pleasure when Karen asked if she, too, would like some wine. She accepted and sat, feeling very grown up, talking about children and the news which no one could forget for long. She blushed when she said the word prostitute. And then, at five, Trot appeared, carrying a parcel wrapped in brown paper.

"This is for the birthday boy," he said, handing it to Karen. "Where is he?" The house was remarkably quiet.

"Upstairs with his cousins. What is it?"

"Ah, ah. Wait and see."

"Come in. Trot, this is my sister-in-law, Sandra. Sandra, Trot."

"So you're the crazy chef?"

Trot glanced at Karen, a mischievous question in his expression. Within minutes he had them laughing, imitating all the chefs and commis chefs with whom he had worked. It was at that moment that Dave arrived and found them doubled up.

"Who's this?" he asked, rather rudely as Karen tried to pull herself together. Dave had never liked it in the past when his wife and sister got a fit of the giggles. He always felt it was at his expense.

"I'm sorry, Dave, this is Trot. I work with him."

Trot stood up and extended his hand. Dave had no option but to take it. "Trot? Funny sort of name."

"Carl Pearson, actually. Trot's a nickname I acquired years ago. It seems to have stuck." He had already explained to Karen that it was earned in his days as a catering student, when his political tendencies had leaned that way. "Before," he added, mocking himself, "I turned to Marxism, communism and every other ism and finally became resigned to the British three party system."

Nevertheless, Karen thought the name suited him. He did look rather foreign and mysterious; he merited a name to match his appearance.

Dave accepted one glass of wine but said he was driving.

"Are you going to have some tea with us?" Karen asked. This had been his original intention, but the look on his face suggested he had changed his mind.

"No. I've got things to do. Where's my boy? He's awfully quiet."

The "my boy", Karen knew, was for Trot's benefit. "Upstairs."

"Can he have my present now or do you want to give them to him all at once?"

"Now's fine." It would be unfair to deprive him of seeing Danny open it. "Come on up." She led the way upstairs, still finding it strange that he had to wait for an invitation in what had once been his own home.

The three children were sitting on the floor, Danny draped over Kirsty's legs as she read him a story. Dean was making something out of pieces of Lego.

Danny only acknowledged his father's presence when he handed him the package. He ripped open the paper with great excitement. Inside was a giant book of well-known children's stories, some crayons guaranteed not to leave stains and a brightly coloured clock in unbreakable plastic, whose hands could be easily rearranged by those of a small child.

Immediately Karen knew the gifts had been chosen by Julie. Dave would have opted for a huge cuddly toy or something extravagant but unsuitable, not these aids to education. She was hurt, and what caused the most pain was they were exactly the sort of things she preferred him to have. She left Dave with their son and went back down to entertain her guests.

They started on a second bottle of wine. "I mustn't, Karen, really," Sandra said. "Whatever will the nurses think if I turn up half-cut? And the baby."

Dave was on his way out when John Turner arrived. They greeted each other cordially, shook hands and made a few comments about the weather then Dave explained he must go and see his mother. Once he had left they settled down to enjoy themselves.

Doreen arrived at a quarter past six and more drinks and the food was distributed. Danny, in his highchair, was soon sticky but happy. The presents were admired and played with then suddenly, as everyone departed, the house seemed emptier than ever.

Karen bathed Danny and washed the jam out of his hair. When she finally got him settled a feeling of anticlimax took hold. It had gone well, she knew that, and everyone had had a genuine reason for having to leave early. She just wished one of them had been able to stay. Still, it was nice seeing Mary flushed with pleasure and hoped she would not be in trouble with her parents for having had two glasses of wine.

Chapter Eight

Karen was sitting quietly, thinking over the day's events and how Sandra had brought up Colin Mitchell's name, saying that everyone knew he fancied her, that the only reason he hung around on the corner was to catch a glimpse of her. Karen had laughed at the idea, but secretly, it worried her. It was this which caused her to jump when the doorbell rang a little after nine.

There, on the doorstep, was Sue Trent. Karen was so surprised she was unable to speak.

"I'm sorry to bother you so late, but I just wanted to tell you I'm sorry about your mother-in-law."

"I, uh, well, thank you." Karen hesitated for only a second before she said, "Come in, why don't you?"

Sue did so, brushing her hair back with her habitual gesture. She was not sure what she had expected, but certainly not a room so clean and cosy.

"Sit down, please. Would you like a cup of something? Or a glass of wine?" There was half a bottle left. Karen saw she was nervous, her hands were clasped tightly together around her knees.

"No. Thank you. I can't stay long." It had taken more courage than she knew she possessed to come at all. "It's just, well I don't want to interfere or anything, but I wondered if you'd found anyone to look after your little boy yet."

"No, I haven't," Karen replied, rather surprised at Sue's interest. "It's quite a problem actually. To be honest, I haven't had a chance to give it much thought. It was his birthday today." Karen still couldn't decide why she had come.

"Well, if you're stuck, I'll do it."

"You!" She hadn't meant to sound so rude but she was completely taken by surprise.

"Yes. You see, Martin, my husband, is going away on a job, and I don't go out in the evenings anyway."

"It's very kind of you to offer, Sue, but—"

"I don't expect any payment," Sue said quickly. Karen must think her mad. She had not meant to blurt everything out so suddenly.

Karen, on the other hand had not thought that far ahead. But she had heard all the rumours about the Trents' past; how they'd lost everything.

"I love children, you see, and it would give me something to do. I'd look after him as if he was my own."

Karen thought she did see, now. The Trents had no children of their own. Perhaps this was another reason for Sue's bitterness. But what could she say? She hardly knew the woman. But the temptation was there. "I couldn't let you do it for nothing. It's not fair to you. What did you have in mind, anyway? Coming here until I get home?"

"I thought perhaps the same arrangement as you had with Mrs Wilkes. He could sleep at my house."

Karen bit her lip. She did not like the idea of Danny staying with a virtual stranger. But then, she was missing work, missing Melissa's bawdy humour and seeing Trot almost every night. She even missed the customers who, however inane their conversation, were at least other adults to talk to. "All right," she said, making a snap decision, "I'll give it a try. We must have an agreement on a trial basis, though. It's not fair to anyone otherwise. You might find you can't cope—"

"Oh, I'll cope, please don't worry about that." It was the first time Karen had seen Sue Trent smile. She seemed genuinely pleased.

"All right. I'll ring my employer tomorrow and see when he wants me back. He's got a temp in at the moment, and I don't suppose they can let her go on the spot. I'll let you know as soon as I find out."

"Thanks, Karen. This is just what I need, you know."

Karen saw her out and decided she couldn't wait until the next day. She rang Leonard Murdoch at the club.

Oakfield Road, in term time, was blessed with six or seven quiet hours. The shrill shouts of children were confined to the school playground some distance away, and the risk of injury from cyclists and and careless skateboard riders was greatly reduced.

On fine mornings housewives gossiped as they hung out washing or shared pots of tea. At this time of year, after several weeks of torrential rain and now, easterly gales, it was even quieter. No one ventured out if it could be avoided. Occasionally a wrapped up, hooded figure hurried to the bus stop. Soggy leaves and bits of rubbish gathered in the alley alongside Karen's house. Not even Colin Mitchell braved the elements, but spent a fair bit of time indoors watching television with his father.

By Thursday, Danny was over his cold and Karen was looking forward to returning to work. Sandra collected her in her car, saying she was going to continue driving until she was too large to fit behind the wheel.

"That Trot, are you serious about him?"

"Hardly. I've only seen him twice, apart from work. Why?"

"I don't know. There's something about him."

"I thought you liked him. He had you in stitches."

"Yes. He did. I can't explain it, but I just felt maybe it was all an act. Be careful, Karen, that's all," Sandra said worriedly.

Karen tried to laugh it off but found it harder than she would have liked. "Well, I'm going to his flat on Sunday. He's cooking me a meal."

Sandra took a quick sideways glance at her sister-in-law then stared back at the road. "At least I know where you'll be."

"Whatever's that supposed to mean?"

"Nothing, Karen, I'm sorry. I'm just a bit edgy. I always am when I'm pregnant."

Karen patted her arm. She loved Sandra dearly, for all her slapdash ways, her mostly scruffy appearance and her dark brown hair which even now she wore in the same style as when she was at school, the fringe cut straight across her forehead, the rest in a ponytail held with an elastic band.

May was making rapid progress and was pleased to see them both, and Danny, who was now allowed into the ward. She had heard about the divorce, Dave having mentioned it. "I suppose he's going to marry that trollop," she said, a comment which caused much amusement.

A more trollop-like person than Julie, Karen could not imagine.

"And your dear father came to see me last night," May continued to Karen. "Look what he brought me." She produced a book of cartoons, some of which were vaguely obscene; not something he would have taken to Doreen were she in hospital. "He cheered me up no end."

On hearing that Sue Trent was going to be Danny's new babysitter, May could hardly believe it. "Perhaps she's human after all. Well, as long as you're happy with it and Danny's well looked after, that's all that matters."

They left May soon afterwards and made their way back to Karen's. As they rounded the corner into Oakfield Road Sandra said, "Surprise, surprise, there's your boyfriend." On the corner, blue with cold, stood Colin Mitchell.

THE SOPFORD MAIL
PROSTITUTE FOUND DEAD

Police are investigating the suspicious death of Katherine Vera Bishop, aged 26, whose body was discovered in her flat in Grenadier Gardens two days ago by a neighbour. It appears Miss Bishop has no known relatives in this country and the public are requested to come forward if they know of any. Neighbours say the victim was quiet and polite and they were not aware of her profession. Bishop was known to the police but has never been arrested. Details of how she died have not yet been released.

Mr David Stonehouse, a police expert in psychological disorders, has suggested that the man responsible for the spate of recent attacks on prostitutes in the area, now referred to as The Carver, may be responsible – now needing to kill these women in order to gain the satisfaction he is seeking. As there was no injury to Miss Bishop's forehead, Mr Stonehouse stresses this is only a theory, but one upon which the police are basing their investigation.

Continued on page 4

"Good heavens, John, look at this."

John Turner neatly sliced the top off his second boiled egg and watched the steam rise, grateful that muesli was out of fashion this week. The granary bread he could cope with. "What is it, dear? Another of those 'Carver' reports?"

"Worse than that. He's started killing them."

"Oh?" John knew well enough his wife's tendency to exaggeration. "Them" probably meant one, and the killer might not be the same person as the one who had done the "carvings".

"Shall I read it to you?"

He nodded. She would do so anyway. Doreen turned over to page four but was disappointed in that it had nothing more to say than in previous weeks. There was only more speculation and more appeals to the public for both help and vigilance. He let her finish the article but his mind was on Karen. He was so close to her, he could not bear the thought of anything happening to her. He had been extremely sorry to hear about May's illness; she was one of his favourite people, but if it had meant Karen had had to give up that job, there would have been some good in it. He had been very disappointed when Karen had rung last night to say she'd found a replacement sitter.

He had hoped for so much for his daughter, but over all he

86

wanted her happiness. Her marriage had not worked out and his feelings about the impending divorce were ambiguous. At the time of Karen's marriage he said that if Dave Wilkes was the man for her, that was all right by him, although he thought Dave a little immature. Marriage and fatherhood had not, as he had hoped it might, altered that fact.

For once on the same wavelength as her husband, Doreen almost voiced John's thoughts. "It's daft, isn't it, but I still worry about Karen even now she's a grown woman. I suppose I always will. I said at the time, didn't I, that that marriage wouldn't last."

It was true, John could not deny it.

"Still, she's going to dinner with some young man on Sunday. I'm a great believer in arranged marriages myself," Doreen said apropos of nothing and causing John to drop his toast on the plate. It was the first time in almost thirty years he had ever heard her mention the subject. It left him wondering who Doreen's parents would have chosen for her. Not him, certainly.

"Parents can see more clearly, John, they'd be able to pick someone from a similar background. I still say she should have married that nice boy from the building society. What was his name, now? Raymond, wasn't it?"

"Um, I think so." He saw it now. The generalisation was no such thing, Doreen only meant arranging Karen's marriage. To get her off the touchy subject he asked if there was any chance of more toast.

"You know where the toaster is," Doreen reproved. She was a career woman and a great believer in equality.

John, on the other hand, knew he was on a losing wicket before he asked, but he liked to put up the occasional show of male dominance.

He realised all their serious conversations were conducted over the breakfast table. Since his wife's business venture had taken off, their evenings were spent jointly preparing a meal and washing up, both of them too tired to discuss anything with enthusiasm whilst they ate. John then slumped in front of the television or read. He'd never been much of a pub man or he might have escaped most evenings. He was content to go along with Doreen's social engagements and to sip the odd drop of Scotch at home while she shut herself in the spare room and did her books.

"I suppose," he said when he returned with a slice of darkly browned toast, and picked up the newspaper report, "that it's one of the risks of being on the game, or whatever euphemism they call it these days. They must get all sorts."

"I suppose so. Still, they don't have to do it."

John tried to imagine what it was like to pay a woman to do anything you wanted. He would not have the nerve to do so himself and suspected this fictitious woman would find his demands very tame. But after Doreen – no, he pushed the disloyal thought away before buttering the toast and pouring another cup of tea.

Doreen, now in the kitchen marinading a large piece of lamb, in turn, wondered what it was like to sell one's body. Such things fascinated her, although she knew how shocked John would be if she said so. Deep down there was a longing to be more adventurous, less inhibited. What stopped her was the fear of being thought unladylike; that John might be disgusted. It was too late to change now.

John carried the remains of the dirty dishes through to the kitchen and sighed when he saw the size of the piece of meat. It could mean only one thing: they had guests for dinner.

He had read the article and knew his luck was in. There were no relatives to make a fuss; to ensure the police kept looking. If they didn't find a culprit soon, they would quickly get tired of looking. But he would let the news die down before he struck again. Each time was better. Each time the mixture of love and rage and violence he felt against the only woman ever to have mattered to him came to a head and was dissipated. Of course, it always built up again. He was certain she knew, not by anything she said, but by a particular look she gave him, a knowing look, followed by a sigh. And if she did know, she would never tell him; she was far too clever for that. He was sure she knew about the knife, though.

She always said he had his father's blood in him and that she had fought against it. She was the one to make sure the police never came knocking on their door.

Cocky now, positive he would not be caught, he was almost tempted to tell her, to boast of his conquests, for that was how he saw them; even threaten to give himself up so he could see the pain in her eyes. It would only be a fraction of the pain she'd caused him.

Carl Pearson, or Trot, had been aware for some time that his feelings for Karen were getting stronger. He wanted her. As much as he hated "Lenny's Place", being at work was a pleasure when Karen was around – yet there was something which prevented him from asking her outright to go out with him – a barrier he was gradually breaking down. He sensed she was terrified of being hurt again, yet instinct told him it was not in vain to persist, that she wanted him to break through that reserve. He had come to love her, to feel happy when she smiled, useless when her eyes were veiled with sadness, although that happened less now than when she had first come to work at the club, over a year ago.

Now, Carl felt again that heartstopping, dry-mouthed sensation he had experienced once before, with Lizzie, whom he had nearly married.

The club was filling up. Burgers and hot dogs did not stretch his talents. He picked up the long, sharp blade and shredded an iceberg lettuce. Murdoch insisted they copy the American idea, more classy, he said, and put lettuce, tomato and gherkin in the burgers. The customers here were no gourmets. The first thing they did was to remove these extras, the only bits that had any nutritional value.

Trot looked at the knife in his hand. There were times when he felt like sinking it up to the hilt in Leonard Murdoch's paunch. Then he thought of Karen and the anger was assuaged as an idea occurred to him; the perfect way to show her that he cared.

Karen finally picked up the 'phone and made an appointment

to see a solicitor. The prospect of being with Trot decided the issue. She found one who would give her a five pounds, fixed fee interview. She sat nervously in the reception area and prayed that Danny would behave. When she was shown in it was not the ordeal she had anticipated. The solicitor reminded her of her father, and was kind. As they had no joint property except the furniture, and as it was Dave who had initiated the proceedings and was unlikely to quibble – Karen knew May would not allow it – it all seemed very straightforward. She returned home feeling quite lightheaded.

Sandra called in, at first deliriously happy, then suddenly bursting into tears. She had had confirmation they were being rehoused. "I'm sorry, Karen, it's just after all this waiting. And Mum, it'll be a relief to her in a way, but I keep thinking they won't let her keep her house – it's too big for one person."

This had crossed Karen's mind. May's whole life was based in Oakfield Road. Would she ever adapt to somewhere new, especially after being so ill?

There was no point in worrying over imponderables. Karen said she'd been to see a solicitor. Before she could give the details, she heard a thud from upstairs. "That's Danny, I'll get him down. He doesn't sleep very long in the afternoons, do you think I should forget his nap?"

"He'll let you know soon enough when he doesn't want to go down. Keep it up as long as you can, believe me, it's a long day otherwise."

"Put the kettle on if you're staying."

"A quick one, the kids'll be home soon."

Karen placed Danny on the floor, his cheeks warm and pink with sleep. Gradually he came round. "Sandwa," he said, patting her knee. Then, "Juice for Danny" as he heard his mother in the kitchen. "Please," both Sandra and Karen said automatically and in unison.

"I know who Trot reminds me of," Sandra declared when Karen mentioned her meal with him, "a young version of Lech Walesa. He's got the same intensity in his face, and the same shaped face, come to that. Is he for-eign?"

"Not unless you count Derbyshire as foreign. No accent though, too busy copying everyone else's I suppose."

"You've got that look on your face."

"What look?"

"The same one you get when you think Danny's done something clever. You can't fool me, Mrs Wilkes. I can't see you taking Leonard Murdoch's offers up any more if this is the way you feel."

"Oh, honestly, Sandra." Karen bit her lip. As she uttered those three words she sounded exactly like her mother.

"What on earth have you got that thing on for?" Gloria wanted to know as Colin headed for the door. She was still clearing up after the evening meal. Colin had not mentioned he was going out.

"It's cold."

"Why go out, then? It's lovely and warm in here. Why do you spend so much time out there, it's not like you're doing anything important?"

"I am."

"Here," Frank said, joining them in the hallway, "what's going on? And that's my cap you've got on. Give it to me, I might need it later. I don't understand that boy," he added to Gloria, "what's he want to be wearing a cap for at his age? And while we're at it, where's my tweed jacket? It's the only bloody decent thing I've got to wear."

"Leave it, Frank, he's not doing any harm. He'll look after it. Besides, when did you last put on a collar and tie?"

"That's not the point." He turned to Colin. "You make sure that jacket's back in the cupboard tonight, do you understand? Or I'll give you something you won't forget in a hurry."

Colin did not respond. It was an idle threat. Frank was a bully and a coward. Colin knew he'd slapped his mother once or twice, and themselves, many times, as children, but now they were all bigger than him he would not have dared.

91

"Go on." Gloria gave Colin a push towards the kitchen and the back door. "What time are you going out, Frank?" she inquired to distract him from the fact that his son had disappeared.

"I didn't say I was going out, did I? I said I might."

But she knew he would. Since he had received his redundancy money he spent most of the day at home then went to the pub in the evening. She could understand it in a way. He must be bored silly. Nevertheless, she had hidden her first extra ten pounds from Bill Haines and tomorrow she was going to open a savings account at the Post Office. God help her if Frank ever found the book.

Gloria was no expert on matters of the mind, nor was she articulate enough to express her thoughts in even pseudo-psychological terms, but she believed she had an inkling why Colin borrowed his father's clothes. She guessed it made him feel better in some way, older, and less shy, as if by wearing another person's things he would acquire some of their personality, although God knows why he should want to be like his father. He did look older, there was no question about that, as he mooched down the road, especially since he had gained some weight. He liked his food but did not get enough exercise to work it off. Already he was developing a slight paunch. Still, the boy was doing no harm, why worry about it?

Colin reached the corner of Oakfield Road and paused, feeling a pang of disappointment when he saw Karen's curtains were drawn. Sometimes she left them open until long after dark. He turned left, into the alley. He wondered if there was someone in there with Karen. He'd seen that flashy man pull up in a big car last Sunday and he'd taken an instant dislike to him, and not just because he was in Karen's company.

Friday night and Sopford was busy. He liked it best then, trying to imagine where all those people were heading, giving them destinations and lifestyles of his own. He had some money in his pocket. Tonight, feeling confident, he was going to find a pub and have a drink. Not like Spike and

Mickey; he didn't want to be swilling lager down his throat for hours, out of the bottle too. He'd tried it once and found he couldn't swallow it properly, either none came out or it gushed, choking him. He was better than that. He was going to order a single whisky and put water in it to make it last. Whisky was a man's drink, and if he was to deserve Karen, he must be a man. He caught sight of himself in a shop window. At least he looked the part.

The Bird in Hand in Halcyon Road had half-curtains hanging on wooden rods. The windows were latticed and there were window boxes, although they only held some ivy and a couple of miniature firs at this time of year. The paintwork was clean and, from outside, he couldn't hear any noisy music. He hated rough places.

It was very busy. The male customers all seemed to be wearing suits and the women were smartly dressed. He guessed they were office workers on their way home from work and wondered how they could wait until eight or nine in the evening before they had their tea.

There were carpets on the floor and plenty of ashtrays. There was no chance of running into any of his brothers here. An extractor was efficiently dispersing the smoke. Colin hated smoking and was glad Karen didn't smoke. He squinted at the price list on the wooden panel at the side of the bar and as he turned back to be served, noticed fluorescent pink stickers attached to several of the optics. It seemed that the cheaper brands of whisky, gin and vodka were only one pound fifty for a double. He ordered one of the special offer Scotches and took a sip. There was nowhere to sit so he remained awkwardly at the bar, not liking to be in such a prominent place. He watched the animated faces as they wound down after work and got ready for the weekend. He was the only person on his own.

A large group who appeared to be celebrating some sort of deal, the details of which he could not make head nor tail of, suddenly drank up as they decided to go elsewhere. This gave him room to edge away from the bar. He liked to be as inconspicuous as possible. Pushing through the crowd he got to the corner and found it was no better. He was almost wedged behind the door. Once, it swung open so abruptly he had to step back to avoid being hit but banged his head on the coathooks behind him instead. It was then the idea came to him. He couldn't help it, perhaps it was the whisky; he wasn't used to it, but he knew he was going to walk out with one of those coats. He glanced around, trying to guess to whom it belonged. There was no way he could have known but chose to believe it was the tall, broad-shouldered man in the pinstripe suit who was ordering a round of drinks with total confidence. Colin placed his empty glass on the narrow shelf which ran around the whole of the bar and very casually picked up the greenish-grey raincoat. Knowing he was one of those people no one looked at twice, he walked out without a backward glance. Only in the fresh air did he realise the enormity of what he had done. He was a thief. He tried to walk nonchalantly, waiting for a shout or a hand on his shoulder. He would say he was mistaken, he thought it to be his own, but nothing happened. He wanted to put it on there and then but it was too soon; it would have to wait until tomorrow. And he could return his father's jacket.

Suddenly alarmed, he stopped in the alley before he reached home. The pockets might contain money or credit cards or something important enough for the owner to call the police. He checked and sighed with relief when all he found were some tissues, which he threw into the bushes, several paperclips made into a chain, a box of matches and a couple of business cards. The raincoat was smart, but not new. It was doubtful the owner would bother the police. They'd probably laugh if he did.

Colin knew he must hide the thing before his parents saw it. His mother would be heartbroken if she thought he was turning out like the rest of them. But this was different really.

For tonight the raincoat would remain at the back of his wardrobe. Tomorrow he'd find a safer place to keep it, out in the shed.

He lay on his bed dreaming about when he would wear

it, how he would become like that businessman, how Karen would admire and look up to him. His hand strayed to his crotch as he thought about her. "No," he told himself, "not here." He dare not under his parents' roof.

Thinking of Karen seemed to clear his brain. He had a better idea. There was no need to hide the raincoat; it obviously wasn't new. He'd tell his mother he got it in the Oxfam shop. It was a good omen. Soon Karen would be his.

Chapter Nine

It was very late, well into the small hours, when he knew he had to get out for some air. Through the window the moon was large and round, only an occasional cloud obscuring it. It wasn't raining but he still thought he'd wear his raincoat. It was a little on the large side, but that was the fashion.

He tried not to let it show but his self-image was poor. When he saw his reflection in shop windows he was always surprised to find himself taller than he imagined and more filled out. As a child he had been shouted at, chastised and belted for the smallest misdemeanour. He had been brought up to believe he would never be as good as anyone else. He would be, though. One day he'd show them all. Look at what he'd achieved so far without being caught.

He pulled up the collar. So much for his amateur weather-forecasting, the raincoat was necessary after all. He'd only been out five minutes when the fast-moving clouds drew together, banking up and blocking out the moon until they formed a threatening umbrella. By the time he reached the shopping centre raindrops were dancing like clusters of jewels beneath the streetlights. There was no one in the street but himself and a solitary dog which cocked its leg against the rear tyre of a car, scratched contentedly then proceeded on its way with a quiet dignity and a sense of purpose which was almost human.

Reggae music thumped steadily from an unknown source. No lights showed from above any of the shops. Wherever the party was, the neighbours couldn't have been very happy.

He reached the part of the town where all the chain stores and supermarkets were before there was any other sign of life. He heard voices, coming nearer. A man and a woman were arguing in a desultory manner.

"Forget it," she said, "it doesn't matter. Anyway, whatever you say, I heard you ask for her 'phone number."

"For God's sake, Sheila, I did no such thing. Why would I go and do that?"

"Look, just shut up about it, will you? I wish we'd never gone to that sodding party." She stopped on realising the man approaching could hear. She didn't want to wash her dirty laundry in public.

He nodded at the couple who stared back but walked on without acknowledging him.

He had been seen. He would certainly be remembered, if not recognized, if anyone was asked. It was no longer safe.

He waited, sitting on the low, brick wall that surrounded the trolley area of Sainsbury's. He would look even more suspicious if he started walking back in their direction, they might even think he was following them. He thought about Katherine, her body discovered only because a neighbour wanted to borrow something. Her age was given as twenty-six. He had thought her older. Perhaps he had done her a favour. Twenty-six, old before her time, missed by no one. It was not much of a life to lose. He wanted to do it again. His nerves were stretched like harp strings.

He waited, still seated on the wall, but his frustration mounted, mixed with anger. He picked up a milk bottle which lay against the side of the bus shelter and hurled it at Sainsbury's window. The bottle shattered and shards of glass tinkled to the pavement. The reinforced window stayed intact. His frustration refused to go away.

Sue Trent lay in bed next to Martin. It was his last night at home. Tomorrow he would set off for his new job, the contract for which was six months, possibly longer if it was not finished by then. He would come home on some of the weekends, but not many, because of the expense.

They had made love, both feeling obliged to, but it was not a very satisfactory experience for either of them. All Sue could think about was Danny and how it was going to be. It was on a trial basis, but she would make sure it worked. Only a couple of days to wait now. She was not sure why she hadn't mentioned it to Martin.

She rolled over and felt the heat radiating from her husband's body and pictured his sad expression after they had finished making love. Guilt churned at her stomach. Why was it so easy to love him when he wasn't there but as soon as he was in the same room she became cold and unresponsive? She put an arm around him and was gratified by the way he moved back towards her in response, even though he was asleep.

Sunday afternoon and the whole family were gathered around May Wilkes's bed. She was regal and smiling in her salmon pink, frilly nightdress, a present from Sandra, and Danny was allowed to sit on the bed as long as he kept still. He wrinkled his nose at the strange hospital smells and ate one of the chocolates someone had brought in for his grandmother.

Dave, on the opposite side of the bed, studied Karen's face. She looked great; relaxed and happy. Was this what the prospect of being divorced from him brought about? It was a sobering thought. He could not know it was anticipation of the evening ahead which made her glow or he would not have been so polite. Julie, of course, was not included in these family visits, but it was a relief to her not to have the child.

Although Karen had squeezed in with Trevor and Sandra and the kids to get to the hospital, Dave offered to drive her and Danny home.

"Did you see a solicitor?" he asked, when they were in the car.

"I did. It doesn't sound very complicated, we've nothing to quarrel over, have we?"

"No. Karen," he hesitated, "it was just like old times there tonight, wasn't it? Mum and Sandra and all, and you and me."

"No, Dave, it was nothing like old times." Her assertive

manner and denial of what he said was like a slap in the face. He remained silent for the rest of the journey.

"Thanks for the lift, Dave. What about next week, with Danny? Do you want to leave the arrangements until we know about May?"

"That's probably the best thing to do."

He saw them to the door. Karen smiled a little as she saw the stiffness of his back as he walked away. Typical Dave, if things didn't go his way he carried his hurt pride like a banner. He did not look back to see Danny waving to him.

Karen gave Danny a cold sausage to munch while she saw to his tea then she put him to bed and read him a quick story. He had had his bath earlier to save time now, and to make sure there was enough hot water for her own ablutions. But what was she going to wear? It would be an insult to arrive wearing jeans if Trot had gone to the trouble of preparing her a meal but she did not want to look overdressed.

She sank into the foamy, scented water of the bath, dipping her head back to wet her hair. The bathroom was full of steam, the mirror cloudy. She soaked for fifteen minutes, listening out for Danny who had been put to bed earlier than usual and might not settle so quickly, although he had missed his afternoon nap. He was at that age when he could almost climb over the gate she had bought for the top of the stairs.

Her hair washed and wrapped in a towel, Karen smoothed on body lotion before pulling on her dressing gown. After she'd blow-dried her hair and put on make-up she would make the final decision as to what to wear.

"Blast, who can that be?" It was too early for Mary. She had heard the bell just as she was tying the belt on her robe. She went downstairs and cautiously opened the door a few inches. Her heart sank. "Hello, Colin. What is it? As you can see, I'm just getting ready to go out."

"I . . . you're not . . . sorry." He was more than embarrassed to see her undressed. He turned to walk away.

After all this waiting, after the indecisions and putting it off, he had finally plucked up the courage to knock at her front door and ask her outright if she would go out with him. He had thought he had timed it well. He knew she would be visiting May in the afternoon. He had also given her time to see to Danny and right now he imagined she would be sitting down watching television. To find out she was going out was a real kick in the teeth. Don't let it be him, he thought, seeing Leonard Murdoch's face again.

"Colin, wait."

"It's all right. It can keep," he answered, dejectedly, as he left.

Karen shut the door and sighed. Why did he always manage to make her feel thoughtless? It was the first time he had come to the house. She hoped he wasn't going to make a habit of it.

There were no longer any possessions of Dave's in the bedroom she had once shared with him. Everything he owned was at Julie's, which meant there should be no wrangling later. Karen did not possess many clothes, there was plenty of space in the wardrobe. When she opened it the choice immediately became obvious. The calf-length, full skirt. In black, rust and red, it would go well with her tan boots and scoop-necked, rust body stocking. She would look as much like a gypsy as Trot did at times. She got out the garmets and put them on then took a bottle of coppery nail polish downstairs to apply at the kitchen table because the light was better there. Her auburn hair gleamed under the fluorescent tube buzzing overhead.

She found the nail varnish difficult to apply because her hands were shaking. She jumped when thunder, which had been rolling playfully around the heavens for most of the afternoon decided it was time to get down to some serious business and gave an almighty clap directly overhead. The small bottle fell over and rolled to the floor as her hand twitched. She took a few deep, calming breaths. This was so different from those occasions when she had prepared to go out with Len Murdoch, but that was because she knew that with Len, there had been no attraction on her side. Perhaps it was unfair to have gone out with him at all.

100

Mary arrived on time. "You look lovely, Karen." There was wistful envy in her eyes.

"Thank you," Karen smiled.

Mary was wearing her black skirt. It was too tight but she had read somewhere that black made you look slimmer. Her plump thighs, unprotected by tights or stockings, were mottled and bulged over the side of the kitchen chair. Her hair, as always, looked as if it could do with a wash, the lank strands falling to just below her ears.

If only she'd make some effort, Karen thought, not knowing Mary had started to do just that.

"Right, I'm ready. Help yourself to anything, you know where things are. Emergency numbers are by the 'phone and this is where I can be reached." She had transferred Trot's home number to her diary. It was the scrap of paper on which he had written it that she handed to Mary. It was the only thing she had with his handwriting on and did not want to throw it away.

Trot, too, arrived promptly. He had said his flat was not easy to find so he'd collect her then see her back in a taxi. His eyes ran swiftly up and down the length of her body but he made no comment about her appearance. As she turned to introduce him to Mary she remembered the two of them had met at Danny's birthday tea. The movement caused her hair to bounce and Trot smelled the sweet cleanness.

"Hi, Mary."

"Hello." Mary said this without taking her eyes off her clasped hands.

With an umbrella over her head Karen made a dive for the car. It was too dark to see what make it was but it was by no means new and the engine was rather noisy.

"It goes, that's all I care about," Trot told her. "God, this weather. Will it ever stop? By the way, what time do you have to be back?"

"Want to get rid of me already?"

He laughed. "No, but Mary's got school tomorrow, hasn't she? It'll just make it easier for me to plan the evening if I know."

Plan the evening? What did he have in mind?

"I said about eleven."

"That's fine. Plenty of time." Another enigmatic remark Karen chose to ignore.

Soon they pulled up outside a large, stone building situated amongst other, similar buildings in a labyrinth of back streets. "This is it," Trot said, pulling in to a space reserved for the occupants. "Home."

Frank Mitchell was on his way to the pub when he saw Karen get into the car. It was six-fifty; the twelve minute walk ensured he didn't miss any drinking-time. He scratched his head in the circle on his crown, unprotected by hair, then rubbed the stubble on his chin. Once, he'd shaved every day; now he didn't bother at the weekends. Even in the rainwashed darkness, in the fleeting glimpse he had of her as she dashed for the shelter of the car, it was easy to see how attractive Karen was. There was something indefinable which made her so; not just her looks. Her hair was almost alive, a colourful cloud, the deeper reds picked out by the streetlight. Not that Frank would try his luck there, or anywhere, come to that. Gloria was enough for him.

Despite the discrepancy in their ages, size and colouring, there were similarities between his wife and Karen. Frank was aware of this but could not see how it could be so. It was the innate sexuality they both possessed which drew men to them, even when they did not look their best.

Automatically he turned to see if Colin was hanging about. There was no sign of him. "Bloody nuisance, that one," he muttered, finding it easier to understand the criminal mentality of his other three sons than Colin's strangeness. And he could have done with his cap tonight, Frank thought. It didn't really matter, he was in quite a good mood. He had enough money to last the evening, and longer. He couldn't understand some of the other blokes; all that redundancy pay and too mean to spend it. After a good Sunday lunch he'd given Gloria a fiver to go to bingo. And not many blokes would've done that, he congratulated himself as he pushed open the door of the pub.

Gloria waited until Frank had gone before turning to the television pages of the *News of the World*. She had not been to bingo for ages and did not fancy it tonight. And, there was an Agatha Christie on, one she hadn't seen. The five pound note would join the ten that Bill Haines had given her.

"How did you get on?" Frank asked when he staggered in shortly after closing time.

"I had a very nice evening, thanks," she answered with total honesty.

Frank grinned and planted a sloppy kiss full on her lips. His wife had no secrets from him, she'd have told him if she'd won anything. And in return for his genoristy he might like to give him a little something in return.

Gloria was already bracing herself.

Colin was recovering from his disappointment. It was his own fault; he should have asked her anyway. He walked, not caring that it was dark and wet, and found himself out on the Bordfield Road before he was aware of his surroundings. He was wearing his father's cap, and his newly-acquired raincoat kept most of him dry. It was waterproof, good quality. He didn't like it here, with the river and trees, he was more comfortable amongst man-made things; concrete and glass was his natural habitat. The houses, on one side of the road only, were detached, hidden behind high hedges, barely a chink of light showing anywhere through expensively-lined curtains. The sounds of water predominated; the small river in spate, the rain hammering down and the occasional swish of tyres as a car passed.

He retraced his footsteps and, when he reached Karen's house, stood, staring at the windows, knowing it was only Mary Langley sitting behind the drawn curtains.

Mary sat close to the fire, legs stretched out in front of her. She had checked on Danny twice already, stroking back his hair lovingly as he slept. His breathing was shallow and even, his cold completely gone. She liked his room with its pastel walls and teddy bear frieze.

Beside her was her third cup of coffee, black and sweetened with two of Karen's saccharin tablets. She resisted the temptation of the chocolate-covered wafer biscuits Karen kept as a treat for Danny. Now she was going out with Paul she was going to lose weight. Five days and it was already beginning to show; not to others yet, perhaps, but her waistbands felt a little looser. On the television was one of those Hercule Poirot mysteries. She loved the women's clothes. When she was thinner she would buy something like that, knee length and straight and slinky. The plot hardly mattered as she could not stop thinking about yesterday afternoon.

It was like a dream. Paul had met her in the foyer of the cinema, as arranged, and they had gone immediately in to see the film because he'd been a bit late. Mary felt sick as she waited, not knowing what she'd do if he didn't turn up. They had already missed the trailers, which she quite liked.

She shook, half with pleasure, half with fear. Paul was a year older than her and so good-looking. She could not understand why he chose her. It was not long before his arm slid across the back of the seat and rested there a few minutes before he dropped his hand and let it lay on her shoulder. When he pulled her to him and kissed her she thought she was going to wet herself with excitement. It was the first time she had been kissed and she did not want it to end.

Inexperienced and unsure in all sexual matters she did not stop him when his hand reached under her baggy sweater. She breathed in deeply, trying to pull in her stomach but nothing would disguise the roll of flesh around her middle. When Paul's hand moved lower she knew she ought to stop him. As he gently stroked her thigh the sensations were indescribable. She tried to part her legs, she was hot now, but there wasn't enough room in the seat. She knew, if they had not been in the cinema she would have allowed him to go all the way.

When the film ended she floated out into the street, red-faced and eyes sparkling.

"See you then," Paul said, with a casual wave. It took several seconds to come down to earth but the pain, and the knot in the pit of her stomach she felt at his sudden departure soon vanished as she recalled what had happened. She knew how strict her parents were, maybe Paul's were the same and he wasn't allowed to go out with girls. She hadn't exactly lied; in fact she hadn't lied at all. Mary had told her mother she was going to the cinema, and as this was something she often did on a Saturday afternoon, Mrs Langley assumed it was with a girlfriend.

Paul had not said when he would see her again. Had she done something wrong? Then she smiled. There was no need for him to say, they would see each other in school on Monday. Tomorrow!

Karen followed Trot up a single flight of stairs. As soon as they were in his large, airy sitting room Karen knew she had chosen exactly the right clothes. Trot himself was in jeans, faded in parts but tight and clean. Under a leather jacket he wore a white, loose-fitting shirt with dropped shoulders. He might have walked straight out of the pages of a D.H. Lawrence novel. There was no particular theme to the room but the combination of bits and pieces picked up here and there seemed to work. A cotton rug in muted shades was flung over the back of the settee. The impression was of life and colour. "It's a lovely room."

"Thanks. I like it. Drink?"

"What've you got?"

"Wine. Beer. Spirits." He indicated a table set in the corner of the room. The selection was impressive.

"Wine, please. Dry white?"

"That's in the fridge." Trot smiled, it was what he was having himself.

Karen drank the first glass too fast because she was still nervous, but the second glass relaxed her. Trot's lopsided smile was back in place when he said he had better see to the food. He refused Karen's offer to help.

"You know what we chefs are like in the kitchen, everyone else is a damned nuisance. It won't take long. Here, put some music on." He showed her how to work the equipment and left her to choose what she wanted.

After a few minutes he returned bearing cork table mats and cutlery. "I like your choice," he said, referring to the gentle classical tape she had put on, hoping he didn't think she'd done it for romantic effect, which was exactly her reason.

Trot pulled out another table and extended a flap before laying it. "If you want to make yourself useful you can pour some more wine." He returned to the kitchen from which, already, delicious aromas were wafting and making her hungry.

Karen went to the table in the corner where the misted bottle of Australian Chardonnay was tilted in an ice bucket. It was an odd feeling, having a man cook for her. Dave had never lifted a finger unless he'd been asked, and then not always with good grace. She studied a couple of prints on the wall then poured Trot's wine.

He stood at the worktop, his back to her, motionless, apparently staring at the wall ahead of him. He had not heard her approach. In his hand was a chopping knife. Without warning he slammed it, point down, into the board which held salad vegetables. Karen gave an involuntary gasp and spilled some wine. Trot spun round, as surprised as she was. His brown eyes flashed and for a second she thought he was furious with her.

"Karen. I'm sorry. I didn't mean to frighten you." He was pale and not fully in control of himself.

Karen wished she hadn't come; this was not at all what she expected.

"Please, forgive me. I don't know what's up with me lately." He shook his head. "I do actually, it's having you here, alone with me at last. And doing this," he indicated the half prepared food with the blade of the knife which he

106

had pulled out of the board as soon as it entered it. "It's just reminded me of what I'm capable of. That bloody club. And Murdoch. It's just all beginning to get me down."

Karen remained frozen to the spot, fear rendering her incapable of speech. Everything Melissa had said about him came back to her. How foolish she'd been not to take more notice. She could not take her eyes off the knife in his hand. It was long and narrow and very sharp. All sorts of wild things rushed through her mind.

"Karen?" Trot took another step closer, laying down the knife before doing so.

She was amazed she did not flinch when he reached for her hand.

"I've ruined the evening, haven't I? And I wanted it to be perfect. I haven't always been like this; it's just frustration, believe me. The sooner I get away from the club the better. I've already starting making enquiries elsewhere. This just about sums me up really. I've looked forward to this for so long, and look what I've managed to do."

"It's all right. Really." What else could she say? She had two alternatives now; leave and forget the whole thing, and find another job, or, believe in her own instincts rather than what Melissa thought and try to restore what had started out so well. Trot, is seemed, had read her mind.

"If you want to go, I'll understand. I'll call you a taxi."

His head was bent but Karen read the disappointment in his posture. "No. I'd like to stay." She, who had been brought up in comfort and safety, had never had to face a moment's danger. She might be taking a risk, but she could not live cocooned for ever. Trot's reaction was enough reward.

"I'm so glad, you don't know how much. Now," he smiled, "I'll take you up on your offer. *You* do the salad." He handed her the knife, handle first. "And I think we could both use another drink."

Karen finished the salad and put everything together in a wooden serving bowl. Trot touched her hand as he passed the dressing. She did not think it was accidental.

Once the food was in front of them and they had put on

107

some livelier music and toasted each other, the mood was altered dramatically. Suddenly everything seemed funny but Karen was very aware she would not get drunk; that earlier fright had sent adrenalin coursing through her veins. They talked about work and made jokes at the expense of the customers who put up with being overcharged. Trot admitted that Melissa scared him. "She'd eat a man alive, that one."

Karen defended her friend but secretly agreed.

When she asked, Trot told her he'd almost been married once. "I lived with her for a while. Lizzie. She was a nurse. It seemed right somehow . . ." He stopped and toyed with the stem of his wine glass.

"What happened?"

He smiled ruefully. "You obviously don't read the right books. Usual story. She married a doctor. She got a better offer; it was as simple as that. Now, look, why doesn't Melissa, who's obviously out for the same thing, make a play for Murdoch? He's not married and he's got plenty of the folding stuff."

"They're too similar. I know they both seem flashy, but I think they're both after constant reassurance. They both need someone calm and quiet, and with plenty of patience."

"Ah, the amateur psychologist. You've been out with him, what was it like?" Trot hoped the question did not sound accusatory.

"He likes to be the centre of attention, especially in restaurants. Well, I've only been to one with him, but that's how he struck me. It's as if he's used to plenty of money and good service, but it's over the top. I think it's all an act." Karen was surprised at her own observations. None of this had consciously crossed her mind until that moment.

"What do you think he'd say about us? He fancies you like mad."

"Us?" Karen ignored the following statement.

"There is something, isn't there? Don't tell me I'm wrong. I hoped, well, surely you must have some inkling of how I feel?"

108

A steady flush of colour spread over her face. Karen did not know what to say. This was it then, this struggling to breathe evenly, an inability to speak was what happened when the man you wanted hinted he felt the same way. But he had only hinted.

"Oh, Trot." She gulped at her wine.

He smiled, watching the blush fade. "'Oh, Trot.' Is that the best you can come up with? Am I wrong to hope?"

"No. It's just . . ."

"I know. You need time. I've rushed into things. It can't have been easy for you. I won't say any more, except I'm always here if you need me."

"Thank you." There was so much she wanted to say but her head was reeling. She wanted to laugh and cry at the same time.

"God, look at the time," he said. "Your babysitter." It was eleven-fifteen. "No, leave all that, I'll clear it up later." Trot went to the 'phone and rang for a taxi. "Ten minutes is the soonest they can do. Do you want to ring Mary?"

She did so and told Mary to ring her parents to say she would be late.

Trot insisted on seeing her back in the taxi. "Can I say something?"

"Of course."

"Be careful of Murdoch, Karen, he's after more than your friendship. It's none of my business, but I don't want you to have any problems, especially now you're coming back to work."

"There won't be any," Karen replied.

"Okay."

The cab pulled up outside Karen's house. During the short journey Karen had come to a decision. She had come this far but she knew she wanted more.

"I won't be a minute," Trot said to the driver, expecting to be returning home in the same cab.

"Do you want to come in for that coffee we didn't get round to?" Karen asked him.

"Are you sure?"

"Yes."

"I'd love to," Trot smiled at her. "I'll just pay the fare." He told the driver his plans had changed. The driver grinned at him and winked.

"I'm so sorry, Mary," Karen said, as Mary, who'd heard the cab pull up, opened the door. "Are your parents annoyed?"

"No, it's all right. So long as they know where I am," Mary replied.

"I'll just see her home, Trot, make yourself comfortable." Karen watched Mary walk the short distance to her own house and once she was safely indoors, went to put the kettle on. There were no dirty dishes anywhere, just one mug soaking in the sink.

They sat, side by side, on the settee and drank their coffee. The empty cups were on the table when Trot leant across and kissed her. Karen responded. The first kiss from any man, except her father, in eighteen months. How she missed physical contact.

"Oh, God, I'm sorry," Trot said later as they lay in bed. "I seem to have spent the whole evening apologising. I don't know what's wrong, it's never happened before."

"It's all right," Karen reassured him. And it was. Trot had been so gentle, it was wonderful, right up to the last minute then, just when she was as aroused as him, his erection had suddenly subsided.

He felt so humiliated. Those other times were never like this. But he had not loved them. Is that what it took, then, a lack of love to make it work? He got out of bed and started pulling on his clothes.

"Don't go," she said. "Please."

"Sure?"

"Positive."

They slept curled around each other, sex, for the moment forgotten, as was the incident with the knife.

In the morning Danny bounced on the bed, apparently unconcerned that there were two bodies under the cover.

110

Karen was grateful he was not a few years older, when explanations would have been necessary.

Colin Mitchell saw the taxi arrive, watched as Karen got out and held his breath as the man with her went to the door. He almost choked when he was let into the house. He waited, saw Mary walk home with Karen watching out for her, then the door closed. The man was still inside. At least it wasn't the flashy one.

The lights remained on for quite some time then the downstairs ones were extinguished and her bedroom light came on. The man was still inside.

There could be only one explanation. He knew the sort of girl Karen was, she wouldn't do anything that wasn't good and decent. The man, whoever he was, had to be a relative. A brother possibly, he seemed about the right age.

He must make his move soon. Too many people were becoming involved in her life.

Only when the heavens opened once more and water began seeping into his trainers, did Colin go home, his feet squelching as he walked.

Chapter Ten

Leonard Murdoch strolled around his empty club. Despite the numerous extractor fans it always smelled of stale smoke, and damp. The damp-proof course he'd forked out for last year hadn't made a damn bit of difference. He abhorred the musty atmosphere but there was nothing further he could do about it. Some establishments, bowing down to the modern phenomena of political correctness which, to him, smacked of "Big Brother", had abolished smoking altogether. He knew if he tried such a move, he'd been left with a handful of customers. Besides, his attitude was, let people go to the Devil their own way. Why should someone else deem to know better? "Might as well have a bloody dictator," he muttered as he inspected the place.

All the overhead lighting was on and, unpopulated, the premises looked what they were: tatty and depressing. Under the disco strobes and subdued side lamps a different atmosphere was created.

The table tops were scored and the flooring would have to be replaced soon before someone tripped and broke their neck and he found himself in the middle of a large compensation claim. He could do without that sort of publicity. The inspectors from the fire service would be arriving any minute. It was a formality. All the extinguishers were in place and in working order, the fire doors and exits clearly marked and illuminated. His certificate would be renewed.

Mondays were such a drag. He liked being here when the place was full, music thumping out, the till working overtime. At such times he was king of his domain – no use being a king with no subjects. The one thing he could not come to terms with was that his mother was unaware of his success; would never truly understand what he had made of himself.

He hardly knew his father whose face stared blankly at him, unsmiling, from the one photograph of him he possessed. Leonard had had to build up his own fantasy of the man, crediting him with virtues and mannerisms which, had he actually had them would have made him a saint.

The fire officers came and went pronouncing everything to be satisfactory; exactly in accordance with the regulations. Leonard saw them out. From his office window, barred against intruders because it was on the ground floor, he watched as rain blew in horizontal drifts across the bleak area at the back.

He picked up his raincoat, double-checked the locks all round the building then went out to his car. The engine purred quietly and reassuringly on the first turn of the ignition. He took the main road towards Bordfield and the private hospital room, for which he paid, where his mother lay dying.

In that building he was treated in the manner which he knew he deserved. Staff made him welcome and offered cups of tea and coffee and listened to what he had to say with deferential respect. Money could buy lots of things, but not the ones he really wanted.

He was praised for his trouble and the time he spent with a woman who was no longer able to recognize him, except at times he thought she did.

The nurses here knew his worth, even if she did not.

"Come on, girl how did it go?" quizzed May.

"Well, it was – Danny, for goodness sake, sit still will you? – it was very nice."

"Very nice. What kind of an answer is that? I want to hear all the details, if you don't mind."

Karen smiled. "All right. It was more than nice. I enjoyed it very much; the food and his company. And, before you ask, yes, I'm going to see him again. Now let's talk about you, did I hear the nurse say you're coming home soon?"

"You did. A few days, whatever that means. I hope it's not on the same scale as their few minutes. I've waited twenty of them for a bedpan before now. I can't wait. I'm going daft in here."

"You'll have to take it easy, May."

"Good God, girl, don't you start. That's all I ever hear. I'll do anything to get out of this place. Anyway, you're back to work tomorrow, aren't you?"

"Yes, and looking forward to it. Sue can't wait either, she's really looking forward to having Danny. Oh, May, I'm sorry, that was tactless."

"No," she patted Karen's hand, "life has to go on. You just make sure you get back safe at night. They haven't caught this lunatic yet. I feel so sorry for those girls, having to earn their living that way. It's such a risk these days. Well, I suppose it always was. If you ask me, they should legalise it, like they do abroad. Still, nothing I can do about it. Anyway, dear, I'm so pleased you've found yourself a nice young man."

If May had decided Trot was her young man, nothing Karen said would alter the fact. She wasn't sure yet, how things stood. Time would tell.

Danny was in the bath, smacking his hands down flat on the surface of the water and half soaking Karen when the telephone rang. She almost left it then decided it might be Trot. She bundled Danny into a large towel and carried him downstairs to answer it.

"Did you have an enjoyable evening?"

"Dave?"

"Obviously it's me. How many boyfriends have you got?"

"He's not my boyfriend." But even as she said it, she decided he probably was. She misread his jealousy, assuming it was on her behalf. But it turned out that it was on Danny's, at the thought there was the remotest possibility someone else might take on the role of his father.

It seemed Dave wanted nothing more than to make her

114

feel bad. He did not comment on May's improving condition or anything else. Karen hoped it would not affect his attitude towards the divorce.

She hugged Danny to her but he was not in the mood for it. Impatiently she put him to bed then rang her mother because she felt the need to talk to someone.

"Actually, darling," Doreen said, "we were just on our way out of the door. Is it important?"

"No. I only rang for a chat."

"Lovely to hear from you. See you soon."

"That's that, then," she told herself when she hung up on a second unsatisfactory telephone call.

Half an hour later John Turner rang the bell.

"Dad! I thought you were going out."

"We were. Your mother's gone on alone. Some ridiculous cheese and wine thing connected with the salon. It's just a sales pitch, I believe, on the part of a supplier."

"Won't she be furious?"

"I expect so. But not for long; not once she gets there. I heard part of the conversation, Karen. You sounded odd. And I know you don't ring up your mother just for a chat. What is it? Oh, by the way, I thought this might oil the hinges a bit." From a carrier bag John produced a bottle of wine and some chocolate buttons. "Those are for Danny. When you think fit."

Karen kissed him on the cheek and went to get the corkscrew and some glasses. The wine was red. Foresight on John's part as it did not need chilling.

"I don't know what's the matter with me, Dad. Just when I think I've got everything sorted out, it's all turned on its head. It's not just May; that was unexpected, I know, but I was lucky enough to get someone else so quickly. It's Dave. I feel sure he's going to cause trouble over the divorce. And then there's Trot."

"Trot? The man who took you out to dinner?"

"Yes."

"What about him?"

"I think I'm falling in love with him. No," she saw the

115

beam of happiness on her father's face, "it's not quite like you think."

"You either love him or you don't, girl, if there's any doubt, forget it."

"I do love him."

John shook his head. There were times when he didn't understand his daughter any more than he did his wife. "Okay. You do."

"Is it possible to love someone you suspect's done something terrible?"

"Yes. I think it probably is. You've only got to read the papers, mothers swearing to stand by their murdering, raping sons, wives sticking with husbands in jail for all sorts of reasons. Why? Oh, Karen, don't tell me you think this Trot fellow's done something?"

"I don't know, that's the trouble. One minute I've convinced myself my intuition is right, that he's a perfectly ordinary bloke – well," she smiled wistfully, "not exactly ordinary – you know what I mean. But the next moment, I'm not sure."

"What is it exactly you think he may have done?"

She shook her head. "No. It wouldn't be fair if I said. I'm almost certain I'm wrong and if I told you it would influence how you felt about him for the rest of your life. Then there's Colin . . ."

"Pour that wine for goodness sake. How many men are there in your life at the moment?"

"It does sound bad, doesn't it? Colin's a neighbour, one of Gloria Mitchell's sons. Don't look so worried, Dad, he hasn't done, or said anything, it's just that he stands over there under the trees watching me. There's nothing for him to see, only me and Danny, and in the day-time the light's against us, so he can't see in. At night I pull the curtains. He just gives me the creeps, that's all. May's known him for years and she says he's all right."

"Would you like me to have a word with him?"

"No. Please, Dad, don't do that. It would make my life here very awkward. It's just me. I'm going through a fit of mild depression. Probably best if you ignore everything I've said, I just wanted to say it, that's all." She had hoped her father would offer to speak to Colin but as soon as he did she knew it was not the way things were done. She must do it herself or put up with the situation.

Once Karen was smiling again John took his leave saying if his own life was to be worth living, he'd better put in an appearance at the Melville Hotel. "You finish up the wine then get a good night's sleep. Ring me tomorrow, at work if you like, then your Mum needn't know about any of this. She does worry about you, even if she's got a funny way of showing it."

"I know she does. Give her my love. Just say, well, I'm sure you'll think of some reason why I wanted to talk."

Just as she was thinking about going to bed, the 'phone rang again. She swore, hoping it hadn't woken Danny.

Dave again. And if she was hearing right he sounded a little drunk, and that was most unusual. He started questioning her again about her night out.

"Dave, we only had a meal together," she said, which, after what happened later was almost true, but she didn't see why she should have to justify herself to the man who had walked out on her for another woman. "Anyway, from where I stand, I can't see that it's any of your business. The sooner we get this divorce out of the way, the better. You were the one who left, remember."

"Didn't have much choice, did I?"

"What's that supposed to mean?"

"It wasn't exactly easy living with 'little miss perfect'. All those fancy table manners and you with never a hair out of place."

Was that how he saw her? It seemed impossible. There were many times when Danny was small when she didn't have time to do any housework, when she lived in jeans for days and muddled through the hours until she could put her feet up. Why had he turned on her?

"Just be careful, that's all. If I thought you were so busy going with other men you weren't looking after my son properly, I might be tempted to do something about it."

"He's my son too." But it was too late. Dave had hung up. She went to bed feeling sick and was unable to sleep for a long time. What would Dave think of Sue Trent looking after him at night?

And then she became angry. Jealousy. He'd always been the same, questioning her as to what she had talked about every time another male came near her. Even now, with Julie, he couldn't stop himself. How clearly she saw him now it was too late. Did he expect her to stay celibate for the rest of her life? No thank you, Dave Wilkes, she thought before she finally dropped into a disturbed sleep.

Monday night. What could anyone do on a winter's Monday night? Even with money in your pocket there was nowhere to go. The pubs were almost deserted and none of the clubs bothered to open.

Yesterday he had bought most of the Sunday papers, combing them for articles about Katherine Bishop. A couple of them had picked up the story but a particularly nasty bomb attack in London occupied most of the headlines. It was a good sign. Her murder was not important enough to carry much weight. How long was it since he had killed her? Over a week. Nine days in fact. Dare he risk it again? Her body had only recently been found; the police might still be on the lookout.

He felt the familiar stirrings of arousal. Just recalling past events was often enough to cause this. Strange, try as he might, he could not conjure up Katherine's face at all, not even as he had squeezed the last breath from her body. His hands found their way into the pockets of his raincoat. Unconsciously he began fondling himself. His breath, as it came faster, misted in the air. He could not wait. It had to be tonight.

He wandered through the back streets of Sopford as he decided how to approach the problem of not arousing suspicion. The girls here would be very wary now. Perhaps they'd been prepared to risk a nick to the forehead. Death was a different matter. Fine, he'd give them some time to get over it. Meanwhile he'd try his luck in Bordfield. He laughed silently at his own cleverness.

With his father's cap pulled well down over his eyes he walked purposefully to the bus stop and checked the timetable. Yes, a Bordfield bus was due shortly.

His reputation as The Carver had gone, he knew that now and he was sorry; he'd quite enjoyed the name. He recalled that some smart-arse police shrink had suggested that The Carver and the murderer might be one and the same man. That was too near the knuckle for comfort.

When the bus came there were only a few vacant seats. He ignored the one beside an attractive woman in her late twenties; someone like that was more likely to notice a man. He chose to sit beside an elderly lady wearing a sort of tea-cosy hat, who was clutching a small dog in her lap. She hardly seemed to register his existence.

As they reached the suburbs the bus began to empty. These people were on their way home from work. When he saw the sign for the clearway through the window he felt a rush of excitement. A new town. After some twenty minutes the larger houses on the outskirts of Bordfield came into view. There was money here, all right. Plenty of it by the cars parked in some of the drives. Here, in reverse, people began getting on at the stops, those who had been home and were going into town for the evening. Good. That way he was less conspicuous. He only knew the main parts of Bordfield so waited until several passengers stood up and alighted with them. A walk wouldn't do him any harm. It was far too early yet for the business he wished to conduct.

On Monday afternoon, after she got home from school, Mary Langley's mother had to tell her three times that she wanted her to run down to the shop for half a pound of butter, and while she was there she might get an extra pint of milk if she wanted some rice pudding. "What's the matter with you?" she said. "You're mooning around like a lovesick cow."

Mary took the money her mother held out but did not reply. She hid the furious blush which spread up her throat by turning away and going out the back door. Her mother could not have chosen a more appropriate word. Lovesick was precisely what she was.

Did she look different? Had her mother guessed, or someone seen her at the cinema with Paul? She had barely been able to hide her disappointment when she had learned Paul was not at school that morning. He had gone off to an interview, some sixth form college or something, where his parents wanted him to go to get good "A" level grades. Paul was clever, she knew that, why couldn't he stay where he was and do them? At least she would see him tomorrow.

"Welcome back, Karen, it's great to see you. Mother-in-law okay now?"

"On the mend, Len. And thanks, for keeping the job."

"I wasn't going to let a good one get away, was I?"

"Hello," Trot said quietly as he slid some burgers onto the griddle later in the evening.

He seemed almost shy. Karen guessed he was still embarrassed about his performance in bed. She was flattered in a way, it meant he wasn't treating her like an object.

"You look tired," he observed.

"I am. Bad night."

"Danny?"

"No, he's fine. His father."

"Oh." But it was obvious to Trot that she was not going to enlarge on this comment.

"Are you going somewhere later?" Karen asked Melissa who had given her an effusive welcome and said she was glad to see the back of that other little bitch. Melissa's hair, dyed blonde and streaked even lighter in places, was piled on top of her head and her blouse was cut an inch lower than normal causing Karen to wonder why she bothered to wear one at all.

"Yep. Another club. Better than this dump. Stays open as long as there's someone drinking. Unofficially, of course. I

120

met a cracker at the weekend. Fortyish, not bad looking – if you don't mind a hint of baldness. Managing director of some company or other, big car, the lot."

"Married?" All Melissa's blokes were. Karen was beginning to think it was deliberate. That way, she was safe from forming permanent attachments and thereby being disappointed.

"Yes, but the wife's sunning herself in some exotic location for a month. Don't look so prim, I've no intention of taking him away from the little wifey. It's just too good an opportunity to miss, that's all. He's loaded. Well, come on, what've you been up to in your absence?"

The conversation had to be postponed as the place started filling up. Between them they kept the drinks flowing while Trot served burgers and hot dogs through the hatch that was fastened closed on Saturdays. No waitress ·service for this lot.

When the evening was over, and before Trot came out to join them for their staff drink, Karen told Melissa she had been to his place for a meal. "He really can cook, you know. It's not just a boast."

Before Melissa could ask about the part she was really interested in, Trot came out from the kitchen having scraped down and scrubbed his equipment.

"You're blushing," Melissa whispered as Trot helped himself to a pint of beer.

"I'm not."

"I really enjoyed our evening," Trot said, making it quite clear to Melissa how things stood. "When can we do it again?"

"Next weekend." Karen was blushing now. "Only I'd like to return the compliment."

"Fine. Now what about Danny, shall I take him off your hands one afternoon so's you can go and see May?"

"If you've nothing better to do, that'd be nice."

Melissa watched in fascination. There was definitely something between these two, she could tell by the way their conversation had changed.

*   *   *

121

In the morning it was a great relief to Karen to know that Danny had slept all night and had been no trouble whatsoever. She admired the little room where he slept with no idea of the efforts Sue had made to convert it, in such a short space of time, from a place where they stored things, into a pretty nursery. The tiny bed had been purchased in a junk shop because she dared not spend an amount Martin was likely to question.

Chapter Eleven

Gloria Mitchell, as she peeled enough potatoes to temporarily satisfy her family's appetite, did not know she was in for a shock. A pleasant one. Tonight she was cooking liver and onions and it would be on the table at six-thirty sharp. Those that were not there to eat it would have to warm it up later. If it was dry, too bad. Frank was already in when she had got back from work and by the state of the living room it looked as if he'd been in all day.

Spike was in the bath, she could smell some revolting aftershave from where she stood. Still, this latest girl must be quite serious if he was taking her to the pictures. His dates usually consisted of going to the pub with his mates where they ignored any females with them until it was time to go home. Mickey could be anywhere, as could Colin.

It was ten-to-six when the back door opened and her second eldest son stunned her into silence by saying, "I've got a job."

"What?" Gloria sank into a kitchen chair, the potato peeler still in her hand. "My God, I can't believe it." She paused. "Is it legal?"

"Course it is," Mickey sneered. "Is that all you can say?"

"No. I'm really pleased for you, son. What is it?"

"Removals firm. Bloke I know's broke his leg, so I went along to see if they needed anyone else. They said if I was any good they'd keep me on because Des isn't up to much. He breaks too many things." Mickey laughed at his own little joke. "Including his leg."

"That smells all right," Frank said, joining the two of them at the kitchen table.

"You'll have to wait for the potatoes. I've casseroled the liver, I'm sick to death of fried food. Well, go on, Mickey, tell your father."

"Tell me what?"

Frank seemed uneasy with the news his son imparted. He hoped this wasn't setting a precedent. He gruffly said he was pleased for him.

Spike eventually vacated the bathroom wearing his best shirt and a new leather belt in his jeans. Gloria did not like to ask where he had got it.

"Where the bloody hell's Colin?" Frank asked as they began to eat. One of these days I'll give him a bloody good hiding."

"Calm down, Frank. You know he's always been the same. He forgets what the time is."

"It's not natural, always being on his own like that." The idea of anyone being able to enjoy their own company was anathema to Frank.

Colin chose that moment to walk in, only a minute or so late.

"Well, well," his father said, "if it isn't . . . remind me now, what's your name?"

"Stop it. I won't have arguments at the table," chastised Gloria. "This is an evening to be celebrating, not stirring up trouble."

Frank saw by his wife's face she meant it and kept quiet. He'd never admit it, but he had a fair idea of what Gloria had put up with over the years, including his own crass behaviour – for which he usually felt sorry, but never thought to tell her so.

Colin had seen Karen today. She had been walking into town with Danny and she had smiled and said hello.

Karen was still dubious about leaving Danny with Sue. The first night might have been a one-off, because she had made sure she had tired him out during the day. Time will tell, she told herself.

That evening Leonard Murdoch called her into the office

during a lull in business. "Karen, I can't tell you how much I enjoyed our outing the other Sunday. Now you've got another babysitter I'd like to take you out properly, you know, the cinema and drinks and a decent meal, something better than a curry. We could get to know each other better. I'd like that, and I think you would too."

It was only then Karen saw him clearly for the first time. He looked sleazy in the pale lilac shirt, his mouth was too slack and his eyes, although a clear grey, were somehow dead. He repulsed her. How had she ever gone out with him at all?

"I'm sorry, Len, but it wouldn't work. And," she hesitated, not wishing to jeopardise her job, "there's someone else."

"Someone else? Oh, Trot. Don't you bother your pretty little head over someone like that. We'll leave it for now, shall we. You'll change your mind when you've had a proper chance to think about it."

She just doesn't know when she's well off, he told himself as he locked up. She was the perfect partner to complete his image. Wait until his mother set eyes on this one. Oh, yes, she'd take it in, he was sure of that, even if she wasn't able to let him know.

Monday night was one of the best nights of his life; one of the lucky times. He knew it as soon as he saw her. He had got off the bus far too soon, still way out in the suburbs. He had to walk almost a mile before he came to any sort of shop. The shopping centre itself was far bigger than Sopford's. He looked in the windows, not that he was interested in their contents, it was just a way of innocently passing time, letting the excitement build slowly, the sexual tension mount gradually until the final release. Except this time he was prepared. This time, whoever's face it was, he would make sure he remembered it.

How to go about it was still the problem. No doubt there were cards in telephone boxes and adverts in corner shop windows, the usual, girls offering French lessons, that type of thing. He could instantly pick out what he wanted.

He was so deep in thought, planning this next move, he

didn't see the girl at first. A soft voice from a shop door-way whispered something he didn't catch immediately. She repeated it. "Are you lonely? Feel like some company?"

He stopped, completely taken aback. The initiation had always been on his side. And right there, in the main street, at this time of night, he couldn't believe it. It was an omen. And it had broken the pattern, a pattern the police may be aware of.

The girl turned away and lit a cigarette. A point not in her favour. But she'd be giving up soon. Permanently. She had thought, by his hesitation, that he was going to pass on by.

"Yes," he said. "Yes, I am lonely."

Without another word she fell into step beside him, smoking furiously, as if her life depended upon it. He hoped she wouldn't take his arm or anything like that, he hated any sort of intimacy. To an outsider they were an ordinary couple out for an evening stroll, or on their way somewhere. "Where are we going?"

"To my place. It's not far. It's extra mind, indoors."

"How much extra?" he asked, for form's sake. He would have no need to pay her. She told him and he said the amount seemed reasonable. He laughed.

"What's so funny?"

"Nothing. Private joke." He could hardly tell her she could have named a thousand pounds as her fee, she would not be around to spend it.

He saw, by the flat, why her price was a little above the average. It was more than a bedsit, having a bedroom, bathroom and kitchenette separate from the living area. She even had her own entrance, up a short flight of metal stairs on the outside of the building. He saw now, with the aid of the electric lights, that she was quite pretty and was dressed almost as if she worked in an office. Her skirt was knee-length and straight, topped with a pink, fluffy sweater which couldn't have been cheap. Her court shoes were of medium height. She threw her jacket over the back of a chair and opened the bedroom door, swallowing nervously. He guessed she hadn't been at it long.

"How do you want it?" she asked.

He couldn't answer. He was almost salivating, the girl was so innocent, not yet having acquired the hardness which came to them all in time. She looked like any nice girl you might meet in the street. And there were no worries any more. It was quite safe to take all his clothes off. "Get undressed," he said. His voice was thick. "Everything."

She did so, revealing spotless white underclothes. Michelle Jarvis was even more nervous than she appeared. She was not afraid of him, or any other man. She had read about the things which had happened, but those other girls were different. She was not really a prostitute, just earning some extra cash. She had never had cause to fear anyone or anything. Besides, those sort of things happened to other people, not her.

Recently, in one disastrous week she had lost her job two days after her parents decided it was time for her to leave the nest. They had spoiled her, provided for her every need and were just beginning to reap what they had sown. It was time Michelle stood on her own two feet. And the rows had become intolerable.

Mr Jarvis was by no means a hard man, he really wanted the best for his daughter. He even went as far as to find this flat for her and pay the first three months' rent and the key money. The rest was now up to her. He had thought he was doing her a kindness.

She had not found another job. The one she had left had been hers only because of her father's influence. This was only her fifth client.

"Tell me what you want," she said, hoping to get it over with as quickly as possible. She had to admit, already it was getting easier. The first time she lay rigid, staring at the ceiling. The client had told her in no uncertain terms she wasn't worth half the money. But he'd let her keep it and went off in disgust.

He did not reply but pushed her roughly down onto the bed. She winced because of her own unreadiness. His hands were either side of her face, caressing her. She warmed towards him. He was probably very lonely. "Look at me," he said, "look me in the eyes." She did so. He was paying.

His whole weight was on top of her, crushing her. She could not have moved if she had wished to. His grip became firmer, then he was squeezing. "Don't," she said. It was beginning to hurt.

"Look at me, you bitch."

She tried to beg him to stop, but couldn't speak. She did look at him, trying to get the message across in her eyes. Soon she was no longer seeing him. There was only a red blur and she knew that she was dying.

But he could see her, the half-smile that faded, the disbelief that turned into panic. Then the terror. Oh, yes, he could see her all right, and he was enjoying every minute.

It was over quickly. She was dead before he had finished. He lay on top of her quite still, at peace, until he could breath evenly again. There was no hurry. She hadn't made a sound. Slowly and carefully he dressed, not looking at that thing on the bed. Then, when he was ready to leave, as an afterthought, he took the knife from his pocket and carved his initial on her head.

Now they will know, he thought, now they'll know for certain it's me, and there's nothing they can do about it.

By Tuesday night the sensation was fading and the calmness was creeping over him. He had seen Karen, too, and that helped. Not long now. Soon he would tell her what he really intended, for her and Danny. Ah, yes, Danny. He was the key to the whole thing.

For now he was content to wait.

Dave Wilkes knew he was being unfair to Karen and despised himself for it. Even his own mother, from her hospital bed, had told him so. He had left her because he'd met Julie, and he was happy with Julie; he just didn't want Karen to be in the same position or his son to become attached to another man. But he had no right to stop her from seeing anyone. If she remarried before he did, he knew there was no chance of getting custody of Danny. He had to stop it happening.

May thought she understood him. He had been the same as a child. When he was given anything, be it a comic or sweets, he would sneak up to his room, unwilling to share the spoils with anyone. Sandra had always been a generous child; his actions hurt her. May felt sure she had not treated them differently yet Dave acted as if he was a spoiled, only child. Anything that was his, remained his. He did not get it from his father; for all his womanising, Joe Wilkes was not materially selfish.

Dave had noticed a slight change in Julie, she was warmer than ever towards him, something he had not thought possible. She was obviously looking forward to being his wife and seemed almost as happy as he did at the idea of having Danny living with them.

Her added affection was, in fact, for the opposite reason. Soon she would be in a sounder position from which to wean Dave away from his son. As she undressed, he commented on her weight loss. "I don't want you getting too thin," he said.

"Oh, I shan't. It's only a couple of pounds." But it was more than a couple and she had no intention of stopping now. She had also made an appointment with her optician.

She had not told Dave yet, but next week she was going out with some people for work for a drink. It paid to mix, it made you a more interesting person. It was a pity Dave did not have any interests. She did not think she had ever met anyone his age who was so content with work and home. Still, if he stayed in he was not likely to meet anyone else.

She had forgotten that he had met her on the shop floor of the supermarket, how they had chatted and he had asked her out for a drink on that first occasion even though she saw he was wearing a wedding ring. They had become involved almost at once. It did not cross her mind it could happen again just as easily.

He had, she noticed, taken to leaving his wedding ring off now.

Spike Mitchell, astride his bike, rode up Oakfield Road on

his way to meet his girlfriend. Having heard what Mickey would be earning he briefly wondered if he should make a bit more effort to find a job. The thought didn't last long. He was happy enough as he was.

As he accelerated around the corner her saw his brother trudging up towards him. Colin had said he was staying in. He must have changed his mind. He did not bother to wave; he knew there would be no response, even supposing Colin saw him. He was weird, was Colin. Even when he was little he had never played with the other kids and he was always rubbishing his and Mickey's girlfriends. It was jealousy, probably, because he'd never had a girlfriend himself. Spike was not one for pondering the mysteries of human behaviour but it occasionally crossed his mind that Colin was some sort of foundling, or at least had a different father. He was nothing like the rest of them.

Colin had seen Spike but chose to ignore him. He didn't like any of his brothers much and preferred to keep out of their way. Having decided to stay in, after twenty minutes in front of the television in his father's company, he had to get out of it. Frank Mitchell could not watch anything without giving a running commentary so there was no chance of really following what was going on. He wasn't even saying anything intelligent, or in disagreement, his comments were on the lines of "he doesn't know what he's talking about," and, "look at that fool". Even the newsreaders were not exempt.

Worse, Mickey kept crowing about his job. He bet it wouldn't last. And there was Spike, off to see that slag of a girlfriend. He wouldn't be seen dead with her, with her too-short skirts and rainbow-coloured hair. No one could compare with Karen. She was always dressed nicely; ladylike was the word, her hair and face so lovely without any make-up. And she spoke softly, not screaming and shouting and using swear words all the time. And it made his heart ache to see how well she looked after little Danny. One day he would share that tenderness. Karen would stroke his head just as she did her son's.

He had come to a decision. For some reason he picked next Sunday as the day. He didn't like Sundays. The town was dead and there was even less to do. It would be something to look forward to. He would knock on the door after Dave collected Danny and whatever happened, no matter what she said, he would ask her to go out with him. Right then, if she was free; if not, they would make a definite arrangement. Or he'd take them both out, Karen and Danny. They could go for a walk. She might even let him push the pram and strangers would think Danny was his. He didn't even mind if she wanted to go down to the stream. He knew they went there sometimes so Danny could throw sticks in and watch them float under the bridge. His thoughts drifted on, picturing the scene, imagining Karen letting him hold her hand.

How on earth could Dave have left them? That showed how stupid Mickey was. Mickey had been to school with Dave Wilkes and reckoned him to be all right. He said Karen probably nagged or he wouldn't have left. No man that walked out on Karen was worth twopence.

He stood in the shadows, watching until it was time for Karen to take Danny up the road to Mrs Trent's and go off to work.

Tonight she was in a hurry. She looked vaguely in his direction and he raised his hand. He could not speak to her, he might make her late for work and if she lost her job how could she afford to live?

Then the realisiation hit him. He was as stupid as Mickey. He had not thought things through. She could not be expected to keep him, too. It was his place to provide for her. He, like Mickey, would have to get a job.

Gloria almost dropped the teapot when Colin burst in the back door not long after he'd gone out. It was unlike him to be so noisy. Mostly he crept about, frightening the life out of you when you turned around and suddenly found yourself face to face with him. "What's up with you?"

"I've been thinking."

Gloria arched an eyebrow.

131

"I'm going to get a job as well."

Instead of putting the teapot away she placed it beside the kettle on the gas. This was too much to take in. She needed another cup of tea. What had Mickey started? If Colin did find work, three out of four sons would be employed. It would be a miracle. There was the problem, though, of who would want to employ Colin.

"Yeah, well," Frank said later, when Gloria told him of this latest development, "I'll do something about it myself soon. After slaving away at the factory I needed a bit of a holiday."

Gloria held her tongue. She was pretty certain the holiday period would last until retirement age.

Mary Langley could not sleep; had not slept much last night either. She thought she might never close her eyes again. She had floated through Sunday, hardly able to wait for school the next day then had had to face the disappointment of Paul not being there. Then came Tuesday and her world had come tumbling down around her ears.

She had been too wrapped up in romantic dreams to notice the whispering and giggles of some of the other girls and the nudges and winks of the boys. She did not see Paul before the start of classes but in the break he was there with a group of his classmates. She approached them shyly. "Hello, Paul," she said. "How did you get on yesterday?"

One of the boys punched Paul on the arm and they all started laughing.

"What's funny?" she asked, smiling herself, wanting to join in with them.

"Now what do you think's funny, Mary Langley?"

She looked at Paul's friend in confusion, blushing because she thought she was missing something obvious. They were still laughing.

"You fell for it, all right, didn't you?" Mary looked beseechingly at Paul who still had not spoken. He gazed into the distance somewhere over her head. "Did you think he fancied you? It was a bet, stupid. To see how far you'd let him go."

It couldn't be true. He was only saying that. It was a cruel joke, that was all. "Paul?"

"Aw, forget it, Mary." He turned and walked away from her.

For the rest of the day she was allowed to wallow in her misery unhindered by the teachers. They often had to speak to Mary, to shake her out of whatever daydream she was lost in, but today it was quite plain the girl was suffering. Later, in the staff room, the reason was discovered. One of them had overheard the playground gossip.

"Oh, poor Mary." That was how she was most often thought of.

Chapter Twelve

"Karen, look at this." Sandra was hardly in the door before she was thrusting the letter under her nose. "They've found us somewhere, I can hardly believe it."

Karen almost tripped over Danny who had come to see what all the noise was about. "Let me read it."

"I only hope we can get in before the baby arrives."

"Where is it? I don't know the address."

"Over behind the comprehensive school, which is another bonus for Kirsty next year. One of those new places."

"I'm really pleased for you, Sandra. I'll miss not seeing you so often though."

"I know. And I'm going to tell Mum tonight. Straight away. So's she can get used to the idea before she comes home. Oh God, I hope she won't have to move."

"So do I," Karen replied, worriedly.

"How's Danny getting on with Sue?"

"It's amazing, they've really taken to each other. It was like he already knew her. I had my doubts but it seems to be working out all right."

"And your young man, as mother calls him?" Sandra asked, grinning.

"Oh, that too. He's having Danny this afternoon, actually; taking him out in his pram."

"You must trust him."

"Yes," Karen said. "I do."

"Now what shall I get for Sunday?" Doreen Turner asked. "How about a nice leg of lamb, or pork? We've still got some apples in the shed for the sauce."

"Whatever you like, dear," John Turner replied. It would be a last-minute decision anyway; whichever piece of meat caught Doreen's eye. "Is Karen coming over?"

"Not this week. She's cooking a meal for Trot. I hope he's all right. It's rather a peculiar name."

"It's only a nickname," her husband pointed out.

"But we don't know anything about him; his background and family, for instance."

"Oh, Dor, don't be such a snob. Karen's quite old enough to come to her own decisions." But was she? John was still concerned about what she had told him the other evening. Supposing this Trot chap was in some sort of serious trouble? He sighed. He had to let go at some point.

Doreen reverted back to her favourite topic, The Carver. She had read every word printed about his activities and was horrified at the murder of Katherine Bishop. "I agree. It has to be the same man. It's too much of a coincidence for all this to be happening in a town as small as Sopford. And this was one was a prostitute too. This'll put us on the map, if we've got our own serial killer."

"He's only killed one so far. And they don't *know* it's the same man."

"One so far. You mark my words, there'll be another one. They can't stop those sort of people. They'll find him in the end. I was reading just the other day how the police can find people now through traces of saliva and semen and things, and if he's having sex with them first, it should be easy."

John, a slice of toast raised to his lips, put it back on his plate. Had he heard right? Had Doreen actually used the word semen? She had never said such a thing in all their married years, using euphemisms for anything she considered to be a delicate subject. As she poured more tea she remained unaware of the jolt she had given her husband.

After she had left for work John stacked the dishes and looked out of the kitchen window. The leaves were building up again on the back lawn. He would clear them at the weekend. It was the last time it would be necessary; the trees were bare now.

135

He would also have another chat with Karen, he hated to see her unhappy.

Doreen Turner was proved right. "There's been another one," Melissa told Karen. "Heard it on the local station this morning."

"Another what?"

"Jesus, woman. What goes on in that head of yours? Another murder."

"Here?"

"No, Bordfield this time. The girl's been dead since Monday. Just like the last one, she wasn't missed at first. They said whoever did it must have known her. But they found out something else, it's definitely The Carver. He left the usual mark, that C or L or whatever it's supposed to be. But, here's the thing; this one wasn't a prostitute."

"She wasn't?"

"No. Which makes it more worrying, doesn't it? I mean, if he's going to go round doing it to just anyone, I shan't feel too happy being out on my own at night."

"God, it's awful. If she knew him, and didn't suspect. And let him into her home."

"Karen? Are you all right?"

"Yes. I'm fine." But she wasn't. Last Monday morning Trot had gone back to his flat about ten, after she had made him some tea and toast. She had told him she'd be going in to see May in the afternoon, leaving it open for him to suggest seeing her later. He need not have said anything, or arranged to see her some other time, but he had made a point of saying he was busy that night. Monday night. The night the girl was killed. And the others; it had all been late at night or when the club was closed. And she had let him take Danny out.

No. I'm wrong. It can't be, she told herself. But the memory of that knife being slammed into the chopping board came back again. She knew nothing about him, other than what he chose to tell her. His last girlfriend had left him. She couldn't hold that against him, or use it as evidence of anything. She was hardly in a position to do so. And yet she felt safe with him, somehow sure he would never harm her or Danny. She thought about him now, tucked up in bed in the tiny nursery in Sue's home. She had that to be grateful for. She had not thought that anyone but herself could handle Danny with such love and care.

"Anyway," Melissa continued, "old skinflint's forking out for taxis for us every night now, whatever time we finish."

"Good." It was a double relief; she would also be able to avoid Colin Mitchell.

Sue Trent had been sure that at the last moment Karen would change her mind, but she had still gone ahead and prepared the room. It also meant she unpacked a few of the possessions they had managed to retain from their lovely home. Looking at them made her sad, but nowhere near as unhappy as she would have been once.

She had been amazed at how easily she coped with the little boy. By the second night he was quite happy for her to cuddle him. On Wednesday morning, when Karen collected him she said she was quite happy to put him to bed, if Karen didn't object. Having him there was bliss. Not once had she thought about Martin. She believed, at last, she might be happy. If only it wasn't so hard to hand Danny over in the mornings.

For Sue, the years of bitter disappointment and frustration had taken their toll. The house, the cars, holidays abroad and her jewellery, these things had been no more than compensation for the child she would never have. Now they, too, were gone. All she had to console her was Danny.

He did not have the radio on that morning, but he heard people talking about it. He dared not seem too inquisitive. He waited to read it in the *Sopford Mail*:

PROSTITUTES PREYED UPON

On Wednesday morning the body of Michelle Jarvis, aged 22, was discovered by her father when he went to visit her at her flat. Mr Jarvis said he called round to make sure she had settled in as she had only recently moved there. There was no response to his knock and, as it was only eight-fifteen, he believed she must be at home. He tried the door and it was unlocked.

According to the police, Miss Jarvis was not a known prostitute and her parents disclaim the suggestion as "utter nonsense" but it might be that she had turned to this way of life as a last resort when unable to find work. Her parents, speaking from their detached home in Bordfield said they were shocked and horrifed. "Her mother is devastated," Mr Jarvis told our reporter. "Her brother will be flying over from Canada for the funeral." Mr Jarvis, obviously extremely distressed, went on to blame himself. "I insisted she stood on her her own two feet. If I'd given her a bit more time, this would never have happened." The Jarvises are being comforted by relatives.

The police are working on the basis that there is a connection between the murder of Michelle Jarvis and Katherine Bishop, the woman also recently murdered. Both were strangled in their own homes and neither was missed for several days. In the case of Michelle Jarvis, further evidence that this is the work of The Carver was found. What looks like the initial C or L was cut into her forehead. The police say the public must not remain complacent. In view of the fact this second victim was not a prostitute and that the first was unmarked, it may be that the perpetrator of these atrocious murders is someone trying to lay the blame at the feet of the man only known as The Carver.

He smiled as he read it. How stupid they were. How very stupid. Even giving them one of his initials they were no further forward. It was four days now since the killing and the euphoria was beginning to fade. The memory was just strong enough to prevent him making the mistake of acting again too soon.

*   *   *

138

On Friday night, after the club had closed, the first of the taxis arrived. To give Leonard Murdoch his due, they were now provided for all his staff, male and female alike. Several of them shared anyway, as their routes lay in the same direction. Melissa went off on the first. Karen and Lorraine, one of the upstairs girls, waited patiently for fifteen minutes then went to tell Len it had not arrived.

"They've never let me down before. I'll give them a ring." He turned his back to do so.

"They're busy. They said it would be another fifteen minutes at least. I'll run you both home, I'm off now anyway. Just let me lock up."

"It doesn't matter," Lorraine said, "as long as we get home safely."

Lorraine was the first to be dropped. She lived so near it hardly seemed worth her while getting in the car but it was just not safe to be in the streets alone at that time of night. Leonard waited until she was safely inside before continuing on towards Karen's house. He started to get out of the car.

"It's all right, you needn't get cold, just wait until I've got the lights on. Thanks, Len."

"Aren't you going to ask me in for coffee?"

"Len, I'm very tired."

As she leant over to open the door his arm went around her and he pulled her to him, more roughly than he intended, because she jerked back in astonishment.

"Karen, don't do this to me. You must know how I feel about you."

"Let go, Len. Please." She did not struggle because she thought he would do as she asked. Only when he tightened his grip and tried to kiss her did she shove him away hard. "No, Leonard. I said no and I mean no." She got out of the car and slammed the door hard, forgetting the neighbours in the heat of the moment. She was shaking as she let herself in.

Len smiled. She was a little spitfire but he knew she had enjoyed it really. She was just playing hard to get. Or she might have been embarrassed; perhaps her neighbours

139

were a nosey lot and she didn't want them to see her in a compromising position. She was, after all, still married.

There was no rush, there would be other times. She'd give in in the end.

The woman behind the desk wore a pale blue blouse under a darker blue suit. Her hair was carefully coiffed. Her appearance was deliberately cultivated because some years ago someone had told her she looked like Margaret Thatcher, a lady she admired almost as much as the Queen. Spectacles swung on a gold chain and rested on her bosom. Her attitude was not always all it should be because no matter what anyone said she still harboured a sneaking suspicion that the unemployed were only so because they chose or deserved to be.

She sighed when she saw who her next applicant was; another one of those dreadful Mitchells.

"I don't mind what I do," Colin told her.

"I've heard all this before, Colin."

"I mean it this time. Mickey's got a job."

Not through us, she thought, as she digested this unlikely piece of news.

As she sifted through the information on her computer screen Colin told her, "I've got to find some work. I've got a girlfriend, see, and she's got a baby."

"Your baby? Only if it is, there are certain regulations . . ."

"Danny's not my baby."

Mrs Prentice was aware that there were few jobs Colin Mitchell was capable of filling but there was an expression of anxious hope on his face. "There's not much around at the moment, but there is one here which might be suitable. Do you have transport?"

"I've got a pushbike." Or rather, his father had.

"It's a few miles outside Sopford. Outdoor work. Would you object to that?"

"I'll do anything."

"The Forestry Commission are seeking someone. You need to be fit. Would you like to go for an interview?"

Colin nodded eagerly. Mrs Prentice made the necessary arrangements with one brief telephone call.

"You can go along this afternoon, about three. They'll be a bit lenient on the time because it's not easy to find. Here's a map and this is the name of the man you should ask for. Don't let me down."

"No, I won't. Thank you."

He was leaning over the desk, eyes shining. For one awful moment she thought he was going to kiss her. "And try to be punctual," she called after him.

But he did not hear. For the first time in his life Colin Mitchell felt like all the other people in the street. One of the crowd. A man with a job. Of course, he hadn't got it yet, but he was determined to succeed. Something in him had changed. He had found a purpose in life, and that was to provide for Karen and Danny.

Mary Langley had no idea how she would get through the weekend, nor could she decide if being at home was preferable to the taunting she suffered at school. The humiliation was almost as bad as the heartache. She was a laughing stock, but how could she have imagined someone like Paul would be interested in her? The diet was already forgotten. Food was her only comfort.

She lay on her bed, her large, unsightly thighs bulging through thick, black leggings, the roll of her stomach concealed beneath the same baggy jumper she had worn to the cinema. She put it on every night after school, convinced she could still smell Paul's smell on it.

On the bedside table lay sweet wrappers. When they were finished she had gone downstairs and made a mug of drinking chocolate and brought a packet of biscuits up with her.

Fridays were what her mother called "treat" days. She and her husband would choose a video to hire and watch it while she sipped a few small Bacardis with Coke and Jim drank a few bottles of light ale. Neither of them were big drinkers. Later they had a Chinese take-away. On Saturdays they went out now Mary was old enough to be left on her own.

Mary never went anywhere unless she was babysitting. Usually she watched the video with her parents and was allowed, if she wished, to have a tiny measure of her mother's Bacardi.

"It's best she learns at home, under supervision," Mrs Langley said. "Everything in moderation. She'll know what's what when the time comes that way."

But she hadn't known with Paul.

"She's in a mood, isn't she?" Jim Langley commented.

"I don't know what's up with her lately, I can't get a word out of her. She'll grow out of it. I hope."

"I'm going up The Cherry Tree."

"What?" Frank Mitchell choked on his meat pie. "On your own? And it's Friday."

"I know that. There's no law against it."

"There is as far as I'm concerned. You're not going up there alone, not all dolled up like that. I'm coming with you. What's it all in aid of anyway?"

"Finish what's in your mouth, Frank, if you don't mind. You're spitting crumbs everywhere."

He did so. "Well come on, tell me."

"You won't believe me."

"Try me."

"Colin's got a job."

"Bloody hell." It took quite a while for this fact to sink in. "Are you sure?"

"Yes. Seems he was serious after all. He starts on Monday."

"Doing what, for Christ's sake?"

"Forestry Commission."

"Never."

"Absolutely true."

Frank thought about it. With Dean married, Mickey and Colin working and Spike at his girlfriend's most of the time, the pressure was off. Gloria would ensure some of the money from their wage packets went towards living expenses. She would not be on at him all the time then. He scraped his plate, licked the knife then even went so far as to carry his plate to the sink. "I'd better have a shave."

"Well hurry up. I'm in the mood for celebrating."

Frank was pleased to be going out with his wife. She looked good tonight, in those shiny ski pants and the leotard top. The loose-fitting, flowing voile shirt over the top disguised any imperfections.

"Mind you," Gloria warned as they walked quickly up the road, "I don't want any of that football talk."

"Listen. Now you're all done up, why don't we go somewhere different, just the two of us, like we used to? Have a bit of something to eat later, maybe."

"That'd be nice, Frank." It was times like this when she remembered why she married him.

"Look, isn't that Colin? It is, and he's got my sodding cap on again."

"Don't get excited. He'll be able to afford one of his own soon."

Colin saw his parents and tried to hide behind the tree. His head was full of his job. He liked the man who had taken him on and he thought he'd be able to cope with the work. It was all manual; other people saw to the paperwork and stuff. And when he got his first pay-packet he'd be able to take Karen out properly; buy her a drink or something. It would soon be Sunday. He had the good news to tell her before he asked her out.

And then, when they were really together, when they were sharing a bed, that other thing would stop.

Sue Trent did not work on Saturday mornings because the sandwich bar only really catered for office workers. When Martin had been here he worked until one so she was used to spending it on her own. Today, however, the place seemed larger than usual, and empty, because Karen had already collected Danny. Sue was always pleasant to her, she would not dream of telling her what she thought of her for entrusting her son to someone else because she would

143

lose him altogether. Danny had only been coming for four nights but already it felt like more. Her feelings towards him were growing steadily, like a consuming thing. It was all right at work because she was busy, but as soon as she got home she found she couldn't wait to see him. And he loved her, she knew that. Whenever she picked him up he put his dear little arms around her neck. Her own child, had she allowed it to live, would be twenty-five by now and possibly have had children of its own.

She was dusting the lounge windowsill when she saw Mary Langley go past. The girl looked worse than usual. Whatever's the mother thinking of, she thought, to allow her to go about like that? Her dress sense was abysmal enough, but the expression on her face was worse.

Mary crossed to Sue's side of the road but did not look up. Sue thought she might have waved. She felt warmer towards her neighbours now.

Sue had no shopping to do, nothing really with which to occupy herself for the rest of the day. As the weather was beginning to clear up she would start work on the garden at the back. She had never taken any interest in it, unlike the grounds they used to possess, but now she wanted to make it nice for Danny, for the summer.

Karen sat down unhappily in the kitchen. Why was it so many things filled her with guilt lately? And why couldn't she think straight? No matter how hard she tried her concentration was poor. She had made a couple of mistakes at work last night; not with money or anything, the till saw to all that, but by pouring wrong drinks because she had not been listening properly. There was no great wastage, she had got rid of them on other rounds.

She had always boasted how she took the job at the club to be with Danny during the day and here she was, snapping at him. She loved him more than she could say but her patience was wearing thin lately.

It was Trot, of course, she knew that deep down. She loved him too. Over the year and a bit she had known him this love had been growing surreptitiously and she thought she would still love him even . . . "No! Stop it!" She had said it aloud, surprised at her own voice. How could she conceivably love a man who might have done something so awful? Because he didn't do it. But I just want to hear him say so, she thought. But how could she ask? She could hardly say, excuse me, Trot, but do you go around murdering people and carving your initials in their heads? She had read some of the reports. The police thought it was a C or an L, but how did they know this was supposed to represent an initial? It could just as easily have been some other sign. The coincidence had not struck her at first because she always thought of Trot as Trot, not Carl.

Oh, pull yourself together, she berated herself. This is getting you nowhere. And it was probably the time of the month as well. And, she was tired. And, there was that ridiculous scene with Leonard last night. She had every reason to be grouchy.

She was in the process of trying to decide whether to call off the meal on Monday, to make some excuse. May had not, after all, been discharged. Karen suspected the news about Sandra's move had distressed her, but she would be home on Tuesday. She could say she needed to get things ready. But she wanted to see Trot badly. Alone. Yet her mind kept revolving around the fact that those girls had willingly let the killer into their homes. And there was Danny to consider. But she had been looking forward to seeing Trot so much it was keeping her awake at night. The doorbell prevented her from coming to a decision.

"Mary? What's happened?" At the sight of so much abject misery her own problems faded into insignificance.

Mary told her, without shame, what had happened; how Paul had only taken her out for a bet. The tears started anew.

Karen put her arms around her knowing how much it cost to admit such a thing, how she would have died from mortification if it had happened to her. But poor, plain Mary had no one else to confide in. No friends, it seemed; no one. The Langleys were all right, quiet and respectable, and they kept their daughter fed and clothed but they seemed to have no idea how to relate to her. They were one of those couples who only really had time for each other and should never have had a child. Life was so perverse when there were people like Sue who would have made a marvellous mother.

Karen let her go through the whole episode several times until the repetition made it seem less real. "I'm not up to much myself today, Mary. Do you fancy taking Danny out?" It was not an entirely selfish suggestion, it might help take the girl's mind off her troubles.

Mary had not imagined that someone as cool as Karen could ever be anything other than all right. "Yes. I've got to go to the shops for Mum anyway." Mary brightened a little. Taking care of Danny gave her a sense of usefulness.

"I'll just get him ready," Karen said. "Come here, you." Danny was in one of his awkward moods; it had probably rubbed off from his mother. He wriggled and struggled until at last his coat was on and he was strapped into his pushchair.

"Here," she handed Mary two pound coins. "Have a cup of coffee or something while you're out." She blew Danny a kiss and said, "But please don't buy him any s-w-e-e-t-s."

Sue Trent, a trowel in her gloved hand, was tackling the weeds which always survived long after the flowers were dead. She had hardly got started when she heard voices. Like the front, the back gardens were divided by low, mesh-linked fences so seeing the comings and goings of neighbours was unavoidable. Karen's kitchen door swung outwards. One of the voices was hers. She heard her instructing someone not to give Danny any sweets, spelling the word to avoid a fuss.

Sue froze. How could she do it? Karen had told her the work was suitable because it left her to be free for Danny in the day. It proved all along what she thought; Karen had no time for her son. She left him at night and he'd hardly been home five minutes before he was being offloaded onto Mary

Langley. And to think he could have stayed there, with her. She felt like crying.

Sue was jealous. It was like a knife, cutting through her body. Not even in the early days with Martin had she felt anything like it, but he had never given her cause to doubt him. She was experiencing it now, and unlikely as it seemed, it was of Mary Langley she was jealous. She put the trowel and the fork back in the shed and threw the weeds straight into the dustbin.

Indoors, she quickly washed off the earth that had dropped inside the gardening gloves and pulled on a coat.

Mary had gone out of the back gate, bumping the pushchair over the step. She was heading down the alley which meant she was going into town.

Sue Trent soon caught up with Mary who never walked quickly at the best of times. She was right behind her when she turned left into the covered shopping precinct.

Mary had the two pounds in her pocket and thought how nice it would be to sit with Danny in a cafe and have a coffee, like an adult. He was quiet now, and chuckling to himself; she didn't think he'd misbehave. First though, with her own money, she was going to buy some sweets. For herself, not Danny, to eat later in secret, in the privacy of her bedroom. And she'd got a True Romance magazine to read.

She went into the confectioner's, one of a chain, large and with a huge variety to choose from. She dared not take Danny in so left the pushchair outside, facing away so he could not see inside the store. She checked the brake was firmly on. "Mary'll only be a minute," she said.

She studied the well-stocked shelves and was reminded of her diet and why she had started it in the first place. Tears welled up behind her eyelids, burning, but she refused to let them fall. She kept her face averted for a minute or two until she regained her composure then selected as many things as her money would allow her to buy. She would not dream of using any of the money Karen gave her.

At the till there were two people ahead of her. A man was arguing about the price of a box of peppermint creams, claiming the shop was practising daylight robbery and asking how they could justify an increase of thirty-five pence in a single week. Eventually, grumbling all the time, he paid for them. The next customer had two bags of "pick and mix" sweets to be weighed before she paid.

Mary paid for her own purchases then she, too, left.

When she got outside Danny wasn't there.

Chapter Thirteen

He knew, throughout Saturday, that he was going to strike again. The closer he got to making Karen his own, the stronger the urge. And he was beginning to believe she really did love him; he was sure he was reading the signals right. It would stop when they were together, he was sure of that.

Karen, staring out of the window at nothing in particular, was suddenly aware of Colin, in his usual spot. Out of sheer bad temper, coupled with tiredness and her anxious state of mind, she yanked the curtains together, shutting out the dull daylight and not caring a damn what he thought.

Colin remained where he was. Tomorrow he was going ahead with his plan and on Monday he started work. Life was beginning to look up.

Mary looked around in confusion. She knew she had tested the brake. Had she, daydreaming about Paul, simply forgotten where she left the pushchair? Even as she asked herself, a sick, sinking feeling settled in the pit of her stomach. She had left him right by the door at the side of the building, facing away so he wouldn't see the sweets, the handle visible from inside the shop.

That left only one alternative.

She was sobbing as she called his name, running frantically, out of breath, from one shop to another. People stared at her but no one stopped to ask her what was wrong; nobody offered to help her.

She had read about such things, seen them on the television, but never had she thought it might happen to Danny. At last, her weight an impediment, she sank onto one of the benches between a couple of tired shoppers. Finally it sank in. She had to contact the police.

On Saturdays a couple of officers patrolled the precinct, as back up to the security men. Today they were not in sight. Mary went into the nearest shop and poured out her story. The assistant immediately realised she was genuine and dialled the emergency number. The other customers, queuing up for their weekend joints, offered to help her search.

"She'd better stay here," the assistant wisely advised, "the police'll want a description and everything."

It seemed hours until the officers arrived, one male, one female, but it was actually only minutes. By then Mary was in uncontrollable tears. "Right outside Grindle's," she said. "I was only gone a minute. I could see him from the shop." But it was longer than Mary imagined. It was certainly time enough for Danny to have been taken.

She described as best she could what he was wearing and told them the colour and type of pushchair. She didn't know the make. "What's going to happen now?"

"We'll start looking immediately." The male officer gave some details over his radio then looked at Mary. She was distraught. "You come with us, love. We've got to let Mrs Wilkes know."

"No. No I can't." How could she possibly face Karen who had always been so good to her. And what if something happened to Danny? "We have to stay here to look for him."

"No, love, others'll see to that. Come on. The sooner you face it the better." He knew that if the worst happened, this girl would never get over it, not even with the counselling she was sure to receive.

The moment Karen opened the door she instinctively knew what had happened, for there was Mary and two policemen and no Danny. Her legs buckled and the WPC took her arm and led her to the settee.

It was a nightmare, worse than anything she had ever experienced, and yet she still couldn't believe it had really happened. All her other worries became nothing more than tiny irritations. Nothing would matter if she didn't get Danny back. She was too stunned to cry, but Mary was doing enough for both of them.

"I'm so sorry, Karen. Please forgive me," she sobbed.

"It's all right." She said it automatically. How could it be all right? And Mary wasn't entirely to blame, she had more or less pushed Danny onto her because she had needed a break.

At last, armed with details and photographs the PC departed leaving the WPC to keep Karen company. First he escorted Mary home because he wanted a quick word with her parents. It would do the girl no good at all if they gave her a bad time.

Suddenly, to Karen, the house seemed full of people. Her father arrived first, followed by Doreen. It was a measure of her love for both her daughter and her grandson that she had left the business in the peak hours of her busiest day. Next came Dave who had the furthest to travel. His face said it all. Karen was not a fit mother for his son. As soon as Danny was safe – he dared not think of the alternative – he would apply for custody.

Time stood still yet now it was dark outside. Karen had pulled back the curtains, wanting the light to shine out, wanting to be able to see Danny the moment he was brought home.

There were trays of tea and more questions when the CID arrived. They wanted to know everyone she had ever known, it seemed, although they were aware it was usually a stranger who took someone else's child.

At one point John Turner went out into the back garden, ignoring the cold. He did not want his daughter to see him crying. He begged and prayed to a God he was no longer sure he believed in. If praying worked, Danny should be on his way back.

Karen was still answering questions, puzzled when they

151

wanted to know about her and Dave's marital arrangements. They also wanted to know about Mary Langley. Karen wondered if Mary was going through much the same thing; if they were questioning her about Karen.

No one mentioned the fact that everyone in the room was under suspicion, including Karen herself. A young, harrassed mother, having to work at night and separated from her husband might easily get to the end of her tether. Mrs Wilkes did not seem the type, but then, who could tell?

Dave left once he knew there was nothing more he could do. He could not bear to be in the same house as Karen. He told the police where they might find him, at the supermarket until six, then at his home address. He did not know enquiries about him were already underway.

"May I ring my employer?" Karen asked.

"Of course you can, Karen," the WPC said, "or would you rather I did it for you?"

"No, it's all right." She could not remember exactly what she said but it seemed no time since she replaced the receiver than Leonard Murdoch was on the front doorstep.

"I had to come," he said. "I couldn't bear to think of you sitting here alone, worrying. I'm sorry, I don't know why I didn't realise you'd have other people here. It might be better if I go."

Karen nodded. The last thing she needed was Len's concern.

"Karen, why don't you have a lie down," her mother suggested. "We'll stay here. If there's any news we'll wake you up immediately."

"I can't, Mum. I'll never lie down again, not until Danny's home."

Doreen put a comforting arm around her and gave her a squeeze. She was not normally a tactile person. She was finding it hard to keep the tears at bay herself.

"I see," said DC Gray when he received a telephone call. "Better pick him up then."

"What is it? Have you found him?"

"No, Mrs Wilkes, a possible lead, that's all. Please, don't

152

build your hopes up too high just yet. These things often take some time."

A PC had interviewed the staff at the supermarket. Anita Frith, aged 51, had given a statement to the effect that once or twice she and Dave had had a drink and a sandwich together in the pub over the road if their lunch hours coincided.

"Oh, nothing like that," she had explained. "I'm more like a mother figure to him. His own is in hospital at the moment. No," she continued when she was made aware of the reason for their visit, "it can't be true. I wish I'd kept my mouth shut now. Oh, God, what if it's all my fault?"

"Your fault?" The officer was puzzled.

Mrs Frith went on to explain she knew how very much Danny mattered to Dave and that she gathered the wife worked in some sordid little club and left the child with a sitter. "I mean, the boy doesn't even sleep in his own bed most nights. Well, I said to Dave, now he's got himself a steady girlfried, why didn't he have him with him all the time? Why didn't he just keep him, not take him back?"

She bowed her head. There was no need to point out the stupidity of this woman's advice, she saw it for herself.

Julie Beechcroft had not long returned from shopping when the doorbell rang. She had bought some steak for their meal, and a bottle of wine, although Dave wasn't that keen on it. At first she thought there must have been an accident. She was stunned and horrified to learn that they thought Danny might be there; that Dave had snatched him. She allowed the place to be searched.

"Whatever do you think we are?" she demanded to know. "Dave and I are getting married. When we do so we'll have children of our own. I have no intention of bringing up another woman's child."

The police were satisfied and they believed her. Danny was not at his father's place, nor likely to be if that was the attitude of his girlfriend. It did not rule out the possibility that the father had hidden the child elsewhere. It might be necessary to search the supermarket. There must be numerous storerooms and offices.

Dave Wilkes found himself being taken to the police station to be questioned. When he was set free his anger against Karen had evaporated.

"Karen, believe me, it isn't me," he said when he returned to Oakfield Road. She did believe him but even through her own pain she was glad Dave knew what it felt like, to be thought of as a bad parent.

The night wore on. John and Doreen insisted upon staying. Sandra and Trevor had called in and stayed for two hours then said they must go and see May.

"Karen, shall I tell her?" Sandra asked.

"No. Think what it'll do to her."

"I know, but suppose she hears it on the news?"

Suddenly it was all real. The news. There would be pictures of Danny and appeals for information. She had sat, almost in tears at other women's similar plights. Now it was happening to her. It was then that she cried.

A little after midnight, Trot telephoned. Karen did not want to talk to anyone. Doreen took the call. "No, there's nothing you can do, thanks. The doctor's been and given Karen some tranquilisers. Yes, quite sure. We'll be all right."

"He sounds considerate," she said as she replaced the receiver.

It had been decided that Sandra would speak to a doctor and see what he or she thought about breaking it to May. Even if she didn't go into the television room, one of the other patients might connect the name or even recognize Danny. The doctor volunteered to tell her himself.

John wished Karen would get some sleep. He couldn't bear to see her looking so ill. He hoped there would be some news tomorrow. He glanced at his watch. It was already tomorrow.

All day Sunday a constant stream of visitors arrived at Karen's house. Doreen began to see why her daughter liked the place. These people were genuinely concerned and the offers of help were numerous. It was harder to cope with than if Danny were dead. At least there would have been something tangible to deal with, to direct their anger and grief towards.

Sue Trent came during the afternoon. The police had already been to see her. Karen saw she had been crying. She seemed at a loss as to what to say. But what could anyone say?

Gloria imparted the news to Colin who knew now, whatever he planned, he could not ask her at that moment. He was far more upset about the child than Gloria expected and he insisted upon going with her when she said was was going to call in.

Doreen, John and Karen had spent Saturday night in armchairs, occasionally talking, but mostly silent, deep in their own thoughts. Yet still they were not tired.

Sunday night passed in much the same way.

Karen realised the only one not to ring or call that day had been Trot.

Martin Trent, settling down to his job in Scotland, was experiencing mixed feelings. Whilst he was there, there could be no more rows, no moods and he was free to act like a normal man, no one knowing anything about his previous background. At the same time he was suffering a keen sense of loss. He had never been away from Sue before, and, despite everything, he missed her.

He had no idea why she worried so much about not being able to give him children. It might even be his fault; they had neither of them been tested. Sue said she didn't want to go through that humiliation, and she knew it was her body letting them down. It really didn't matter, he was not one of those men who only felt real if there was someone to carry on the family name or line. Maybe she was just plain scared of pregnancy. He hoped, for her sake, she had an early menopause, then the question could not possibly arise.

Odd that he had adapted to a way of life so alien to his previous one. And he was so much fitter; he felt good.

Mrs Darghie, Martin's landlady, looked after her lodgers

as if they were her own sons, both of whom now worked down south, an irony in itself. There were three of them from the building site there and Martin got on well with the other two.

The rooms were clean and the breakfasts good. Mrs Darghie went out of her way to please them. She'd had a rough lot last year, too fond of the drink, and one of them had wet the bed. These three were different.

Martin started at seven and worked a twelve hour day. They all did, but the money was terrific. He'd be able to save quite a bit.

After work they returned to Mrs Darghie's and showered, trying not to leave too much mess in the bath, then they had their evening meal. It was optional, but they'd got into the habit of eating there. There was a television room downstairs if they wanted but she had no objection to them having their own in their rooms if they provided it themselves. She'd had aerial points put in especially, some time ago. Most nights they had a couple of pints after their food and fell into bed exhausted. The lifestyle was so uncomplicated and there were lots of laughs at work.

Gloria kept her doubts to herself over the weekend but Danny's disappearance made her forget them altogether. On Monday morning she heard the alarm go off in Colin's room just after six-thirty. She lay in bed, Frank's bulk resting against her. There was the familiar creak of Colin's bedroom door opening, shortly followed by the flushing of the lavatory cistern. He had meant it. He was going to work. She just hoped it would last.

When the bathroom was free she got up herself, first waking Mickey who never bothered to set an alarm. She boiled the kettle and started breakfast. Later, when the boys left, she would take Frank a cup of tea. He was not at his best on Monday mornings. It was the same when he was in work. He always drank more on a Sunday night, as if he was making up for the shorter drinking hours.

Colin was pale with lack of sleep. He had been worried

156

he'd sleep through the alarm and had woken at regular intervals throughout the night. He had also been worrying about Karen. "I wish I could do something for her," he confided to his mother.

Gloria looked at him. So that was how things were. That was why he hung around there all the time. She had been a fool not to see it before. She did not have the heart to disillusion him; to explain he was not in Karen's league. This was possibly the reason for the job. She said nothing, she could not hurt this awkward, self-conscious boy of hers. He would find out for himself in time.

He set off on his father's pushbike, having remembered to ask if he could borrow it. Frank did not object. It was another excuse for not finding work if he couldn't get there easily.

Gloria did not mention the boys' jobs to Bill Haines. He might think that there was enough money coming into the house and change his mind about their unofficial agreement. Besides, who knew how long either of them would last in their new jobs?

Sandra took her two children to school then went straight to Karen's. She had told Mrs Turner that she would come and sit with Karen, insisting she and her husband went home to sleep or back to work. "It's best to keep everything as normal as possible," she said, endearing her to Doreen who smiled at the way she was taking over the parental role.

Sandra was right. It was no good them all just sitting there. Whatever they did would not change things. "I'll call in tonight, darling," Doreen said. "So will Dad."

A sort of numbness settled upon Karen. It was a defence mechanism, the only way she could keep going. She changed the sheets although she had not slept in her bed for two nights, then put them in the washing machine. She could not bear to go into Danny's room and kept the door closed. When Sandra spoke she answered her but had no idea what they talked about.

Sometime during the afternoon Trot came. Karen had

flown to the door, each time expecting to see a WPC with Danny in her arms.

"Karen? Oh, love, is there anything I can do?" She had not moved out of the doorway to let him in. "Shall I go?"

"No."

"Hello, Trot. I'll make some coffee. Sit down." Sandra broke the silence. She remembered it had been Danny's birthday when they had met.

"I won't stay long, Karen, I just wanted to see you. I guessed your family would be here yesterday, I didn't want to intrude. Oh, God, there're so many things I wanted to say but they all seem inadequate now." He saw she was not up to talking, was unable to take in what he said. "I'll go now. If you need me, I'm there at the end of the telephone. Any time. Day or night. Don't forget that." He kissed her on the top of her head, a gesture which did not seem to register, then he left.

"Where's he gone?" Sandra asked. "Did you ask him to go?"

"I don't know what to say to him."

"It's all right. Really it is. He'll understand. Here, drink this." They sat drinking another cup of coffee just for something to do.

Martin arrived back from work on Monday tired and dirty. More than anything he wanted to feel those hot needles of the shower on his back. It had been bitterly cold at work. Mrs Darghie waylaid him.

"Martin," she said, very quietly, "would you come into the kitchen for a moment, please?"

He had been about to say he was too dirty but she put a finger to her lips. "Shh, in a minute."

He followed her down the passage. "Shut the door, would you?"

He did so.

"And I think you'd better have a seat. I waited until you got here. I hope I did the right thing."

"Mrs Darghie . . . ?"

"Your wife's here."

"Sue? Here?" He stood up.

"Just a minute. She's fine. Physically, that is. Look, Martin, this isn't easy to say, but she has a child with her."

"A child?" Martin's head was spinning. "What're you talking about?"

"Did you see the news over the weekend? Only there's a child missing. A little boy. His name's Daniel Wilkes. They showed a picture of him."

Martin vaguely remembered seeing something about it in one of the Sunday papers but one of the others had taken it to read before he could finish the article.

"He was taken from outside a shop in Sopford. That's where you live, isn't it?"

Martin nodded dumbly. A coldness washed over him. He believed Mrs Darghie. It fitted. No wonder Sue had sounded so cheerful when he rang her. "You'd better call the police. I'll go in to her."

"She's in the television room."

Sue's face lit up when she saw him. He had not seen her smile like that in years. His heart melted but it was no use. "Sue, what the hell have you done?"

Her face fell. "His mother doesn't want him."

"Of course she does. Are you mad?"

"It'll be a relief to her. She's busy, she lets anyone take him out." She was gabbling; she had not expected this reaction. She thought Martin would somehow help her keep Danny. "You always wanted a son."

"No, Sue, I didn't. I tried to tell you so many times, it was never important. All I ever wanted was for you to be happy." He sat down. It seemed a stranger's child was capable of providing what he'd tried so hard to do.

There was a knock at the door.

"Ay, that's the wee laddie," the first officer to step inside the room said. He was smiling incongruously considering the situation, but it made a change to have happy ending in the city of Glasgow. "Mrs Trent? Would you give me the child,

159

please?" He approached her cautiously; he didn't want her to do anything daft now.

Danny went to the man without a murmur. He had seen many strange faces today and now he was cold and tired and hungry and he wanted his mother.

"Are you Mr Trent?"

"Yes." Martin offered up no excuses. He knew he might be suspected of being a party to it, but he was going to stick by his wife; get her the best psychiatric help he could, although he assumed the police would see to that. But he dared not think what a prison sentence would do to his already unstable wife. He could only hope it didn't come to that.

"May I use your telephone, Mrs Darghie?" the policeman asked.

She nodded.

Still holding Danny the police officer picked up the receiver and craddled it between his neck and shoulder as he dialled headquarters. It was up to them to relay the message to Sopford. The sooner Mrs Wilkes knew, the better.

There were cheers from the other end of the line before he replaced the receiver.

Monday was the worst day of all. The waiting, Karen realised, might go on for ever. Danny might not ever be found. Exhaustion had taken over about four o'clock and she had slept, but for only two hours. She had lost track of who came and went. None of it mattered. When she saw Danny's face on the television it was too much to bear.

Dave had been kind to her, their differences forgotten. Julie had not telephoned once.

At seven-thirty the 'phone went again. The WPC answered it. Karen took no notice.

"Mrs Wilkes?" Karen stared at her blankly. "Mrs Wilkes, I think you'd better take this call yourself."

Listlessly, Karen took the receiver from her. "Hello?" There was a long silence while someone spoke. Karen's knees gave way. Choked with emotion, all the feelings she believed were dead washing over her, she was unable to

160

speak. Her father, who was sitting quietly on the settee having come straight there from work, watched her face and feared the worst, until he realised it was not the sort of news they would impart over the 'phone.

"Karen?"

"They've found him. He's all right. They've found him."

"Oh, Karen." Tears were running down both their faces, and that of the WPC.

"Mum, we must tell Mum." Karen picked up the 'phone again.

Doreen's shriek of delight was heard by them all.

"Everyone," Karen said, "I want to tell everyone."

"Karen, hold on. Where is he?" her father asked.

"Scotland."

"Scotland?"

"He's on his way back right now."

"Who took, him, Karen?"

She looked puzzled. "I don't know. They didn't say." She didn't know anyone from Scotland. Who cared? Her son was safe. That was the only single thing that mattered. "I'm going out."

Her father was laughing at her happy face.

"Where?"

"I'm going to tell the neighbours."

And she did, knocking on the doors of everyone she knew in Oakfield Road. The reception was the same everywhere, one of joy and thankfulness.

Sandra, who had left when John had arrived, hugged her. "It'll be such a relief for May, you can't imagine how worried she was."

"I can," Karen said, only now able to consider anyone else's feelings.

When she got back to the house no one seemed to know what to do. It would be hours before Danny was back. John Turner solved the problem. He picked up his car keys. "If your mother gets here before I'm back, tell her I won't be long."

Doreen was wiping away her tears when John came back

with a bag containing champagne. Even the WPC had a glass before she left. Her superiors wouldn't begrudge her that under the circumstances.

Dave had been informed simultaneously and had come over as soon as he heard. He, too, raised his glass and smiled at Karen. Having witnessed what his ex-wife went through he wondered how he could have doubted her feelings for Danny. He knew, beyond any doubt, he could no longer consider taking him away from her. He had left; he must bear the consequences and make do with regular visits.

"Do you want to ring Julie and tell her?" Karen asked.

"No. It'll keep. Besides, I want to go and see Mum first. She looked dreadful again yesterday."

"Sandra's already gone up there with the news. Do you think they'll still let her home tomorrow?"

"They won't be able to stop her now."

"You're right."

"How did Mary take it?"

"God, you should've seen her. She was ecstatic. That poor girl, I forgot how she must have suffering too."

Leonard Murdoch, when Karen got around to ringing him, was more than pleased. Hopefully Karen would be back at work again.

Later that evening there was more police presence in Oakfield Road when they came to inform Karen who had taken Danny. At first she couldn't believe it, though the more she thought about it, the more obvious it became. But they had interviewed Sue. The realisation hit her that Danny had been only doors away for two nights and nobody knew. How on earth had she got away with it?

Karen's feelings fluctuated. One minute she hated Sue Trent; the next felt only pity for her. But neither mood lasted long, all she wanted was to see Danny, to feel his plump flesh and never let him go. Every other thing in her life had become of minimal importance.

"And to think," Doreen said to John when they at last went home to get some rest before Danny was returned in

162

the morning, "all the time we were worried about Karen and this Carver. I never imagined something might happen to Danny."

"It's over now, love, and I can't see her going back to the club, not after this."

Karen's reunion with Danny was tearful but almost anti-climactic. Once he had been in the house for an hour, it was almost as if he had not been missing. And she felt strange, as if the world was spinning slightly off axis. She did not know that it was reaction to the events of the last three days coupled with a lack of sleep. At times she wanted to find Sue Trent and beat her to a pulp. It frightened her that her emotions were stronger now that it was over.

That first night that her son was back in his own bed, where, she vowed, he would be every night from now on, when well-wishers had stopped ringing and calling in, she lay on the settee, a great lethargy making her unable to move. The last thing she needed was Leonard Murdoch turning up at nine-thirty, bearing flowers and champagne.

Uncaring whether he went or stayed, she allowed him to squeeze past her into the living room and on into the kitchen. There, quite at ease, he opened cupboards until he found glasses, then ransacked the cutlery draw looking for a corkscrew before he remembered what they were to drink.

"I'm as excited as you," he said, expertly opening the bottle without spilling any. Dully, Karen noticed it was an expensive brand. Typical Len.

"Look, like before, there's no need to worry about work. You seem to be going through a bad patch; it happens to lots of people. Things'll start looking up again, you'll see."

"Len, it's kind of you, but it's no good. I can't come back. I took a chance leaving him with a person I hardly knew and . . ." She stopped. The police had asked her not to mention Sue Trent's name in connection with Danny's disappearance yet. She shook her head. "I won't be coming back."

"What will you do?"

"I've no idea. I need a few days before I can start thinking straight. You'd better find someone else, Len."

He saw she was serious and let the subject drop. It was better really; if she wasn't working in the evenings, she'd be free occasionally to go out with him.

Seeing that she was not up to conversation he did not stay long. It was enough. She had invited him into her home at a time when she was alone, apart from the child, and had sat drinking champagne with him. This scenario was a lot different from when she had pulled away so violently in the car. Satisfied with the way things were going, he said goodnight and left.

Colin Mitchell cycled back from work on Tuesday night exhausted. He knew it would get easier as he became fitter, but it was more hard-going than he imagined. At least he'd had the sense to take some sandwiches today. He'd felt such a fool on Monday. Whilst the others had flasks of soup and tea to go with their sandwiches and pies, he sat in a corner of the hut they used for their breaks and pretended he wasn't hungry. No one was cruel enough to laugh at him and between them, they gave him enough to make a meal.

Colin locked the bike in the shed. It was rusty and squeaked but if it was stolen now he could not get to work.

"I'm starving," he said as soon as he got in. But he wasn't cold. Cycling and hard work had put an end to that.

"Well there's stew tonight; that should stick to your ribs, and I've got some nice ham for you tomorrow." Gloria did not mind making up a packed lunch for him; she felt almost proud to do it if he would stick with the job. Already she sensed a slight change in him, something so small as to be indefinable, and there wasn't that hangdog look about him. An added benefit, if it lasted, was that he was too tired to go out last night.

There were only three of them for the evening meal. Spike was out and the family Mickey's firm were moving were going some distance It entailed an overnight stop. Gloria's fingers were tightly crossed. She hoped there was nothing in the removal van which took her son's fancy. "Oh, fancy me forgetting. Sandra popped in. Danny's back."

Food had never tasted as good as that stew did to Colin.

He was cold, bitterly cold by the time he reached the town centre. A heavier coat was more in order than the raincoat, but the temperature had dropped without warning; a real taste of winter. There was not time to go back and change, the urge was too strong. Maybe hearing the good news about Danny had brought it on. Whatever it was, no matter how strong the stimulation, it would have to wait. There were other matters calling tonight, someone he had to see. Naturally, he would say all the right things, like he loved her. Conditioning had seen to that. It would be a lie; a necessary one, of course, a paradoxical way of breaking that final tie.

When he arrived he was welcomed warmly and with great sympathy. It wouldn't be long now. Soon, everything would be all right.

Chapter Fourteen

Wednesday morning dragged. Karen felt she was walking through treacle. She and Danny both needed some fresh air but she didn't want to go out. Most of the time she didn't want to leave the living room. She felt sick when she heard a doctor had examined Danny. "What for?" she asked. "Anyone can see he's all right."

"It's routine, Mrs Wilkes. Like you say, he's just fine, but we can't be too careful these days."

The police constable did not need to be explicit; she knew they had examined him for signs of sexual abuse.

"I still don't understand. Someone went to see Mrs Trent. Danny must've been there, why didn't they find him?"

"I can't answer that. My superiors are looking into it." And someone was going to get a severe rap on the knuckles for that little lot.

Was it never going end, Karen thought, people coming and going all the time? Would she eventually have to appear in court and go through the whole thing again? If she had some money she would have taken Danny and gone away somewhere for a week or two.

She still couldn't take in the fact that Danny, for two nights, had been only yards away, and no mother's intuition had come to her aid. She would never forgive Sue, no matter how mentally ill they said she was.

And then, on Wednesday afternoon, Trot came. It was the one visitor she had been waiting for.

"Karen? Are you all right?"

She nodded. "Come in, it's freezing out there."

She followed him into the living room. They both seemed

tense and anxious. "Tea?" she said, to break the silence. "Or coffee?"

"Where's Danny?"

"Asleep. Upstairs." She had to force herself not to check him every five minutes.

"I've brought this, if you're in the mood." Trot produced a bottle of wine from the pocket of his baggy raincoat.

Karen smiled. "Everyone's been bringing booze; I shall be turning into an alcoholic next. That'd be fine, wouldn't it?" Her voice rose an octave. "If I did they'd take Danny away from me." She covered her face with her hands. Scalding tears ran down her face and between her fingers. It was as if all she had been holding back was pouring out at once. Still standing, she continued to cry, her shoulders heaving, until Trot gently led her to a chair.

He said nothing, just watched her, his face pale, knowing the stress she had been under.

Finally she stopped, an odd tear escaping now and then.

"Shall I open this?" he asked.

"I think I need it."

"Where are your glasses, Karen?"

Not like Len, Karen thought; not making himself at home without an invitation. She told him where she kept them.

They sipped the wine for a few minutes without talking.

"I found it very hard to stay away," Trot said at last, "but I felt sure you'd be surrounded by people, and the police. The last thing you needed was an extra body around the place, I imagine." He paused. "Karen, you haven't been out of my thoughts for a single second. Nor Danny. I just wanted you to know, that's all. Right. I've said my piece. Hello, do I hear the patter of tiny footsteps?"

"That's a bit of an understatement." Karen smiled. Danny had landed on the floor with a thud. His bedroom door swung back easily and they heard it hit the wall before he stomped across the landing and began his precarious descent down the stairs. They were carpeted but Karen rushed out in case he fell. She could not bring herself to put the gate across the top since his return.

"Twot," he said, rubbing his eyes, as he was carried in. "Present."

"No, Danny, not this time." Ever since his birthday, when he had grasped the idea of presents, he hoped for one each time anyone came. Karen had had to be firm because almost all the neighbours had bought him something with which to welcome him home.

Danny wriggled, demanding to be put down. Karen went to get him a drink. When she came back he was sitting on Trot's knee. Children know, she thought; Danny likes him, he was just shy at first. But Danny had liked Sue . . .

"Am I in the way? I expect you've got things to do."

"No, it's too early for his tea." She poured them more wine, already feeling the effects, but uncaring. It might help her sleep.

"I was thinking, how would you like it, if I came here and cooked you a meal? You need a bit of pampering."

She almost said yes. How easy that would be. Her mother had brought over a few necessary groceries, and other people had turned up with drinks and gifts. She was getting too used to it and she had not been out of the house since Saturday. "No, I shall, as I said, return the compliment, and cook for you," she replied."

It meant going into Sopford town centre. It meant going into the precinct where the best butcher was. It had to be done. Sue was no longer a danger, she was not sure where she was, but the police had told her there was nothing to worry about. But in her mind everyone out there had become a potential threat. Trot no longer seemed one. Her imagination had got the better of her. Danny going missing had put certain things into perspective.

"All right. When?"

"Well, it'll have to be Sunday or Monday, won't it?"

"You decide."

"Sunday, then." Presumably routine would be established by then, and Dave would have Danny on Sunday afternoon. It would give her chance to prepare things. She was dreading it, not wanting to let him out of her sight, but she could not deprive his father of his rights and Dave, too, had suffered. Surely he must feel the same way.

"Fine."

"Come about seven." That way he would avoid meeting Dave.

"You'd better stay off today as well, I think," Mrs Langley said after taking one look at Mary on Wednesday morning. "She doesn't look at all well, does she?"

Mr Langley raised his head from the paper and stared at his plain daughter. "No, she doesn't. One more day, then back or you'll be missing too much work."

It had all been too much for the girl. First she had scaled the heights when Paul had asked her out, and there had been that one, magical afternoon, followed by so much pain. Then Danny. She was so pleased he was safe but she would never ask to take him out again, and that was something she was going to miss.

Her mother believed this was the sole trouble, having no idea about Paul. School was the last place Mary wanted to be. *He* would be there, a reminder of the humiliation, and soon people would know of her part in Danny's disappearance. It was bound to be in the paper. They would think her more stupid than they already did.

"Eat this." Her mother put some buttered toast in front of her. She ate half, each bite sticking in her throat. Since Saturday Mary had lost more weight than when she was on a diet. She went back to bed and spent the day reading.

Later, when her mother returned from work, there was a knock at the door. They had few visitors.

"It's for you, dear," Mrs Langley called up the stairs. "Put your dressing gown on."

In the sitting room stood Colin Mitchell, red in the face and ill at ease. His mother insisted he should come, that Mary would be very upset and probably thought everyone hated her. "She's a lot like you," Gloria told him. "Just pop over and say hello. Karen and the baby are getting all the attention." He had done as she had said but now he was here, was tongue-tied.

Mary stared at him.

"My mother said you're upset and that I was to say no one's blaming you," he blurted out, wishing he had been able to put it into his own words. "I just wanted to tell you. I'd better be off then."

Mrs Langley chose that moment to appear. "Would your visitor like some tea?"

Mary did not know why she couldn't ask him herself. She looked at Colin.

He nodded, still flushed. "Please."

They sat with their mugs, trying to make polite conversation until Colin mentioned his job. Mary smiled, pleased for him, and soon he was able to talk more naturally although he had no real experience of chatting to females. But Mary was all right. Had she been pretty, or clever, it might have been different. In turn, Mary was flattered that someone Colin's age was interested in her at all. He wasn't good-looking or anything, like Paul, but he seemed quite nice.

Only when he left did Mary wonder at her mother letting him in; she was always saying the Mitchells were a rough lot. But Mrs Langley was at a loss with Mary and thought Colin might cheer her up.

He had done it. Gone to see her. But he had not been able to bring himself to say what he intended. Alone, he would practice little speeches which sounded perfect, but when the time came to open his mouth, these words were not what he said. Why could he not bring himself to express the most simple of things? This problem was nothing compared with the greater one, but he must not think about it for the moment.

He had done the right thing, gone to see her. He had, as always, done what his mother expected.

Later he would be free to pursue his activities again.

Julie Beechcroft had shown no emotion over Danny's disappearance. She made the right noises and sympathised with

Dave, but it might as well have been a stranger's child as far as she was concerned. She had not minded him spending time at Karen's; it was natural under the circumstances, but she was hoping that Dave would see what a useless mother she was and want nothing more to do with her after it was all over. Now Danny was back and she had Dave to herself again.

When Dave came in from work on Wednesday, he looked at Julie properly for the first time in many days. "You've lost more weight," he said.

"Yes. I'll need to buy some new clothes soon." She reached up to kiss him.

He pulled back. Something else was different. "Your eyes. Where're your glasses?"

"I've got contact lenses. I've been practising with them when you weren't here." This was a good sign. His thoughts were no longer permanently on the boy. "Much nicer, don't you think?"

But Dave wasn't sure. Julie was not the same girl he had met. She was certainly more attractive, but there was an edge to her that was only just beginning to show. He was not sure he liked these changes.

Leonard Murdoch was pleased with how well the club was doing, and there was the run up to Christmas to come. Business was good. Life was good. Mostly. And it would be perfect once Karen Wilkes was on his arm.

Thank goodness his ex-wife had remarried long ago, and, married well. Their marriage had been a disaster, but thankfully short. Another stroke of luck was that he had not been making any money at the time of their divorce. They had each walked away with basically what they had started with. That was long in the past. It was over ten years since he had last heard from her.

He was making steady progress with Karen. If only he could get to meet her family. They were sure to be impressed by his standing and they might help talk her into it. They would want good things for their grandson, surely.

171

And as for Trot, she'd soon see he wasn't up to much. A two-bit chef who probably lived in some squalid little flat. No, Leonard Murdoch felt his luck was in.

On Friday, Karen ventured as far as the parade of shops. She was nervous, glancing behind her several times, unable to shake off the remnants of the nightmare.

When she got back she shut the front door quickly and breathed a sigh of relief. Danny seemed unconcerned. She was, she knew, in danger of becoming neurotic. Tomorrow, come hell or high water, she had to go into Sopford.

She sat at the kitchen table, chewing the end of a biro as she planned what to cook for Trot. Dave liked simple things; chops with potatoes and vegetables, and stew, or something with chips. These days she was more used to preparing children's menus. At least her mother was adventurous and their diet had consisted of Italian, Indian and French recipes as well as English food. She would ring her and ask for some suggestions.

She did so later, allowing Doreen enough time to get home and have a cup of tea.

"Oh, keep it simple, dear. If he's a chef you won't be able to compete. How about some sort of salad starter, pasta – you can always cheat with a packet sauce, and fill him up with garlic bread. Fresh fruit to follow. All very healthy, and easy."

"Great. I'll do that."

Doreen replaced the receiver with a slight tremor of anxiety. Karen wasn't herself yet; she seemed unsure of everything, which was unlike her. It might be best to let her get on with things now, rather than offer to help. This man she was seeing might prove to be a godsend, it would take her mind off things.

As soon as he was able, he got hold of a copy of the *Sopford Mail*. The headline this week was, "PUBLIC OUTCRY OVER REFUSE SITE." He read the article, not wanting to turn the page, willing there to be no further news of the killings. At first he thought it had died down, then, on page 5, he saw the small paragraph:

The police are continuing their investigation into the two recent murders, one in Sopford, the other in Bordfield, of two women in their twenties. So far no one has come forward with information and the police are renewing their appeal for help. Someone, they say, must be aware of the identity of this man, or men, and might possibly be shielding him.

A psychologist is building up a profile of the type of person who might be responsible. He is being aided by the help of two prostitutes who received injuries at the hands of the man known as The Carver who now feel they are able to give a basic description. It is still being considered as a possibility that there is more than one person involved.

The last but one sentence bothered him. Was it possible to build up a profile? And those girls, how much would they remember? He thought back carefully. No, at that time his face had been hidden. His description, he knew, could fit hundreds of people. Average height and weight, medium to dark hair. He had spoken as little as possible and when he had, he had snapped out commands, keeping his voice low and gruff. It was not the way he normally spoke.

His confidence was shaken, the first niggling doubts were creeping in. But the desire to do it again was increasing, the length of time in between shortening.

Would those girls he had marked become terrified he might go after them now that they were helping the police? Would the fear be enough to jolt their memory enough to find something about him that would lead them to him? No. There was nothing.

Two deaths so far. As he finished reading the article he knew there would soon be a third.

Trot rang once a day but did not push his presence on Karen, much as he wanted to. She needed time and space to come to terms with what had happened. He knew from his own experiences that it was the thoughts of what might have happened which caused the most turmoil. He would see her on Sunday, as arranged. By then she would have had almost a week to get over it.

May was safely home from hospital. Despite her protests they insisted on keeping her in for observation for a further two nights. They understood her impatience to see her grandson but it had been a great shock, quickly followed by the relief of his return.

Trevor went to fetch her on Thursday evening. Tears filled her eyes when she entered her house and saw all her familiar things. "There was a time," she said, "when I didn't expect to come back here." Surprisingly, she said she would wait until the next day before she saw Danny. She was exhausted, not realising how much a hospital stay had taken out of her.

On Friday evening, with Sandra fussing by her side, she walked the short distance to Karen's house. "Stop it, girl, will you? The doctor's told me I've got to take some exercise, walk more. It's good for me."

May was disappointed. Danny's reception was cool until he got used to the smell and feel of her again. "Out of sight, out of mind with you, young man, isn't it?"

"Present?" he said.

"Oh, Karen. I still haven't got him anything for his birthday."

"Ignore him. He's been thoroughly spoiled since he's been back," she replied. "I'd forget it, or wait for a while."

"And you? How are you? Really, I mean."

"Tired. No matter how much sleep I get, I still wake up feeling shattered."

"Reaction, my girl," May said. "It'll take a while. What a lot we are. Still, it hasn't affected his lord and master here. He's probably forgotten all about it."

It was a welcome change for Karen. May was the only one who was not afraid to approach the subject directly.

174

The others all skirted round it, or avoided it. Though she knew they were only trying to be kind; trying not to rekindle memories or cause her pain.

"And what about – I've forgotten, the one with the funny name?"

"He's coming over on Sunday night," Karen replied.

"Good. Give him a slap up meal and plenty to drink and everything will be fine."

Karen smiled. Life was so simple to May yet she was so often right.

"And I shall have the peace and quiet the doctor ordered, this lot'll be off my hands," May continued, nodding at Sandra. "Can't say I'll be sorry."

Sandra and Karen exchanged a glance.

"What's up with you two? Oh, I know. I'm not an invalid, you know and if you think the council are going to shift me, you're very much mistaken."

"But, May . . ."

"No buts. I had a long chat with the social workers or whoever they are. Never had much time for those sort of people before, always thought them interfering old spinsters, but this girl was all right. I told her I'd lived here most of my adult life and if they moved me I'd lose all my friends and have no reason to live."

"You didn't?" Sandra was amazed. Her mother was not prone to confiding in strangers. She saw the smile. "You put on an act, didn't you?"

"Best one of my life so far." May chuckled. "She said if they try anything she'll get in touch with them and write to my MP, whoever he is. Anyway, I'm quite used to the idea of having the house to myself now. I'll be able to spread out."

Sandra's moving date was a month away. It was almost perfect; time enough for May to be properly on her feet and six weeks before the baby was due.

Saturday morning arrived. The sky was blue, the bare branches of the trees a stark outline against it. Karen took it as a good omen. The sun shone but gave off no heat. There

175

might even be a frost later. Danny was in his new quilted jacket, his birthday present from Karen, a bobble hat pulled firmly down around his ears. She walked slowly but found it was too cold to linger. When she reached the precinct nothing happened. It was just like any other Saturday. There were no strange sensations when she passed the sweet shop, although she did so quickly before Danny saw where they were.

"Wonderful to see you, Mrs Wilkes, and young Danny," the butcher said. He had not known her name before but it was from there the call had been made to the police. "I saw your picture in the papers. Now, what can I get for you?"

"A pound of best mince, please." She would have to get used to it, but it would pass quickly. News was soon stale. The nationals had carried the story. When the knock had come early on Tuesday morning and Danny was handed over to her, she had been aware of photographers. The picture they had chosen was not very flattering, but she had not looked her best at that time. The Sopford Mail, coming out on a Friday, had not carried the story of the disappearance, only Danny's safe return. Their photographer had telephoned first and asked if he might come round with a reporter.

Her words, in print, seemed trite and bland, the kind of thing she supposed people expected you to say. But how could you put into words what had gone before?

Now, with this journey into town over with, the fear no longer haunting her, Karen had nothing more to do than look forward to Sunday evening.

On Saturday afternoon, just after Trot 'phoned, Melissa turned up. It was the first time she had been to Karen's house. "Here," she said, thrusting a bunch of not-too-healthy chrysanthemums towards her. "I'm sure Danny's been getting all the attention. This is him then, is it?" She peered down at him but seemed unsure what one was supposed to do with small boys. Danny poked out his tongue and received a slap on the hand.

"Are you staying for coffee?" Karen asked.

"Yes. Nice place you've got here."

"It suits us."

"Len's getting on our nerves," Melissa told her. "He keeps asking us if we can talk you into coming back, or put in a good word for him. You could do worse, he's got plenty of the folding stuff."

"He's not my type," Karen replied.

"Looks aren't everything."

"You should know."

"Cheers. He said he came round with champagne. Cosy little tete-a-tete, was it?"

"Nothing of the kind!" Karen exclaimed. "He didn't stay long. Anyway, I'm seeing Trot."

"Ah, the crazy chef. Whatever turns you on, I suppose."

"How's your balding lover these days?" Karen said teasingly

"Who? Oh, him. I gave him the elbow. He wouldn't know the truth if it hit him in the face. Wifey was not in some sun-spot at all and he'd borrowed the car. It's his own fault; he said he wanted to show me off. Took me to some pub where a couple of his mates drink. They put me wise. Still, there's plenty more where he came from."

Melissa chatted on for another half an hour then Karen said she had to get Danny's tea.

"I've got to go anyway," she replied. "Time to get ready for work."

Melissa looked quite nice in jeans and a jumper, Karen thought to herself. Perhaps if she didn't try so hard she would have more success with men.

Chapter Fifteen

Colin Mitchell's resolve to wait a further week had evaporated. Tomorrow was Sunday, only another twenty-four hours, but he felt confident today because he had survived a whole week at work and was beginning to enjoy it.

He walked boldly up to Karen's door and rang the bell.

Danny was in his highchair at the time; he was almost too big for it now. Peanut butter was smeared across his face.

"Stay there," Karen told him as she went to answer the door. She had had more visitors in one week than in all the time she had lived there.

"Oh, hello, Colin."

"I brought this for Danny." He held out a brown paper bag. "It's only a colouring book, but I got it from my wages. I've got a job. I started last Monday."

Karen stared at him. He was speaking fast, getting it all out at once, but it wasn't that. She did not think she had heard him utter one whole sentence before.

"Thank you. It's very kind of you. And I'm pleased about your job." The equilibrium had been restored, she was able to feel for other people. She was genuinely pleased. And it would stop him hanging around all the time. "Look, why don't you give it to Danny yourself?"

Colin's face lit up. This was too good to be true, he was being invited into her house. He stepped inside, noticing how much tidier it was than his own.

Danny glowered from his highchair. He had been caught in the act. He was half standing, facing away from the tray, his hands on the back as he tried to squeeze out of it.

Karen swung him round by his arms and placed him firmly into position. "Hold on, I'd better wipe his hands."

Colin shyly handed him the package.

Karen sighed. Yet another present, but she didn't want to hurt Colin's feelings.

Colin watched as Danny shredded the paper bag and studied the glossy cover of the book. It was now or never, he wasn't going to leave without saying it. But Karen was already showing him towards the front door.

"I want to take you out," he said without preamble.

"Pardon?"

"I want you to go out with me. And Danny, if you like. Tomorrow?" It was over. It may not have come out as he had intended but already he felt better for saying it.

Karen swallowed hard. "Look, Colin, I appreciate your offer but I'm older than you, with a child. You need someone unattached. And besides, there's someone else." She hoped she was handling this right but it felt as if she was in some surreal landscape where nothing had been normal for some time.

Colin's body stiffened. Someone else? She was making it up. Not that man in the flash car, she wouldn't fall for someone like that. "You don't understand. I want to look after you. I'll never let anyone harm you or Danny." He was getting more and more agitated. "I think about you all the time. I love you."

Karen took a step backwards, blocking the kitchen door, putting her body between Colin's and Danny's. She was frightened; there was such intensity in his eyes. "No," she said as calmly as she was able. "You don't love me, Colin. You can't when you don't even know me. It's nice to think you'd look after us, but we can manage."

Rejection hurt more than he could have imagined. He had to prove to her that he meant what he said. His voice was husky. "You can't. Someone took Danny. I'd *never* let that happen. You need me to take care of you. Look," he reached into his jacket pocket.

"Oh God." Karen steadied herself against the door. In

Colin's hand was a knife. It all flashed through her mind again, just as it had with Trot. All the things Sandra had said, about him watching her. Colin. He could be The Carver.

"This'll stop anyone hurting you," he continued, unaware of the terror he was causing.

Danny began to grizzle as if he sensed something was wrong. Karen ignored him.

"I'll make everything all right, really I will." He was sweating with the effort of trying to convince her.

"Colin, give me the knife, please." Karen heard her voice. It sounded as if it came from a long way off. "Give it to me. If you get caught with it you'll be in a lot of trouble." Fear for her son kept her from collapsing. After what she had already endured she was amazed she could cope with more. "Colin, please. You're frightening me. And Danny."

Danny was crying harder now.

"I'm sorry." He bowed his head and did as she requested.

Karen took the knife. "Thank you." Without being aware of what she was doing her hand reached out to the sideboard where her handbag sat. She slipped it in through the open leather top out of sight.

"I wanted to find whoever took Danny. I wanted to bring him back to you."

Karen saw it then. How pathetic he really was, how much he wanted to appear a hero, yet there he stood, almost in tears.

"The police are there to do that, you know that. And it might have endangered Danny's life." Keep talking, she told herself, keep him calm.

"Will you tell the police, about the knife?"

"No, Colin, I won't. But you must promise not to even think of anything like that again."

"All right."

Please go, she thought, please just get out of my house.

He went quietly, wearing an air of utter defeat.

"Goodbye," she said.

He did not answer.

As soon as he was outside she pushed down the snib on the

180

Yale lock, threw both bolts and slammed the chain across. Then she ran to the kitchen and bolted the back door. Only then did she sink into a kitchen chair as she realised she was shaking from head to foot. "How much more?" she asked, aloud. "How much is anyone expected to take?"

When she felt able to move she went to the sideboard and reached to the back. There was some brandy her father had given her last Christmas. She did not like it much, unless it was with a mixer, which John Turner thought was sacrilege, but she poured some out and gulped it down. Her throat and chest felt on fire but when it hit her stomach she saw why it was used for medicinal purposes. She began to feel calmer.

Ought she to tell the police? No, she had had enough dealings with the police. The more she thought about it the more certain she became she was wrong. They wouldn't believe her anyway; they would say she was imagining things because of what had happened to Danny.

She slept fitfully that night, wondering if it was worth mentioning to Gloria. Then she remembered that the girls who had been killed had been strangled, not stabbed. She began to relax a little.

Danny climbed in beside her before it was light. She cuddled him for a while as she thought of the evening to come.

Dave arrived at two, as arranged. "You're looking better," he told her, which was odd, considering her disturbed night. "I'll have him back by six-thirty."

Karen waved as they went to the car. There was no sign of Julie.

As he opened the car door, Dave turned back to her. "Oh, about the divorce; there won't be any problems. I'm sorry, Karen, for what I said that night."

"It's all right." Karen smiled. "Forget it." Some of the old fondness reasserted itself but at the same time she knew it would never work between them again.

As soon as they left Karen started to prepare the meal, leaving as little as possible to do after Trot's arrival. Suddenly she realised she had not bought any wine. It was twenty-to-three. She would just make the off-licence in the parade if she hurried.

As she turned out of Oakfield Road she saw Colin Mitchell walking towards her. Her heartbeat quickened. Keep calm, keep calm, she told herself.

Colin looked across and waved but he did not stop.

She had grabbed her purse from her handbag, and her keys were in her pocket. She rarely used a bag now, except as a place to store letters and bank books; it was too much of an encumbrance with Danny and the pushchair and shopping. Mostly it lived on the sideboard.

It was peculiar, this change that came over him when he wore something which belonged to his father. It became easy to take on a different persona; a confident one that did things that he could not.

He had made no mistakes so far; it must remain that way. Tonight he would be extra careful; find out a bit about the girl first, pretend to take an interest, maybe, ask about her family. That way he would know if she'd be missed. Luck had been with him so far, now it was time to make his own.

There would be no telephone calls, no chance meeting in the street. He would go down by the railway station where one or two girls hung around under the arches. They were rough, he knew that, but so what?

As he approached the area he changed his mind. No, he remembered now they sometimes went about in pairs, and there were taxis flying about, meeting trains. It had been a stupid idea. At first everything seemed so easy; now there was danger in whichever direction he turned.

Then he saw her. He chuckled. Luck was more than on his side. Why had he worried?

She was about twenty yards ahead, walking slowly in the direction of the bus stop. The short, tight skirt and high heels might not mean anything, but it was far too cold for that sort of outfit, unless she had something else in mind. And she had no coat, just a shiny emerald green bomber jacket with a dragon on the back. She stopped at the bus shelter. No one else waited. He stood beside her, a harmless enough action. She looked at him boldly, her eyes travelling down the length of his body as if she was assessing his worth or judging the thickness of his wallet. The nondescript raincoat and cap gave little away. She smiled, having come to some sort of decision. "It's getting very cold now, isn't it?"

"Very. Going to Bordfield?"

"Yes. Are you?"

"Um. There isn't much to do round here at night, especially on a Sunday."

"No. Look, if you're not doing anything in particular, it seems daft to waste the bus fare. We could have a drink, then go to my place. I've got some wine there."

Wine. Once or twice he had been offered a drink, usually beer or whiskey. "Your place sounds fine." If she insisted they went to a pub he'd have to forget it. He could not risk being seen with her somewhere where people would remember them. They might not be able to recall his face, but there would be no forgetting that emerald jacket.

"Okay. You don't want a drink first?"

"No, I'm not bothered, unless you want to." If she said "yes", he'd buy her one them dump her. No harm done.

"No, we might as well go straight there." The girl told him her name was Joanne. He told her his name was Phillip. Once or twice she stopped to gaze in shop windows and point out items she liked. He knew what she was doing. He would not be buying them for her, nor would she be around to wear them. "Do you live alone?"

"Oh, yes, I couldn't stand someone else around. I moved here a couple of years ago."

"Away from your family?"

"Family?" She snorted. "Some family. Dad's inside, my mother pissed off years ago and God knows where my sister is."

"Oh dear. I'm sorry." Perfect. Couldn't be better.

Her bedsit wasn't up to much, it was pokey and badly in need of redecoration. The tiny bathroom had been converted from what seemed to have once been a lean-to. Her Midlands accent grated.

"Here." She handed him a glass of red wine. It tasted sour. A thought crossed his mind. Was she on the game or had she simply taken a fancy to him and thought they would spend the evening having a cosy little chat? No, she would not have invited him home so quickly.

Joanne, seeing his glass was empty, took it from him and placed it on the floor. "The payment is in advance, Phillip."

His breathing returned to normal. Now he knew where he stood. "How much?"

"It depends what you want."

"Straight sex. Apart from one thing."

"Which is?"

"I want you to look at me. All the time. Do you understand?"

"Fair enough." Strange request, but not exactly hard work. She bent forward, tossing her long hair over her shoulder to enable her to undo the zip of what turned out to be a mini dress rather than a skirt. He saw the tender nape of her neck and was erect at once. In minutes now his hands would be around her throat. And this time he was going to kill her before he orgasmed. This time the girl would be dead before it was over.

He gave no thought to what that would make him.

Chapter Sixteen

Sunday evening provided exactly what Karen needed to soothe her nerves. Dave brought Danny back on time. Having been running about in the park, kicking a football, he was exhausted and was asleep as soon as he was in bed.

The food was ready and would be presentable, at the very least. The wine was open and Karen was bathed and changed.

Trot looked handsome and brought more wine. She knew no one else thought him good-looking. Sandra had said he was merely "all right" in the looks department, but there was something about Trot which appealed to Karen.

They ate and drank and talked. And Karen found herself laughing as they each described their own sets of parents. "My mother, Doreen, runs a beauty parlour. Salon, she calls it. When you meet her you'll realise she could do no other. She tries to be hard, you know; a businesswoman, but underneath, she's soft as anything. And Dad, well, he's just great."

"Mine are divorced. No, nothing to get upset about. No dreadful tales of a broken home or anything. They should have done it years ago. They're nice, both of them. They just don't belong together; probably did the decent thing, stuck it out for my sake and that of my sister. Dad's retired now, ex-Civil Service. He lives down on the coast in an immaculate bungalow – he likes things neat and tidy – and potters about in the garden, growing far too many vegetables, but it keeps him in with the neighbours. He also plays golf and bridge and chats up rich widows. I think he's happier now than he's ever been. Now my mother," he grinned, his eyes sparkling, "she's something else. You'd have to meet her to understand. She's the epitome of middle-class living. You know, the house, with the family silver and dinner parties, the car, the smart woollen skirts and high necked blouses, the sensible flat shoes. I could go on and on. Leading light in the W.I., naturally. Well, after the divorce, out of the blue, I received an invitation to go and visit her, there was someone she wanted me to meet. The house had been sold by then and she'd got a flat in London." Trot was laughing at the memory. "The flat's large and airy, lovely place," he continued. "But not at all her style, or so I thought until I met Tom."

"Tom?"

"An artist. Fifteen years her junior and a little bohemian, to say the least. They are, to coin a phrase, living in sin. And apparently loving it."

"A bit like you. Bohemian-looking."

"Me?"

Karen nodded. "Go on," she said.

"Well there was mother in a flowing dress, happy as a pig in whatsit. But old habits die hard. She accepts Tom exactly as he is, paint-smeared jeans and all, but I got a reprimand for not dressing up for the occasion."

"They sound lovely."

"They are, and I wouldn't want them any other way. Now, here's the thing I've been saving to tell you. The other week, Monday, when I said I was busy, I was making some inquiries. I've got a proposal to make to you, but hear me out first. I went to look over some premises on the edge of town. Not great, but there're possibilities. Planning permission's already been granted to convert the place into a restaurant. I'm going to chance it, Karen, go out on my own. I've already signed the papers. I shall need help, of course, and that's where you come in."

"Me?"

"Yes. There are two ways of looking at this, either I employ you, which was my initial idea, but after what's happened, I can't see you leaving Danny with anyone other than family, or, well, never mind. It was just a thought."

"Or what?"

"Oh, nothing. Hare-brained scheme, that's all."

Karen saw he would not be pushed but there was a tenseness about him which unsettled her, as if he felt he had said too much.

Between them they washed up and when the kitchen was once more tidy, they took the last of the wine into the living room.

When the bottle was empty Karen knew she had to make a choice: offer to call him a taxi or invite him to stay the night. She chose the latter.

Gloria Mitchell heard the back door close. Good, Colin was in. She could relax now and go to sleep. He had not been going out much since starting his job. Tonight, though, he had left straight after his meal and had stayed out late. She hoped he would not oversleep tomorrow. It was ridiculous to lay awake until the boys were in, but she did so. Spike's possessions were gradually disappearing over to his girlfriend's place. Hopefully the arrangement would become permanent and she wished Tina all the luck she would need to put up with him.

She would be happier if she knew what went on inside Colin's head but suspected he wasn't always certain himself. The memory came back, unbidden; the scene she tried to forget. Once, not long ago, she had seen, through the crack of Colin's slightly open bedroom door, her son, sitting quietly on the bed, a knife in his hand. He was almost caressing it. She dismissed the thought that entered her head. She had to.

She turned over and moved into the warmth of Frank's body. His chest rose and fell steadily, and for once, he was not snoring.

"Has she said any more about the divorce?" Julie Beechcroft always referred to Karen as she, as if, by not giving her her name, she was less of a person.

"No, but we're all sorted out. There won't be any prob-lems."

"So, in that case . . ."

"It's sorted, Julie." Dave did not wish to discuss it. Having decided Danny would be better off with his mother, he no longer saw the need to hurry things, in fact, there were times, lately, when he thought he was better off remaining married as that way he could not be pressurized into a second one.

"Are those new?" Dave nodded towards Julie's legs, encased in vividly coloured leggings. He thought her thighs still too heavy to get away with them although they were nowhere near as big as they once were.

"Yes. I'm glad you noticed. Do you like them?" She gave a twirl and curtsied.

He thought her rather silly. "I liked you as you were. What's for tea?"

Julie sighed. Dave was solid and seemed so reliable but they were young. She was sure she loved him very much but since her weight loss and acquiring the contact lenses, her confidence had soared. She wanted to spread her wings a bit before they settled down to night after night of television and going to bed at ten-thirty. She had to start organising a social life for them both.

"What did I tell you?" Doreen exclaimed.

"I don't know, dear. What?" John Turner waited for another of Doreen's revelations.

"Read it for yourself. It was obvious to me."

John took the *Sopford Mail*. He couldn't argue with her, Doreen had mentioned serial killers.

SOPFORD MAIL
SERIAL KILLER STRIKES AGAIN?

The body of a third woman has been found, once more in Sopford. Police say the circumstances of this woman's death are similar to those of the two previous victims. Joanne King, aged 24, had a record of arrests. Miss King also lived alone and had no relatives nearby. Despite the appearance of the initial L or C on her forehead, it still

188

remains some matter of speculation as to whether The Carver and the killer are one and the same man.

Interviewed earlier this week, the police psychologist said, "I find it hard to imagine that in a town the size of Sopford, or even Bordfield, there are two men wishing to harm these girls, and there are too many similarities for it to be coincidence. These similarities are not being made available to the public for obvious reasons, suffice it to say, there is a definite connection between the latest three incidents.

"My own view is that he bears some grudge against a female, or females; that he has perhaps been dominated by one particular female and wishes to take his revenge. This would, to me, explain the initial: they will bear his mark for ever. It is possible that he needed to move on to further violence to achieve whatever satisfaction he is seeking. Having turned to murder, there is no further step to take and my only hope is that, if he is not soon apprehended, this man will realise he has reached the end of the line and give himself up."

"They've got to be joking, haven't they? Pass the teapot, John. Why should he give himself up? He can just keep on doing it. I'll be a bit late tonight, I'm calling in to Karen's on the way home."

John smiled. Since Danny's disappearance, Doreen no longer found Oakfield Road such a no-go area and she seemed to be forming some sort of relationship with the Wilkes family at last. Not quite friendship, it could never be that as far as Doreen was concerned, but at least appreciating some of their worth.

He smiled even further after she had left, as he guessed her ulterior motive. She wanted to meet this Trot fellow and was going to issue an invitation for Karen to bring him for lunch or supper.

Karen was pleased with her mother's new-found interest in her life but wondered, a little cynically, how long it would last once the dust settled.

"It's quite serious, actually," she told Doreen over a cup of tea. "He's buying his own restaurant and he wants me to go in with him. Not financially, he knows I'm not in that kind of position. Well," – Karen stared at her hands wrapped around her mug, waiting for her mother's reaction "the thing is, he wants to marry me."

"Marry you? Good God, girl, you're not even divorced yet. And what about Danny?"

"He wants Danny too, he wants to be able to give him a good life. And I know I'm still married, but I won't be soon."

"But Karen, I haven't even met him yet."

Karen smiled fondly. So that was it. Trot had not yet received the necessary approval, therefore nothing must be allowed to happen until it was given. "I've been through it once, Mum, I know what I'm doing. Of course you must meet him, but don't worry, I'm not rushing into anything. Dave's agreed we go ahead on mutual consent, then we shall see. You're not going to like it, but I shall probably live with Trot first. I can help him with the business, there's living accommodation over the top."

"Oh, Karen, think about it. If it all goes wrong you'll have lost the house."

"I know that. And I have thought about it. I've thought about nothing else since he told me. I've always been sheltered; I have to take some risks."

"But you hardly know him."

"But I do. I've worked with him for over a year. I've seen him in good and bad moods. And the main thing is, I love him."

"Well you'd better ask him over to meet us one evening," Doreen said as she buttoned up her winter coat.

"I will."

"I don't know what your father's going to say about all this."

"'Bye, Mum." But Karen knew. He would be happy for her. Unless he remembered the doubts she had expressed.

*   *   *

190

Until that conversation with her mother Karen had still not come to any definite decision. As soon as she had spoken the words, however, she knew it was the right one. She couldn't wait until Trot came over the following afternoon; she rang him immediately, just as he was setting off for work.

"Oh, Karen," was all he said, and he repeated it several times. "Look, I'm going to be late. We'll talk about it tomorrow. Are you sure? One hundred per cent certain?"

"Yes."

Trot replaced the receiver, pure joy rendering him incapable of movement for several seconds. Between them they would make a go of it. They would have the best restaurant in Sopford. They already knew they could work together and Karen would have no worries about Danny because he would be just upstairs, and when things got going she would no longer have to work. He had been surprised at her enthusiasm over the project when he had finally gotten around to telling her what he hoped for. It had been the morning after she had cooked him the meal, when he no longer felt humiliated about his performance in bed. That first time had been nerves; wanting to impress, wanting to make Karen happy, not wishing to spoil things by doing something wrong. Once he and Karen were finally together everything would be alright.

Karen had spoken of how she hoped to do something with her life when Danny was older. He had not expected her to think of his venture as doing just that. Later, if she still wanted, she could go back to college or whatever.

When he got into work he told Leonard Murdoch. He had already warned of the possibility of his leaving. "I can give you a month's notice, is that okay?" Trot knew it would be. He had known situations where chefs had walked out halfway through an evening. He was playing fair.

By the end of the night Murdoch also knew of his arrangement with Karen. Trot had not been able to keep it to himself, although he did not inform his boss. It was Melissa who passed on the news.

*   *   *

Leonard Murdoch planned his move with care. He went to his office and flipped through the Yellow Pages. First, having met the Turners briefly when he called in to see Karen, he took a chance and rang them. She had given their address and telephone number as next of kin, as opposed to Dave's. He turned on all his charm and asked his favour. Yes, John Turner said, they would be pleased to look after Danny for one night.

"It's the least I can do," Len said. "She's been a great asset to the club, always on time and a good worker. I couldn't think of a suitable present, to be honest, so I thought a slap-up meal was the best way of showing my appreciation."

"That'll be nice for her," Doreen commented when John relayed the contents of the conversation. "That Dave never took her anywhere decent. And if she's going to be living in a restaurant, she probably won't want to visit others very often."

"Karen? It's Len Murdoch here. Now don't say no, because it's all set up."

"What is, Len?"

"My leaving present to you."

"You don't have to do that. Besides, I let you down at the end."

"No, I insist. Now you'll probably think it a cheek, but I've spoken to your parents . . ."

"You've what?" For a second she imagined it was to ask their permission.

"I knew you'd think twice about any other babysitter but they've agreed to have Danny for the night. It's all fixed for Monday. Buxton Manor, with the best of everything you can eat and drink. You know how I feel and I know it's useless, Trot told me, you see. Do this small thing for me, Karen? Let me take you out, just the once? We might not even see each other again."

"All right, Len. Thank you." Buxton Manor? What on earth could she possibly wear?

*   *   *

192

"Trot," she said the following afternoon. "Len wants to take me out for a meal. My farewell gift, apparently. I've said I'll go, do you mind?"

"Let's get one thing straight from the start." Trot sat down.

Karen's heart sank. With Dave she could not have considered accepting the invitation. She was sure Trot was not possessive.

"If you want to go somewhere or do something, you do not, nor ever will, need my permission, or even approval. We start as equals. We have to trust each other and as long as we always talk, tell each other things, it'll be fine. Now, for heaven's sake, woman, make me a cup of coffee." But even as he spoke he was on the way out to the kitchen to make one for her.

Len grinned. It was that easy. He would do it right. There would be flowers, something classy, an orchid maybe, and an aperitif and wine and champagne. He could afford it. Karen would be impressed, she'd see he could make her happy. He would also give her a reason to seek his protection: he would tell her about Trot. Even if she did not believe him, the doubts would be there. She would not move in with a man who might, just might, be a murderer.

The article in the paper scared him further. They were guessing but they were right. And what did they mean, there was a clue which linked the three murders? Keep calm, he told himself. Clues they might have, but they are no use unless they know who I am. The fear excited him. He wanted to stop, right now, before they got any closer. Just once more. The last and the best. Tonight then.

Night descended quickly now. There were more hours of darkness than daylight. And it was cold. Bitterly cold. Exposed features or fingers became blue with cold in seconds. It would not stop him, nor did it ever seem to stop the girls he stalked.

That night he followed one. She turned around, glanced at him nervously and hurried on her way. He had made a mistake. She would not recognize him. The raincoat was buttoned, the belt tied around the middle. With a thick jacket underneath it made him seem bulkier, and his cap was pulled well down over his forehead.

He no longer had the knife. That psychologist was too smart. No more initials; that would confuse him further.

He tried a telephone box. There were a couple of numbers there he might use, but the 'phone was out of order. Was it a warning? Things didn't feel right. Of course, he also had Karen on his mind but it was not just that. It was his mother. He knew she had seen the knife.

A police car, its blue light flashing, raced past. His heart beat faster. No, it was not him they were after. A group of drunks staggered towards him, laughing and jeering and bumping into him as he tried to avoid them. He apologised. He was not afraid of them but he could not risk being involved in a situation where someone might call the police.

He went home to his solitary bed. Tomorrow then. He lay, imagining what he would do, what the girl would look like. A slow smile played around his mouth. He no longer looked the the ordinary, average, man in the street. Just then he looked exactly what he was.

"You are not to hang around there any more. Do you understand me?"

Colin Mitchell had confided in his mother his feelings towards Karen. They were alone in the kitchen. He would not have dared spoken if his father was in the house.

"Not under any circumstances. Do you know what it makes you look like? That girl's been through enough. And she's not interested in you, Colin. I don't mean to sound hard, but it's true. You want to find someone your own age. There're plenty of nice girls out there."

"That's what she said."

"Then she's every bit as sensible as I took her for. Look,

if you're that fed-up take Mary to the pictures or something. She's lonely, you know."

"She's only fifteen."

"I know that. I'm not suggesting you ask her to marry you, for God's sake. Women can be friends as well, you know."

Colin thought about it. He might do that. He liked the cinema but would not go on his own. And next week, on Friday, he was going to have a drink with two of the men from work. He had almost burst with pride when they had asked him. Nothing like that had ever happened before.

"You need to get out more – I don't mean hanging around the streets. Come on, I'll make us some tea and we'll watch a bit of telly. There's no one else in."

Colin was surprised, now that his mother had finally made him understood just where he stood with Karen, that he was not more miserable. It was a sort of relief, really, knowing for certain she would never be his.

In the middle of the day, as he was putting invoices in date order ready to deliver to his accountant, Leonard Murdoch received a telephone call. Without hesitation, leaving everything just as it was, he pulled on his raincoat and ran out to the car.

Once before he had been told his mother was dying. It had been a false alarm. However, he had his image with the staff of the private nursing home to consider.

Only the good die young he reminded himself as he drove out of town. His mother was only sixty-one. She was in the early stages of senile dementia and her body was weak, invaded by several diseases, yet she still continued to exert a hold over him. Her opinion still mattered more than anything else. "Please let her be dead when I get there," he prayed. He did not think he could bear to watch the actual dying.

Last week when he was summoned to her side she had rallied, a glint of something which might have been malice in her eyes when she opened them briefly and looked at him.

For three years now he had visited her at least once a week, sometimes twice. The nurses understood he had a business to run and praised him for his devotion. They had warned him that no matter how much you cared for someone, when they eventually died, you still carried a burdon of guilt, that you felt you could have done more. Not Len. He wondered what the cheerful, pleasant sister would make of him if she knew what was going through his mind.

"Ah, Mr Murdoch, I'm so glad you're here. I'm afraid your mother's condition is deteriorating. I know you've been expecting it, but it doesn't make it any easier, does it? Come along, she'll be pleased to see you."

Len's throat tightened. If she was going to be pleased to see him, she could not be that bad.

He went down the corridor towards the door behind which his mother lay. His feet felt as if they were being dragged through treacle.

"Oh," he said, startled at the dramatic change in her appearance.

"Would you like some tea?" The young nurse at the bedside stood up to give him her chair. A cup of tea seemed to be the answer for everything here. He shook his head. The nurse left.

"Hello," he said.

His mother made no response. She looked smaller, as if she had shrunk since his last visit. His flesh crept at the idea of being alone with the dying woman.

Her body shifted slightly. He had to stop himself from screaming when a thin, claw-like hand touched his. He flinched. Her eyes opened and she looked at him. With the total lucidity of those near death she said, "You know that only I understand you, don't you, Leonard?" Then her eyes closed and her face caved in as the muscles relaxed in death.

He was unable to move. The relief, the lifting of that heavy burden from his shoulders he had anticipated since she was first hospitalized, did not occur. He felt only numbness. She was dead. It was over.

What had those last words meant? Was it her way of saying that even in death she still had power over him, or were they an absolution? Her way of saying she knew what he was trying to do? He would never know. That, in itself, was a hold over him from beyond the grave. He could not forgive her that.

"Mr Murdoch? I'm so sorry. You should have called me."

He looked up. He had not heard the sister enter.

"There was nothing you could do." Only as he turned in her direction did he realise he was crying.

Chapter Seventeen

He could not ever remember being so cold; not through the horrendous winter six years ago; not when he fell through the thin ice of a pond when he was a child. He couldn't wait. Not now, the urge was stronger than ever. He was like a junkie needing the next fix.

It must be Bordfield. No prostitute in Sopford was going to take another chance. His breath steamed and his eyes watered. He had altered his appearance. No more cap, and a leather jacket instead of the raincoat or the bomber jacket.

There were only two taxis by the railway station, perhaps the other drivers decided it wasn't a night to pick up any business. This time he was going to catch a train.

Before he reached the station he saw one woman plying her trade. She was old and worn out, bare-legged, even in this weather. She did not interest him.

The cold had activated his bladder again, he didn't think he'd make it to the gents which was on the opposite platform at the station. He pushed open the swing door of the pub on the corner. The gents was at the back. He would have to order a drink. People didn't like you coming into their premises simply to use the lavatory. He did so, then went out to the back.

When he returned he realised what sort of pub it was. The customers were young, some obviously underage. The air was thick with smoke and he guessed by the tang that not all of it came from cigarettes made with tobacco. Males and females wore a sort of uniform of leather, their hair spiked and dyed, rings in their noses, ears and one girl with a stud through her lower lip. The noise from the jukebox was deafening. He was out of place here.

At a table in the corner was a large man with a half-shaven head. He wore only a vest, tucked into jeans, and a leather waistcoat. There were several other people with him. The girls in the party were young.

He turned his back, aware of the danger of staring. After several minutes one of the girls approached the bar clutching a twenty pound note. She ordered some drinks. "Haven't see you in here before," she said to him.

"Never been in, that's why."

"Oh. I'm here most nights. Gets boring though. Same old thing." She paused, glanced across at the table in the corner then said, "Where do you go for your fun?"

"Here and there."

"Fancy taking me somewhere exciting?"

He did not want any trouble. Supposing she was the large man's woman? She guessed his thoughts.

"I'm a free agent. I just drink with them, that's all. Hold on, I'll be back." She carried the drinks over to the table.

He could not hear what she said but they all laughed.

"Aren't you going to buy me one then?"

He did so, refilling his own glass. They drank in almost total silence, conversation impossible over the music. They left together and he was glad to be out of the place.

"Aren't you cold?" he asked for something to say.

"Nah. I don't feel the cold." She was wearing very little. "Where're you taking me?"

He had not thought about it, assuming she already had somewhere in mind.

"We can get another drink," she suggested. "I know a place that does afters."

"Would they sell us something to take out?"

"Impatient, aren't you? Yeah, I expect so. You'd better wait here, they might not if they see a stranger. Give us the money then."

He handed her a five pound note.

"What? You won't get anything for that."

"Get some wine."

"Oh well, please yourself."

She returned after a few minutes with a bottle in a carrier bag which bore the name of a shoe shop. She did not give him any change. "Here, what's you name?"

"Brian."

"I'm Josie. Well come on, Brian, let's have ourselves a party."

"Party?"

"Forget it, it's just a saying."

"Here we are," she said a few minutes later. "It's a dump really, but it's all I can afford."

She was right. It was a dump, and a not very clean one either. She took the bottle from the bag, found a couple of tumblers and opened the wine. She was fortunate it was a screw-topped bottle, she had no corkscrew.

Josie's eyes were glazed. He guessed she had already had a fair bit to drink. He let her finish the glass of wine then reached across her. She leant forward, offering him her lips. He never kissed them. Never. He pushed her down on the single bed which also acted as a settee. She was pretty drunk; he realised that by her lack of control as she toppled on one side and took several seconds to right herself. He pulled her T-shirt out of her jeans.

"Hey, what the hell do you think you're doing?" She tried to push him off, wishing she had not drunk so much. She did not have the strength.

He groped for the zip of her jeans, undid them and yanked them off at the ankles. As she tried to resist he slapped her hard across the face.

She saw he was not to be reasoned with, that she had made a dreadful mistake, that he had taken her to be a different sort of girl. She was stone cold sober now. Anger gave her added strength. She swung an arm, fist clenched tightly, through an arc of ninety degrees.

He felt the stinging blow to the side of his head. She had hit him. The little bitch had hit him. Momentarily stunned he loosened his grip.

She lashed out again, twice, and kneed him in the groin. He fell to the floor on his knees, sure he was going to vomit.

Josie picked up her jeans. He was gasping and heaving. He saw her move and looked up but was not able to speak. She spat straight in his face. Revulsion achieved what the pain had not. He was sick on the floor.

Josie ran for it. She flew down the stairs and did not stop running until she reached the pub. It was shut but they were still serving behind locked doors. She hammered on the window. The seconds it took for the barman to come around and open the door seemed like hours. She looked behind her but she had not been followed.

"Someone been bothering you?" The man with the shaven head looked her up and down and grinned. "Better get your strides on, girl. Bit too cold for that sort of thing."

"Want him sorted out?" another of the men inquired.

"No. No point. I don't even know his name. Never seen him before, he probably doesn't even live here." And she couldn't go to the police. None of them could. With the amount of drugs they possessed between them none of them were in a position to do so.

It took him some time to recover but he had to get away as quickly as possible. Supposing she went back to the pub and returned with her friends?

As his heart began to beat at a more normal pace he began to walk home. He knew it now, that telephone box that was out of action had been an omen. She could describe him. If he was caught, if the police came after him, he would tell them the truth. She had asked him to take her out and invited him back to her room. He had not actually done anything, it wasn't as if he had raped her. There was nothing to connect him with the other things.

But he knew his time was running out.

Colin Mitchell stuck it out; each day he became a fraction fitter.

Gloria noticed the changes and began to think one of her

family might make something of himself. She had seen him speaking to Mary Langley. He must have taken her advice.

Frank had taken to watching the soaps. She knew, from wives of other men made redundant, that was the beginning of the end. He would never look for another job. But her own little nest egg was growing. It wasn't a huge amount, but each week she managed to save most of the extra tenner.

She mashed a panful of potatoes, adding milk and seasoning and a large knob of butter. Colin came in through the back door. "Just in time," she said. Then more loudly, "Frank, it's ready."

"I'll have it in here."

"No you bloody well won't. You eat with us." Lazy bugger, she thought to herself.

They ate in silence, Colin too hungry to stop to make conversation, and Frank, Gloria assumed, was sulking.

"I'm going out, Mum." Colin caught her look. "It's all right. Really."

None of this meant anything to Frank who pushed his plate away and left the table.

Colin picked up his jacket, shrugged it on and left by the back door. It was seven-fifteen. He had come to a decision. He was going to knock on Karen's door, apologise for upsetting her, which his mother said he must have done, then give her the box of chocolates, promising not to watch her all the time. First he had to buy the chocolates. The off-licence in the parade sold Black Magic and Quality Street.

He passed Karen's house. The downstairs lights were on, so was the one in her bedroom.

Karen was looking forward to the evening out, but more for the food and the surroundings than the company. She wished it was Trot she was going with. Her mother said people did not dress up quite so much these days for dinner; smart, rather than glamorous, was acceptable.

"Here," Doreen had said. "Go on, take it. I can afford it." She had handed Karen a twenty pound note.

"I couldn't . . ."

"You can. Take it. Put it towards a blouse to go with that skirt I love so much. That tan and black one."

The skirt she had worn to Trot's place that first time.

She had done so, choosing a black, silky, loose blouse which only cost a little more.

She was brushing her hair when Colin walked past. Len was due to arrive at seven-thirty. She sprayed perfume on her inner wrists and neck and went downstairs. Her winter coat was royal blue and did not really match but she assumed someone would take it from her before they went through to the restaurant.

Just as Colin returned from the off-licence, where he had hesitated before making his choice, he saw the car pull in. His stomach sank. It was that man again, the one he didn't like. He got out of the car and looked at Colin as if he was dirt. Colin watched him go up to the house. He stepped back, into his usual place, hidden in the shadows and by the trunks of the trees.

Karen came to the door and let the man in. Suddenly, without warning, Colin knew what he had to do. He ran home, able to do so now that he was fit, and burst into Mickey's bedroom.

"Oh, I decided it was easier if Danny went to my parents' house rather than one of them come here," Karen explained, when Len asked after Danny. "It'll do him good." She had been overprotective recently, it was time to let go a little.

Len thought this was a good sign. If they came back here there would be no one else in the house.

"Just a minute. My handbag." She went to get it, throwing in keys and purse. It was tan leather and matched her outfit. Doreen had given it to her last Christmas and she would not be ashamed to have it seen in the dinning room of Buxton Manor. Even the gold clasps matched the buckle of her belt.

"Oh, Len, how thoughtful." He handed her an orchid in a cellophane box. Was she supposed to wear it or keep it?

"Put it on," he said. "Here, let me." He pinned it to her

blouse. She thought she might feel a bit silly wearing it, but it would be unkind not to. She knew how expensive they were.

They had gone out to the car then.

Colin Mitchell was nowhere in sight.

Buxton Manor had been converted from the home of a wealthy family into a luxury hotel and restaurant. The owners had not succumbed to the modern idea of putting in a swimming pool or health spa. It was a place to go to be pampered, not worry about diet and exercise.

It was a mile or so out of Sopford, down country roads, and approached by a long, sweeping drive. The car park was at the side so as not to spoil the view from any of the windows.

Leonard saw immediately that Karen was impressed. "Have you been here before?"

"Oh, no," she said. "Never."

He held her arm as he led her up the steps into the entrance. Doors were held open, coats magically disappeared. They walked across the deep-piled carpet, the hallway lit by chandeliers hung on chains.

In the bar the music was soft. At the grand piano sat a man in evening dress playing all the tunes Karen knew her father loved. Settees and easy chairs were grouped around low tables. On the tables were tiny vases of flowers and dishes of nuts and olives and home-made crisps.

Len ordered their drinks. "Don't eat too many," he said as Karen picked up a pimento-stuffed olive with a cocktail stick. "You wait 'til you see the size of the portions here." He picked up the wine list. As the waiter returned with their drinks on a silver tray he said, "I'd like a bottle of champagne. This one I think."

"Now, sir?"

"Please."

Karen thought it a bit much.

"You'll see," he said. "It's quite a wait for the food. Everything is prepared only as it's ordered. Ah, here come the menus."

It took Karen some time to decide on what she wanted. Almost everything sounded delicious. The menu was extensive and contained many exotic dishes. There were no prices on her copy.

"Take your time," Len told her, "we have all evening."

As Karen knew Danny was safe and that she did not have to get up early to collect him, she allowed herself to relax. Either her mother or father would bring Danny round on their way to work in the morning.

At last, their meals finally chosen and ordered, Len poured the champagne. "Here's to us, Karen." He raised his glass.

"Us?"

"Yes. You with your new venture, me with continuing success at the club."

"Oh, I see. Well, to us then." She reciprocated the toast. "Mm, this is lovely. I've never been that keen on champagne before, it's usually too sweet."

"And it's usually not champagne. Champagne method, probably, or one of these cheap substitutes. If you want the good stuff, you have to pay for it. No," he held up a hand, "sorry. I shouldn't have said that. I didn't want to make you think about the cost." But of course, that was exactly what he had done. Karen would guess at the amount, would, perhaps, feel she owed him something in return, or, better still, wish to live this way a little more often.

They were shown through to their table. Karen thought she had never seen such a beautiful room. The coving was ornate and there was a mural in the centre of the ceiling, lit from an invisible source. Wall lights and individual candles on each table provided the rest of the illumination.

A second bottle of champagne was brought to them.

"Were you ever married, Len?" The drink was making her less inhibited. She would not normally ask personal questions.

"Yes. Briefly, and a long time ago." He told her of his ill-fated marriage. "And now you're going through the same thing. Time heals, as they say. I expect you'll marry again."

205

"Oh, I don't know. It's too soon to think of such things. I'm not actually divorced yet."

"Dave being all right about it, is he?"

"Yes. No problems. This is wonderful, Len, I don't think I've ever eaten food like this."

"Anytime you want to repeat it, let me know. What does Dave think about Trot? Doesn't he mind?"

"I don't know. And I don't think he's in any position to object, do you?" she challenged.

"No. It's just, well, you know Trot. Of course you do, what am I saying? But don't you think there's something, well, odd about him?"

"Well, perhaps he's a little unusual," Karen conceded. "But it's just the way he is. He's a very nice man, though."

"Um." Len left it at that as the plates were being cleared. "So tell me all the plans. There's one thing I don't have to worry about."

"What's that?"

Len laughed. "Trot won't be setting up in opposition."

"No." Karen laughed too, surprised Len could be such good company, and equally surprised that he could make fun of himself, as he was obviously referring to the poor quality meals he served in the club. She wondered if Trot's food would be up to the standard of Buxton Manor.

The main course arrived. The fish Karen had ordered because she had thought it would be lighter, seemed enormous, even though there was nothing else on the plate apart from some garnish. The vegetables arrived in their own dishes. Counting three sorts of potato, there were nine in all.

Karen's eyes were wide. "We'll never eat all this."

"We'll try our best. Go on, help yourself."

For a while they ate without speaking, enjoying the food. As they began to fill up the conversation resumed; they needed a break. Karen glanced at her plate thinking she might have to leave some.

"We haven't discussed menus, or anything," Karen said, "only how the place will run, opening hours and the finances. I suppose Trot'll have to think of a suitable name."

"And that will depend on the type of food, and it needs to be something people will remember. 'Lenny's Place', well that's dead simple, something kids won't forget. Sounds as if there might be a party going on. To the older ones, the customers my age and over, it sounds comfortable."

"I'd never thought of that."

"That's the sort of thing you'll have to consider. Small things, but important. And you're quite sure about all this, Karen? I mean, just how much do you know about Trot?"

"Well, I've worked with him for over a year, as you know," she answered. "And he's good to Danny. I don't mean he spoils him; he's firm but gentle."

"Gentle."

"Pardon?"

"Oh, nothing. It's just that I've seen how he wields that knife around. You know, it crossed my mind once . . . no, I don't want to spoil a wonderful evening." He gazed over Karen's head as if something was worrying him.

"What did?"

"What's that?"

"What crossed your mind?" Karen played with the stem of her glass. She thought she knew what he was going to say.

"All this Carver business. It's nonsense, I don't know why I brought it up. Sometimes my imagination goes into overdrive. I just got to thinking one day, it was always at times when he wasn't at work, you know, very late at night, Sundays or Mondays, and he's got his own set of knives, well, all chefs have, I expect, and even our dear Melissa says he's crazy, and we all know her views about men. I'm sorry, Karen, it was tactless of me to mention it. You know him far better than me, you must do." He rested his hand over hers where it lay on the table. She did not resist. Her face was pale but what pleased him most was the flicker of doubt which passed over her face.

"Now, I can see you can't finish that. Don't worry about it, it's always too much. You must have some pudding, though, I insist."

207

"No, Len. Honestly. I can't eat another thing." Her belt was tight now, and uncomfortable.

"No. I shan't either. I think my stomach must've shrunk, although they say it doesn't really do that. I haven't been eating much lately." He held her eyes. "You see, my mother died last week."

"Oh, Len, I'm so sorry. Why didn't you say before? We needn't have come tonight."

"I never break my promises, Karen."

"Was it sudden or had she been ill?"

"Very sudden. It was such a shock. It hasn't really sunk in yet. The funeral's on Wednesday."

Karen realised her hand was still covered by his. She turned it over and gave a quick squeeze of comfort.

"What makes it worse is we never really got on. I feel so bad about that."

Karen recalled her conversation with Trot about parents. It seemed no matter how old you were there was no getting away from the emotions they inspired.

Trot. Len had thought the same. But could someone capable of speaking of his parents so fondly, someone planning a whole new life, be responsible for taking the lives of others?

She wanted to go home but it would be rude to suggest Len take her yet. They would have coffee and then she would thank him and say she was tired.

It was interesting, seeing this other side of Leonard Murdoch, a man who did have feelings, after all.

"My mother was humourless, you see," he continued. "Eventually my father found someone else and left us. Mother took it out on me, blamed me for being a son instead of a daughter, then, to cap it all, she found out he was a thief. She made it far worse than it really was. A spot of teenage trouble really, no more than that, but to a pillar of society like my mother it was more than she could bear."

"How did she find out?"

"A kindly neighbour told her after he left."

"How awful."

"I know. Still, I had to admire her courage, my mother's that is. She went to see this other woman, I think she half hoped to get my father back. She said, and I quote, she was a painted whore and that they were welcome to each other. She wasn't going to let me go the same way. She said she would knock the devil out of me rather than that. She tried. My God, how she tried."

Karen thought of Danny and winced. How could any mother beat a child? She knew it went on all the same.

"I hated her, but at the same time I loved her. Does that make any sense?"

Karen nodded.

"I tried so hard to please her. I'd run her bath, make her cups of tea, anything. There were times when I wished it was her who'd gone, not my father. I never left home until I was married. Looking back, I think she almost chose my wife for me. They were very similar women. Still, it's all in the past now, all behind me."

Len ordered coffee and two brandies. He sighed. "She blamed me for the break up of my marriage, said I was just like my father. I wish I was. He was strong and confident."

"There's nothing wrong with your confidence, Len."

"Ah, it's mostly an act. I hide it well. Let's forget me. I've done what I didn't want to do, spoiled the evening. Drink your brandy and we'll have another."

He had spoiled the evening and she did not want any more to drink. He was supposed to be driving her home. He did not seem in the least drunk. It would be rude to suggest a taxi, but she had to make sure he didn't have any more.

Karen looked pointedly at her watch. "No more, Len, I think I'll really have to be going. My mother's bringing Danny round at the crack of dawn." Not strictly true, but tactful.

"Sure?"

"Positive. It was very kind of you."

"All right." He raised a hand and a waiter appeared. "Could we have the bill, please?"

209

Whilst they waited for it to be made up he reached into his jacket pocket and pulled out an envelope. "This is for you."

"What is it?" She took it and opened it.

"No." She tried to hand it back.

"It's yours, you're entitled to it. Holiday pay."

"You were more than good to me when I had time off," Karen argued. "You paid me for two weeks of that, anyway."

"One week, you came back after a week. Take it, Karen, please. Look, think of it as an investment for Danny's future if you like."

She hesitated then put the envelope into her handbag. "Thanks."

Len smiled. She did not see the cynicism in it. He signed a credit card slip and they went outside.

"God, it's freezing." It was, literally, a thin layer of ice forming on the windscreen, leaves and grass stiffening as the first grip of winter took hold.

Karen strapped on her seatbelt. She was a little nervous but when she saw how expertly Len backed the car out, turned it and drove carefully down the drive she began to relax. He negotiated the sharp left hand turn onto the main road with ease. After several hundred yards he slowed down, seeing what he was looking for. He pulled into a gateway.

"Why are we stopping?"

"Why do you think? I've told you often enough how I feel, can't you like me a bit? Don't you think you owe me something?"

So this was it. That old adage about no such thing as a free lunch sprang to mind. Leonard Murdoch thought he had bought her.

"No," she said, "you promised. You said no strings. And you also said you don't break your promises."

"Did I?" He placed a hand behind her neck and pulled her head towards him. Before she had time to think he was kissing her. She gagged as he tried to force his tongue between her teeth.

"You're mine," he said. "Right from the start I wanted you. We belong together, you must know that. Forget Trot. He's a nothing. A nobody. Think of all the things I can buy you. And Danny. I wanted to tell you before, all the things I planned. I could send Danny to a good school, give him the right start in life. You and I, we could enjoy ourselves."

"Never." Send Danny away to school? Was he mad? Didn't he know her well enough to see she would never do that?

"Please, Karen, please. It's only you I want."

A trickle of fear ran down her spine. Len was sweating, his eyes wild. Suddenly she saw the cruelty in the set of his mouth.

"I'll never let you go. If I can't have you no one else will. You're mine. The others didn't mean a thing, none of them. I hated them. You're different."

"Others?" Her voice was a croak. "What others?" With one hand she undid her seatbelt and let it slide up before she released her arm with as little movement as possible. She had to get out of the car, away from this man. He might drive after her, run her down, but anything was preferable to this. In one motion she flung open the door and was out on the grass, her boots sinking in mud the frost had not had a chance to harden.

She started to run, hearing his door slam.

"You're no different!" he screamed. "You're just like all the rest of them. You still took the money, you bitch!"

Her heart was thudding against her ribs, already she was short of breath. He would outrun her in seconds. There were no lights in sight. The world was a cold, dark place. She was oblivious to everything except her own ragged breathing and Len's loud footsteps pounding the ground behind her.

"No!" She felt his hands on her arms as he grabbed her from behind. His hot breath parted her hair and cooled on her neck. She did not have the strength to fight.

"You filthy little whore! You've slept with him, haven't you?"

She did not hear what he said next, her knees gave way

211

beneath her. How much could one person take in the course of a few weeks? Danny, she thought, oh God, what's going to happen to him if I'm dead?

The stinging slap he delivered brought her round. "You're worse than them! Worse, do you hear me?"

He flung her to the side of the road. Her handbag flew out of her hand, its contents scattered in the road.

Leonard Murdoch was on top of her, panting, reaching down, ripping at her tights. His whole weight was on her chest as he lifted his lower half to undo his own clothing. She could not scream. She could barely breathe. She felt the warmth of him, some part of him which was naked, and she wanted to be sick.

As his hands closed around her throat, as he said, "Look at me, Karen, look at me!" there could be no doubt as to who he was.

There was a blackness before her eyes. Suddenly nothing else mattered but her own life. And then Len groaned, one long, sighing groan. He rolled off her and she could breathe again. Something was wrong. She knew he had not penetrated her. Her vision cleared. She heard someone shouting and turned to look.

"You fucking bastard, you dirty murdering bastard!"

"No!" she shouted. "No, Colin, don't."

Colin Mitchell stopped at the sound of her voice.

He droped the knife he was holding. There was blood on its hilt. The knife was his own.

Len moaned.

Colin kicked him hard, under the chin and he lost consciousness again.

"The Manor," Karen stuttered, "we'll go to the Manor for help."

They made their way up the long drive.

"The police," she said to the doorman who eyed them suspiciously, dishevelled as they were. "Please call the police. Something terrible's happened." And then she passed out.

Chapter Eighteen

SOPFORD MAIL
LOCAL HERO

Despite all efforts of the police it was Sopford man, Colin John Mitchell of Oakfield Road, who finally apprehended and brought to an end the reign of terror of the man known as The Carver, who has injured many women and killed three of them.

Mr Mitchell was interviewed at his home by our reporter yesterday. He said, "I thought he was up to something. I don't know why, I just didn't trust him. I borrowed my brother's motorbike and followed them. When he stopped the car I watched from behind. I saw him try to kiss Mrs Wilkes then she got out of the car and started running. He was trying to hurt her. All the stuff from her bag was all over the road. I saw the knife and I picked it up. He had his hands around her throat. I stabbed him through the shoulder."

Mrs Wilkes was taken to Sopford General where she was treated for shock. Only recently her young son was abducted, but was returned safely after three days. Her parents are looking after the child until she has recovered, and are then taking them both on holiday.

She said the knife came to be in her handbag because she had put it there some time ago, out of her son's reach, and had forgotten about it as she rarely takes the handbag out with her.

The man who attacked Mrs Wilkes is in police custody but cannot yet be named for legal reasons.

We at the *Sopford Mail* congratulate young Mr Mitchell for his foresight and bravery.

The article then recapped the stories of the injuries and murders. It covered the whole of the front page, apart from a photograph of a smiling Colin, taken in his front room.

"Well, bugger me," Frank Mitchell said, scratching his bald spot when he learned all the details.

Gloria's heart had sunk when she had received a telephone call from the police at twelve-thirty that evening, to say that Colin was down at the station. Then she had learned, with surprised relief, that her son was being hailed as a hero. She, too, found it hard to accept what had occurred.

"I always said there was something good about that boy," Frank continued. "And I was right."

Gloria winced. Frank was going to live off this for a long time, and he would expect a drink every time he told the tale.

Colin did not talk about it much, nor did he ever question Karen's explanation about the knife, but he was a different person now, he stood straighter and no longer feared his brothers. No one would ever know how much he had been shaking when he realised he would have to go to Karen's aid.

Mary Langley came across the road to express her admiration. He asked her to go to the pictures and she accepted.

Nothing would ever be like that time with Paul for Mary, but it didn't matter. She would be seen out with a hero; people might start being nicer to her.

Although the paper had not mentioned Leonard Murdoch by name, it was soon common knowledge that he was the man. For a start, when the staff, including Trot, turned up on Tuesday night they were unable to gain entry to the club. There was a PC on guard outside.

Most of Murdoch's possessions had been taken away by forensic experts. Once the tests were complete, even if he denied the charges, they would be able to match the samples taken from the dead girls with his own.

Trot was aware that Karen had been out with Murdoch on the Monday night, but there was no mention of the incident until the evening news on Tuesday. He had not heard it as he had been in the bath at the time.

Karen had not answered the telephone on the two occasions when he had rung during Tuesday day-time, but he did not expect her to be sitting there waiting for him to ring. Only when he arrived at the club and heard about the evening news report and shocked conclusions of the others, did it hit him. He did not think he had ever moved so fast in his life. He ran to the police station but they would not tell him where she was and he did not know where her parents lived.

"The phone book," he said. There were five Wilkes' listed. He got the right number at the third attempt.

"Yes," Doreen said, "she would like to see you very much. And so would I."

"I'm going away, Trot," she said when he arrived. "With Mum and Dad and Danny. It's only for a week, but I have to do it."

"Of course. Karen? About us? Has anything changed?"

"No." And it hadn't. Despite everything, that was one thing she was certain of.

"It was Murdoch, wasn't it?"

"I'm not supposed . . . oh, what does it matter, everyone knows already, I expect. Yes."

"The club's closed. This'll give me a chance to get things moving my, I mean our, end."

Karen smiled then. She told him exactly what had happened. "I can't keep his money now. I don't want anything to do with it. I'll have to give it back somehow."

"He won't be needing it any more. Keep it, put it away for Danny, like you said. After what he's done to you, go on, do that."

She would think about it. There were lots of things she would need to think about. Suddenly her priorities were a little different, but seeing Trot's anxious face, hearing his words, she knew that when she came through all this there would be a lot to look forward to.

When the court case was over and when Karen and Danny finally moved in with Trot, Oakfield Road appeared no different from the day it was first built. A bit tattier maybe, nothing more. It was the residents who had changed.

May Wilkes, once Sandra and Trevor and the family were rehoused and she no longer had to look after Danny, found a new lease of life. Karen, she knew, was strong enough to survive her experience. Dave would undoubtedly marry Julie, even if he didn't know it yet, for Julie had made up her mind it was to be. May shook her head. He had walked away from a lovely woman; he was going to find the replacement much harder work.

The Trents' house was taken by a young married couple with a baby. No one ever heard what happened to Sue and her husband, except she was having some sort of treatment and he was sticking by her. As soon as the new family moved in they became the centre of attention, the Trents forgotten.

The Mitchell family was the only one to remain unaltered. Except for Colin. He stuck at his job. And he was really a man now; he didn't need to wear his father's clothes to know that. He had been horrified when he read how that Murdoch man had done the same. Dressed up in his dead father's clothes, using them as a disguise and to pretend he was someone else.

He would never forget Karen, but he no longer fantasized about her; no longer felt the need to go down the alley alongside her house and do that awful thing he dared not do at home in case he made a mess and his mother found out.

In pride of place, on the mantelpiece over the blocked-in fireplace in his bedroom, was the invitation for him and all of his family to attend the opening of Karen and Trot's new restaurant. And Karen had said he could bring Mary.

Mary was sixteen now, and a bit slimmer, and Mrs Langley was going shopping with her to buy her a dress for the occasion. He wondered, if they walked home together, if she'd let him hold her hand.